CHAINS OF STONE

BOOK ONE IN THE *CHAINS OF STONE* TRILOGY

JAYSEE JEWEL

THE FIRST BOOK IN THE *CHAINS OF STONE* TRILOGY
JAYSEE JEWEL
CHAINS OF STONE

This is a work of fiction.
All of the characters, organization, and events portrayed in this novel are either products of the author's imagination or are used fictitiously.

Book cover designs by Victoria Chevalier

For Victoria and Anyaeleh,
who supported this book
through all its different stages.

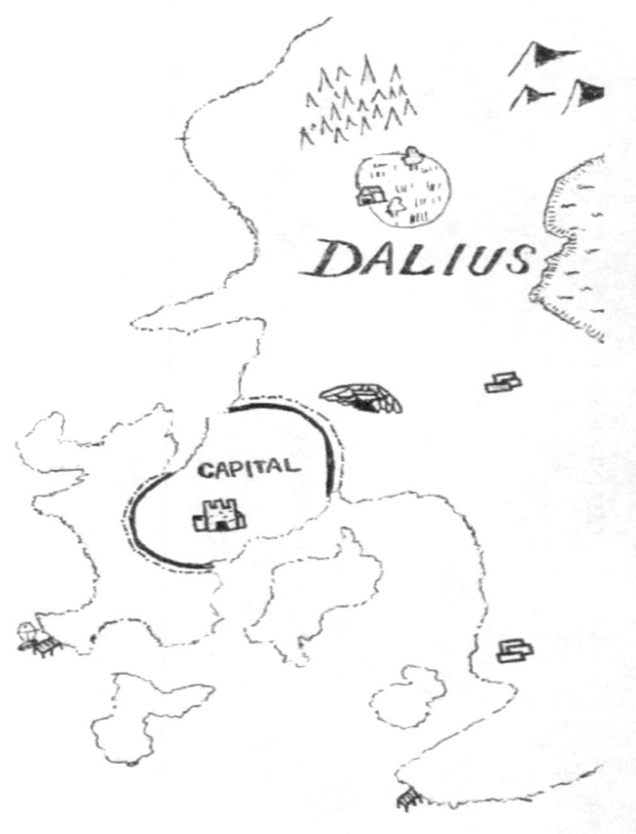

NORTHERN
ISLANDS
DALIUS
CAPITAL

ANTALIUS
MINES OF
DAIKHANDER
CLOSTRUM
CAPITAL
MINES OF
VALHANDER

INTRODUCTION

ELEVEN YEARS AGO

Cassandra Payne passed through the crowd of bloodied slaves, some of them already bleeding out on the ground but a few standing tall, glaring at their young mistress as she dared to walk amongst them. They would soon come to regret looking down on her.

Her tall and filled out body stood out among their emancipated ones. The slaves were strong from their labor in the mines hauling up stones for her and her mother, but they were so cut up and malnourished that they were thinner than her.

Cassandra's eyes darted about the crowd, studying each face. She was searching for someone amongst these doomed men: her husband. He should stand out with his handsome face and height but there were so many of these rebels that she couldn't find the one she sought.

"Come back, Cassandra!" her mother called from the edge of the crowd, hidden behind the empyrean barrier with the other soldiers. Once Cassandra was gone, all of these men would be led into the mines where they used to work before they escaped and massacred the citizens of the nearest town. The men would be locked inside and left to starve as punishment for their crimes against the country and its people.

"I'm coming," Cassandra said under her breath, weaving past the men and ignoring their stares and curses. She didn't care what they thought about her. She didn't even care what her husband thought anymore. Theidre had lost his role as her lover. The only reason she'd gone after him was to hear him apologize for abandoning her and her daughter. He was a traitor and she wanted to hear him admit it.

"Cassandra! There's no time!" her mother shouted.

Cassandra ignored her. Her blonde hair caught on one of the slave's rag clothes and it jerked her head back. Cursing, she turned and slapped him across the face, shoving him away from her with her other hand. The men standing nearby moved to defend their comrade until the soldiers on the borders pointed red empyrean arrows at them, threatening them with a fiery death if they didn't step back. It worked.

These slaves still believed they'd survive this. They had no idea Cassandra planned to starve them to death. They still held onto stupid, blind hope that they'd escape again. She could see it in their eyes. That's why she had to end them. A message had to be sent to the remaining slaves who shared these sentiments.

"Cassandra?"

Theidre's familiar voice met her ears and her determination faltered for a moment as she turned to him, beholding his beautiful face again and the jagged cuts lining his jaw. He had a black eye too, likely from one of the soldiers who recaptured him.

She wished her first thought when she saw him was of his betrayal, of the look on his face when he left her behind to free his brothers toiling away underground. He had given up a perfect life with her just so he could pillage and destroy in the country. He had abandoned his own daughter for this selfish escapade.

But the memories that flashed through her mind were happy ones. She saw him holding their daughter on his shoulders, laughing; Dinner parties with him by her side, drawing stares; Walks in the garden behind her mansion, admiring the butterflies she'd shipped in just for him.

His evil acts weren't foremost in her mind. *He* was. The man she loved.

No. That wasn't right. He was the man she *used* to love.

Now she felt nothing for him.

Her heart hardened as she stood before him, her face a breath away from his. Her hairline was only high enough to reach his chin.

"Why did you do it?" she whispered as his brown eyes searched hers. "I want to hear you tell me why you deserted Evelyn." She saw his jaw tighten and his eyes water. "She was your own flesh and blood. Did she mean nothing to you?" *Did* I *mean nothing to you?*

She hoped he would say something cruel. He could mention all the slaves her family owned and the harsh decisions she made during her thirty-one years. Bring up her potential marriages to other men, as was common in high society. Accuse her of spending so little time with him and Evelyn.

Those insults would have been acceptable. She could have easily ignored them.

Instead, he did the opposite.

"I loved you and Evelyn more than anything," he whispered, leaning down so he could look her in the eye. He always did that when they spoke.

Cassandra could feel her mother's eyes on her, waiting to give the order to kill all these men.

"I still do," he continued as she clenched her fists. "But I cannot sit by and live in luxury while my brothers starve."

"They weren't starving," she countered but he cut her off with a raise of his hand.

"Is Evelyn—"

"Cassandra! Enough!" her mother screamed, her voice filled with fear Cassandra didn't feel.

She turned away from her husband, ignoring the tear slipping down his cheek and how his voice broke when he mentioned their daughter. He *chose* to leave. She wouldn't pity him for facing the consequences of his *own* actions.

"Are you sorry for leaving me?" she asked, taking a step away to let him know this was goodbye.

"For leaving you and Evelyn?" he asked, his voice breaking again. "Yes. For coming here?" He turned to all the men by his side, at their gaunt faces and empty eyes. "Never."

Cassandra wrinkled her nose to prevent her own tears from forming. "That's all I needed to hear."

She turned toward the soldiers, motioned for them to move forward, then stepped away from the slaves. It was time to end this terrible rebellion and go home to her child. "Send them in."

The exodus back into the mine where the men served was slow and quiet at first, but as the female soldiers and their empyrean weapons cut through any who resisted, male screams filled the air. Cassandra kept her back turned as their painful shouts surrounded her. Theidre's voice wasn't among them. He was stubborn like her. He wouldn't go down screaming like a child.

As the last of the slaves went down the tunnel into their grave and the soldiers placed pillars of red stone along the entrance to prevent any survivors from digging their way out, Cassandra ran a hand over her wet eyes and finally turned toward the mine. It was little more than a hill with a hole in the front, hiding a large tunnel system underneath.

Her daughter's face filled her mind as she raised her hand, instructing the soldiers to begin the cave-in. If she backed down now, her daughter would need to deal with these rebellions forever and would likely be killed as a result.

It was Cassandra's responsibility as a mother to make sacrifices so her child wouldn't have to.

This was all for Evelyn.

If only Theidre felt the same way.

CHAPTER ONE

PRESENT DAY

The sun peeked through the branches of the trees along the dirt path, shining in Evelyn's eyes. Her ears rang from the pounding of footsteps and clanging of swords against armor.

Evelyn had been given the option to ride in one of her mother's carriages during this journey, as was customary when moving from the city she grew up in to the mines, but she wanted to spend the last hour of her trip on foot to enjoy what little fresh air she had left before going underground.

The young noble, who had just turned twenty a few weeks ago, walked along the forest path with quick steps, trying not to fall behind the soldiers and servants ahead of her. She sometimes detested being heir to one of the wealthiest women in Clostrum, as it offered little privacy, but the added protection was always a comfort.

Her silk dresses from back home had been replaced by a deep crimson uniform with silver buttons, the fabric cheap and scratchy to help her blend in with the other mine employees she would be joining.

Her blonde hair, which used to be curled by heat and styled into the most fashionable updo the capital could offer, had been tied into a tight bun to keep it away from her face. Her skin was also bare, feeling damp without powders to hide it.

"Watch your step, my lady," one of the soldiers warned her, dressed in the purple-tinted threads of her family tree. "The ground is uneven here."

Evelyn nodded, stepping over a fallen branch and wondering why the ground hadn't been paved with stones as the city streets were. Her family spared no expense in the construction of Clostrum's mines, so it felt odd that they hadn't done the same to the road. Perhaps it was because slaves and commoners were the only ones who used it.

When the mines came into view, the reality of Evelyn's situation became all the more unbearable. The mountain, more like a hill in her eyes, was covered in foliage, but the entrance was little more than dirt and the barest of grass. Two rows of stone pillars marked the entrance, standing guard over the tall doorway into the mines.

Evelyn would spend the next two months inside that horrid place, disguised as a regular employee so she could, in her mother's words, "learn to appreciate her privileges and improve the mine's efficiency".

Two towers rested on either side of the mine, filled with two soldiers each, all of them holding long-barreled guns and using binoculars to examine their surroundings. Their weapons could send empyrean stones into a man's back from nearly a mile away.

Below the towers were even more guards. They straightened as the daughter of their leader approached.

Evelyn wiped any remaining dirt off her uniform and held her head high as she walked between the pillars, knowing she had to leave a good impression on the people inside. They may not know who she was now but they would eventually, so gaining their respect was crucial if she was to continue her mother's legacy.

"Welcome, Lady Anita." A deep female voice echoed up the stairs and Evelyn raised her chin as the speaker emerged from the dark doorway. She was one of the tallest women Evelyn had ever seen, over six feet tall. Evelyn had only seen one taller woman in her life—a foreigner from Dalius where women were generally taller and stronger.

This woman had long black hair woven into a brain wrapped around her shoulder and her eyes were the most striking feature, dark and judgmental. Evelyn could feel the woman examining her, studying the state of her uniform, before addressing Evelyn again.

"Welcome to the Mines of Valhander," she said, her booming voice softening as Evelyn reached her. "We have long anticipated your visit."

Once Evelyn was the only one within earshot, the lady lowered her voice. "Your mother informs me you are to inherit the mines, should you impress me."

So this woman knew her true identity after all. The use of her fake name, Anita, was for the sake of the guards nearby, then.

"Thank you for your warm welcome," Evelyn said politely, bowing slightly as she was unsure who had the higher station here.

"No need for politeness with me, Miss Payne." She wrapped an arm around Evelyn's shoulder and led her toward the entrance, the ominous darkness making the young woman shiver.

Evelyn glanced over her shoulder at the guards and servants she was leaving behind but didn't say goodbye. She would be alone from now on until she had proved herself to this woman and, in turn, her mother.

"Allow me to give you a tour," the commander continued as they started down the stone steps. "I'll show you the more…hospitable areas on the first level so you won't get scared away. Then when you're ready, I'll have one of my most trusted slaves take you into the tunnels."

"Are you afraid of entering the tunnels yourself?" Evelyn asked.

"No, I'm not afraid. I am getting old, though, and the air down there doesn't agree with me." The woman gave her a knowing look, but Evelyn wasn't sure what she was referring to. "I forgot to introduce myself. My name is Lady Fiona Drestana, though you will call me Commander. I will address you as Anita until you decide to reveal your identity."

Evelyn didn't plan to. This mine wasn't meant to merely test her but also serve as an investigation into the mine's management. It was Evelyn's responsibility to ensure the mine was operating as it should. This would be easier to do from the inside if the other employees and slaves believed she was one of them.

"Thank you. I…look forward to your instruction."

The woman smirked. "My, you are polite. It must be a habit by this point, I assume."

"Something like that."

"Good. The other guards like being talked up to so it should make you a favorite among them."

"I see." Evelyn cringed. She had never been a fan of sucking up. One of the few benefits of being at the top was that you rarely had to do it, though it was annoying to know that everyone else never spoke honestly around her.

"This is the foyer," the commander explained as they entered the first room. It was large, equal to the size of her dining hall back home. The walls had been cut into the mountain without care for decoration. There were no tapestries or artistic carvings down here.

At the far end of the room were several furnaces. They were large holes carved into the walls with giant red empyrean bowls lining the bottom. The mystical god-given stones could only be activated by the minds of women, so there was a female guard standing next to each one. Evelyn watched as the guards made the runes on the red stones glow with a single thought, lighting the entire bowl so it heated whatever it touched.

Several rows of male slaves carried heavy stones from the tunnels to the furnaces. They strained to dump them into the bowls, then slumped back into the tunnels while the female guards effortlessly melted them down. Evelyn couldn't tell what kind of minerals were being transported but knew it wouldn't matter for now. Her job was to focus on the *people*, not the materials.

Thankfully, the furnaces gave her the first glimpse of both the male slaves and the female guards she would be overseeing in the future. She considered it her responsibility to ensure everyone cooperated and the slaves were treated humanely. While males were generally considered lowly in high society, Evelyn still thought they should be given basic respect. Besides, if the men were beaten or malnourished, they wouldn't be able to work competently.

The male slaves who walked past were of varying heights but every single one was thin—too thin. Some were muscular but she could see their bones clearly. Their skin was covered in dirt and soot and their clothes were torn and ragged, barely covering anything and offering zero protection from the heat.

The worst part was their eyes. They were dull and devoid of emotion. She used to think *she* was expressionless but these men— some of them barely above ten years old—had the life drained out of them years ago.

The female guards, on the other hand, looked like they'd been eating all the food the slaves were missing. The women were fit but had a lot of meat on their bones. The only difference between them and Evelyn now were their silver and crimson uniforms, which were as filthy as their surroundings. Evelyn dreaded looking the same in a month's time.

The eyes of the women were eerie as well, though for different reasons. Some of the guards looked normal, like civilians or servants she had seen in the city streets. They held no animosity nor respect for anyone around them. A few of the women, though, looked down on the men with spite, searching for a mistake they could punish with their whips. One of them, likely an overseer judging by her empyrean whip, had the worst expression of them all.

Empyrean stones had existed since the beginning of Clostrum's history. They were elemental rocks sent down from the stars to help the mortals survive. In the past, both genders could wield this power, but a hundred years ago the gods decided the violence of men should be tamed by granting only women the ability to control the stones. That's what history said, at least, and the books often contradicted each other.

Each empyrean stone could be activated to grant a certain element. White empyrean stones became cold and red stones created heat. Green and yellow stones also existed, granting accelerated plant growth or decay, but they were more popular in Antalius to the west, so Evelyn never used them.

There were also black empyrean stones but Clostrum's religious leaders and the queen herself collected most of them, so Evelyn rarely bothered buying them. The main preoccupation of Evelyn's family was the collection and distribution of the red and white stones, as they were the most useful in Clostrum. The black ones were of little concern.

Each empyrean stone had an opposite element that could weaken the stone and make it malleable. White stones could be molded in heat, red stones in cold, green in water, and yellow in soil. Only black stones were a mystery, seemingly changing on their own without reason.

The mountain she currently stood below was said to previously house an entire city that was later destroyed by a manmade landslide. There were supposedly hundreds of empyrean stones to discover down here, alongside other useful minerals for building. This was how her mother made her fortune and how Evelyn would continue building upon it.

Evelyn appreciated the empyrean stones for their usefulness and the power they granted, ranging from basic cooking to forming guns and arrows. However, seeing the stones used against slaves made her uncomfortable.

The guard's whip was formed from two long strings of empyrean stone melded together. One was white empyrean and the other red. If both were activated at the same time, they would lose their rigid form and lash at their victim, freezing and burning skin at once. Evelyn hadn't seen the weapon used on humans before but heard the pain was excruciating. The fact that this woman had such a hungry look in her eyes and kept tapping the whip with her pinky as a warning to the passing slaves disgusted Evelyn. She made a mental note to demote the woman as soon as she took over. She wanted that whip to serve as a last resort—not an invitation.

The final thing in this room that Evelyn abhorred was a look some of the women were making toward the men—a lusty one. It looked like they were undressing what remained of the men's clothes. The fact that some of the slaves were still boys and most of them looked ready to collapse from exhaustion made Evelyn recoil. "Disgusting."

"Is something wrong?" the commander asked. She had been in the midst of presenting the two tunnels beside the furnaces to Evelyn and explaining where they led but Evelyn hadn't been listening.

"I was just commenting on the soot. It looks disgusting."

"You'll get used to it," the commander whispered with an amused chuckle. "Just wait until you're assigned to the lower levels. I recommend a mask if you want your throat to survive." The foyer's tour complete, she pointed to their left. "If you'll follow me, the kitchen is this way."

There was a doorway to their left and it led into a large dining area, though it was devoid of tables. The empyrean stone ovens and ice boxes in the far corner were well manned. There were two women surveying the kitchen and keeping the empyrean stones lit but most of the cooks were male. It was strange to see such thin cooks overseeing so much food. They looked like they hadn't eaten in days.

"What does he do?" Evelyn pointed at an old man sitting in a corner on the stone floor next to a box of bread loaves. His legs were uncomfortably crossed beneath him.

"That is a...cripple." The commander crossed her arms and watched as the man handed out tiny loaves to a line of slaves receiving bowls of soup. "He's useless down in the mines so we assigned him here."

"Why would my mother purchase a cripple? Out of pity?" Her mother didn't normally do such things.

The commander pursed her lips. "I'll explain later. For now, just focus on the tour. I don't want you to become overwhelmed." She kept her voice low, letting Evelyn know the answer would likely put her in a bad mood.

The young heir was at least relieved that the commander seemed to take pity on the slaves, if she was judging her tone correctly. The tall woman didn't have the same look in her eyes as some of the guards on duty.

Past the kitchen was the slave barracks, covered by a large stone door with two very muscular females armed standing guard. They opened the door a crack so Evelyn could see inside but there wasn't much to see. It was just a large stone room with no beds or pillows and only a few thin blankets on the floor. It also stank of sweat and other unsavory things she didn't want to think about.

"You won't spend any time in here so don't pay this area any mind," the commander said. "Not for a few months, at least," she added.

The barracks for the guards, on the other hand, felt like a spa in comparison. The rooms were still small but had warm bunks for two to four people in each room. The beds were draped in thick blankets and pillows made of dirty fabrics that couldn't compare to Evelyn's silk ones back home. It would be difficult to sleep on such things but she reminded herself they weren't designed for *her* but for women who had never felt silk in their lives.

"One of our guards recently died from infection so you'll be alone in your room," the commander said, leading her to a room with only one pair of beds that would be her home for the coming months. "I'll keep the room empty for as long as you like."

"Thank you." Evelyn's servants had already moved her traveling cases inside the room, along with a mirror she would probably cover so she wouldn't have to see her filthy skin in the future. "I think I'll keep it to myself for now."

"A wise choice."

"Tell me if the other guards start complaining, though. I don't want to bring any attention to myself."

"Another wise choice."

"And please don't butter up to me. I hate when people give compliments they don't mean."

The commander smiled and bowed her head. "I'll be in my office if you need me. Head back to the entrance once you're settled in. A dark-haired slave should be waiting there to escort you into the tunnels."

"Why not one of the guards?"

"I've known this slave since he was a young boy. He's as trustworthy as they come and, if I'm honest, I prefer him to most of the women in this facility." She lowered her voice again. "He can also tell you everything that occurs in this mine, including what happens behind my back. No one is afraid to show their true colors to a slave."

"Noted." Evelyn raised an eyebrow. He might be a fine source of information. "Thank you. You may go now." She waved her away, wanting to organize her things before beginning her work.

"Watch your tone, lady Anita. You are still under my employ," the woman said, still smiling to show she was obeying Evelyn's command to be informal but reminding her of their temporary stations. "I look forward to working alongside you."

CHAPTER TWO

It took Evelyn longer than expected to work up the courage to leave her room. The smell in this place was getting to her. It stank of dirt and soot and human waste. Evelyn had grown up in nothing but perfume, soap, and powder. Her mother had ensured she had every necessity and want growing up, so long as it didn't reach the point of spoiling, so now Evelyn feared having to tolerate the opposite.

She had to remind herself that this was how most people spent their entire lives. What she tolerated for two months was the only thing others knew. If she was to pay and command these people, she had to know how they felt. She didn't want to become the sort of selfish, cruel ruler so many other women in her mother's circle had become.

The former queen was a pristine example of this. She drank and slept her way through so many drinks and people that it weighed on the country's economy. If she hadn't died of a supposed accident, someone would have killed her eventually for her mismanagement of the country's wealth and borders. Her excess had taken Clostrum out of its glory days.

"The guards do not wait for their nerves to disappear, so neither should you," she told herself. Her hand had been pressed against the door for five minutes now and she hadn't worked up the courage to push on it. "You are not a coward."

She willed it to be true and forced herself forward.

The long stone tunnel led her back through the guard barracks and into the foyer again. It was just as she left it, with rows of slouched men passing by and female guards barely giving her a second look. She was a novice in their eyes, far below their station. If only they knew how truly low they were in comparison to her.

After looking around the room and not finding the commander, she finally spotted the slave she'd been instructed to meet. He stood next to the exit stairs.

The man was young, maybe even similar in age to Evelyn, and only a fist taller than her. The outfit he wore was the same as the other males' but his was a little less torn and covered more skin. Said skin was just as filthy, hiding most of what was likely pale flesh behind several layers of grey grime. Even with it, though, she could tell he had a plain face, a larger than average nose, and sharp features that made him look malnourished. He would be considered plain by civilians but ugly by most of Evelyn's friends.

As she got closer and he made eye contact for the briefest moment before looking down, she realized his eyes were different from the other slaves in this mine and even back home. He didn't bear that empty look of giving in to life's miseries. There was a sparkle there that even *she* lacked.

It made her curious how he managed to retain so much energy and life in a place like this. The commander had been wise to assign him as her escort.

"You may speak," she told him, studying his face without shyness. She had never been nervous around men.

Once given permission, he made eye contact again and she got another good look at those grey eyes. "Lady Anita?"

"Yes," she lied.

"I'm to escort you through the tunnels and explain your duties," he said, speaking in an expressionless tone. She was sure he'd been instructed to speak emotionlessly but, while his voice was monotone, his eyes and brow moved with his words, filling them with life. She had never seen a slave do that before, especially when addressing a lady.

She allowed the man to lead her through the foyer and kitchen again and didn't interrupt as he explained a few things she already knew. He added more of a personal touch to the descriptions than the commander did, so she was willing to listen again.

"The slaves eat in the kitchen twice a day, once in the early morning and again at the end of the shift."

"The shifts last twelve-hours, correct?" she asked.

"Yes. Curfew is ten minutes after the final meal, then we are sent to the barracks and locked inside. After that, you are free to do as you wish."

"Understood."

He glanced at her, as though checking to make sure she really did comprehend what he was saying. Seeing him do that made her wonder if he had more to tell but was afraid to.

"You may speak freely," she prompted. "I don't care for formal language."

There was a slight raise of his eyebrows, then he nodded. "In that case, I will hold nothing back. If you have any questions, feel free to ask. I grew up here, so I know this place like the back of my hand." His tone had immediately become livelier.

"You grew up inside the mines?" she asked as he led her back to the foyer.

"Indeed. I was dropped off at an orphanage as a baby and they lacked the space, so I was sent here when I was old enough to walk. I started by carrying pebbles, then rocks, and now empyrean stones."

"I see." She could tell he enjoyed talking and was glad she had given permission to do so. It felt like there was no class difference at all now. He wasn't avoiding eye contact either.

She kind of liked it.

Once they reached the front of the tunnels, the slaves weaving around them with their burdens, the young man leaned a little closer to Evelyn. "I must warn you. Without a mask, the air below will destroy your lungs. You should ask for one before we go."

"...Thank you." He wasn't wearing one either but neither of them commented on it as she asked one of the guards for one. She considered getting one for him too but since the guard didn't offer one, she didn't bother.

"What was your name again?" Evelyn asked as she rejoined the slave.

"My name?" He smiled slightly. "I am...surprised you would ask."

My, he was informal. "I'm curious. I may come to ask you several questions in the future so I would prefer to call you by your name."

"In that case, my name is Francis."

"Francis." She gave a curt nod, not particularly liking the name, and finished tying the mask over her nose.

"If you have any questions, I would be happy to answer them," the slave repeated, his voice completely cheery by this point. "The other guards tend to ignore new employees so I will take it upon myself to help you in any way I can."

"The guards ignore new employees?" How unprofessional. She made a mental note of it and planned to write it down later. It might be useful two months from now.

"To an extent, yes. If something inconveniences the women, they don't bother with it. Most new guards have to learn the ropes themselves." He waited for her to protest the casual language but when she didn't, he continued. "I am happy to answer any questions they will not."

Now she was suspicious. Why would a slave care to help his superior if it didn't benefit him?

Ah. She knew why. He was being nice in the hopes that she would give him something in return, like his freedom. It was common for lower class women to bring slaves out of the mines with them as they left, some to be wed but most to serve as concubines or maids. He was probably after the same thing. She thought she had gotten away from that mentality when she hid her family name but to the men down here, any female was a high enough figure to seduce.

"Don't expect anything in return for your efforts," she told him in a cold tone. Perhaps that would drive him away.

The slave looked surprised for a moment, those thick eyebrows shooting up, but he seemed to catch on quickly and smiled again. She was sure it was a real smile this time. "Don't worry. I have no intention of taking advantage of you."

His voice sounded genuine but she had met good liars before. "Just…show me the mines and make it quick. I don't want my throat to give out on my first day."

"As you wish." With a polite nod, he led her into the tunnels.

CHAPTER THREE

Just as the commander described, the tunnels were the worst part of the facility. Not only were they cold and dark, but they stank of sweat and possibly dead bodies. The air felt like it was burning her lungs, eating away at her eyes, and muffling her ears. She now understood why the slave casualties in the mines were so high. While Francis explained to her that guards only worked in the tunnels a few times a week, the slaves would often spend their entire twelve hour shifts down here.

Evelyn knew these tunnels were a necessary evil, since the empyrean stones and minerals they mined were what kept Clostrum's economy afloat. Their neighboring countries didn't have such ruins on their land, so this was the queen's main bargaining chip in negotiations.

But despite knowing how vital her work down here was, Evelyn breathed a sigh of relief once her hour was up and she dreaded her next shift down here. There was a constant and ominous sense of being watched in the tunnels, one she'd never experienced before.

Her escort spent most of the tour explaining what the slaves did and what her guard duties would entail. As they reached the end of the hour, though, he started shifting his tone from obedient and monotone to personal.

"I mean no offense, but the shift changes the guards receive should be implemented for the slaves as well," Francis told her quietly as they headed back up the stone tunnel to the foyer again. "Especially for the old and young."

Evelyn squinted at him. "I don't have the authority to do such a thing," she lied, not wanting to be discovered. Had he already figured her out?

"Oh. I meant no offense, my lady." Francis raised his hands in defense while bowing his head at the same time. "I merely hoped you could mention it to the commander."

"The commander doesn't have that authority either. My mo…Lady Payne makes those changes."

He furrowed his brow and she once again wondered if he'd somehow figured out who she was.

"We'll discuss such things later," she told him, quickening her pace. "I'm eager to get out of these tunnels first."

"Of course."

They didn't speak again during their walk. As soon as she was back in the lobby and removed her mask to get a breath of fresh air, a bell rang from the barracks. If she recalled correctly, the first bell let the guards and slaves know it was time for their final meal, then curfew would come into effect immediately after.

Francis bowed and waited for Evelyn to give him further instructions but after she ignored him, he moved to the kitchen and she didn't see him again.

Free of any more obligations, Evelyn was heading back to her room to get some much-needed privacy when a young guard grabbed her by the arm. The girl who touched her was young, barely twelve by the looks of it, and clearly excited to see her. For what reason, Evelyn had no idea, since she'd never seen this girl before in her life.

"You're the new girl, right? Anita?" the young girl asked, her brown hair pulled back into the same tight bun they all had to wear. Her cheeks had brown splotches on them from the dust in the air.

"Yes, I am." Evelyn looked down the hall for an excuse to leave but there was no one else around to interrupt. "Can I help you?"

"I'm Cecil. I was the new girl until you arrived. I'm so glad. They always made me go to the lower levels because I was a rookie but now, you'll have to do it instead." She said the words with such a wide grin that Evelyn forgave the child's lack of empathy.

"Cecil. Nice to meet you." Evelyn pulled her arm out of the girl's grasp and forced a polite smile. "You're a little young to be a guard."

"My mother's one of the most notorious criminals in Clostrum. I'm just here to pay off her debts."

"Oh." That sounded horrid.

"It's not all bad. The guards here treat me better than my parents."

"I see." Evelyn waited for the girl to explain why she had stopped her. Perhaps she was lonely.

"I came to invite you to the games," Cecil finally explained, pointing down the hall at one of the other bedroom doors.

"The games?"

"Yes, the nightly games. It's tradition."

Evelyn had never heard of such a thing. "What exactly happens in these games?"

"You'll see. Come on." Grabbing Evelyn's arm again without permission, the girl led her down the hall and into the room. Evelyn was surprised to find several more guards seated inside the large space in a circle on the floor. She recognized most of them. They were the ones with venomous or lustful eyes and they were the last people she wanted to spend her free time with. The few guards she had come to like during her shift were nowhere to be seen.

"I brought her!" Cecil announced and pulled Evelyn to the back of the room. "Since we're new, we sit at the back," she informed Evelyn in a whisper as the door closed behind them.

Evelyn studied the room, not answering the child. What exactly was going on here? She had a foreboding feeling and knew even if she didn't like what was about to happen, she'd have to remain because everything would need to be reported to her mother.

Please just let it be gambling or some other harmless card game, she thought.

Her heart sank as the door opened again and several male slaves were led inside, their arms bound behind them. They were forced to stand at attention against the stone wall despite looking half dead. Some of them even had their eyes closed and were sleeping standing up.

Evelyn knew exactly what was going on as soon as she saw the lineup. The men were all covered in soot but their features were still easy enough to discern. Every one of them had a somewhat handsome face and good build, emphasized by the absence of their shirts. One in particular stood out among the rest, a taller man with strong arms and long hair. She could tell he used to be blond before he became covered in soot. His sharp facial features made him look mysterious and handsome, though they were worsened by malnutrition and scars covering his nose and jaw.

One of the guards, an old woman with a short stature and wrinkled face, brought in some cups and started splashing water on the men's faces, ordering them to scrub until their skin was visible again.

"This is barbaric," Evelyn muttered under her breath. The slaves and servants in her own home were never treated so inhumanely.

Her legs were aching to push off the ground and escape this room.

The only consolation right now was that the young man Francis who had escorted her earlier was not here. He must not be handsome enough to satisfy these women.

Once the men were clean and the guards had spent a few minutes ogling them, elbowing each other and giggling in each other's ears, the short woman brought out another cup. This one was full of dice, which she poured onto the floor in the center of the circle.

"This is the game," little Cecil explained breathlessly, thrilled to be here. The child's age only made Evelyn feel more repulsed by the women around encouraging her to participate. "Everyone guesses what the number rolled will be, then the game leader rolls the dice. Whoever's guess was the closest gets first pick of the men."

"But you can choose any man you want," a woman sitting nearby added after listening in. "The ones brought in today are just the pick of the litter."

"So I see," Evelyn growled. "Does the commander participate in these games?"

"No," Cecil whispered, laughing under her breath. "She's a prude and says she's married, like that matters. She often comes in and threatens to shut down the games if we don't behave."

Well, at least that was a small consolation. Once Evelyn came into power, though, these games would be shut down for good. While not illegal, sex trafficking was not why the mines were created. Not only did she personally find it abhorrent, but it also detracted from the slaves' productivity. The men were already exhausted. Forcing them to stay up half the night would only make them more useless.

Her stomach shriveled in revulsion as she watched each woman say a number, guessing what the dice would add up to.

When it came her turn to guess the number, she raised her hands in an X. "I wish to observe for now," she lied. She was already memorizing their faces and once she learned their names, she would remember who had and hadn't participated in this game.

"You sure you don't want to try? Do it while John's still here. He's usually taken first," Cecil warned.

"Who is John?" Though she could already guess. As expected, Cecil and a few other women pointed at the handsome, golden-haired man. John wasn't the most attractive person Evelyn had seen in her life, since she was often forced to meet with princes and nobles who were pruned from young ages to be beautiful, but he was certainly good looking. If he was cleaned up properly, he might even be able to compete.

The slave was currently facing forward, his hands clasped behind him and his jaw tight. There was a hint of blood lust in his eyes, which she couldn't fault him for having.

"I take it all the girls are vying for him?" she asked Cecil, tired of this whole affair. There were several nods, as though that should be obvious. "Very well." She sighed and ran a hand through her hair, giving herself time to scan the row of men again. "And I can choose anyone? Even from the barracks?"

There were several more nods.

"Very well. I choose…five."

The woman holding the cup of dice laughed. "There are six dice," she said, shaking her head. "The chances of getting a five is impossible."

"Yes, I know." Regardless of the number, she knew the one she planned to summon would not be taken, so there was no need to win.

Several of the women mocked her but she could tell a few of them understood her intentions. As the rest of the guards gave their guesses and prepared to roll the dice, she approached the door, ready to retrieve her former escort from the barracks.

"Twenty-six!"

The woman who guessed twenty-seven cheered and pointed at John. She giggled as she pulled the dead-eyed man behind her, sticking out her tongue at the other guards and receiving curses in response. Evelyn couldn't help feeling sorry for the man as his legs dragged along the ground.

"I'll put an end to this as soon as I leave," she promised herself under her breath.

After receiving a nod from the dice roller, she walked to the slave barracks at the other end of the mine and commanded the two women standing guard to open it for her. The door was so heavy that the women had to work together to push it.

The stench from the room was even more rank than it had been last time, and she had to cover her nose with her sleeve, her eyes stinging. The only light came from the hallway so all she saw inside the room was blackness. If Francis was in there, it would be impossible to find him.

"I'm looking for Francis," she told the guards. "I...wish to summon him to my chambers."

Both guards glanced at each other, then gave her a blank stare in response. "If you want him, go get him. That's not our job."

Of course. Rolling her eyes, she grabbed one of the torches and stepped inside. Her second step almost made her kick someone and when she looked down, she noticed a man sleeping beneath her, curled up like a newborn. He was shivering, as were most of the other men.

She changed her mind. She refused to go in here. Entering a room full of tired, hungry, and angry slaves who could snap her neck was suicidal.

Backing away and ignoring the judgmental stares of the two guards, she raised her voice and addressed the sleeping slaves inside. "Tell Francis to enter my bedroom within the hour."

She could hear movement and a few male voices in response but couldn't make out what they said. All she could do was hope they were more obedient than the women behind her and walked away, her steps quickening the further she went.

This entire mine made her uncomfortable. The only people who didn't fill her with revulsion were the commander, the few kind guards she had spoken to on her shift, and Francis. What made it worse was her mother was responsible for all those slaves being trapped in that claustrophobic, pitch black room. She remembered the few thin blankets she had seen during her tour and knew they would do little to prevent the stone floor from stealing the men's body heat. It was a wonder they didn't die in their sleep. Maybe some did.

Not ten minutes later, Francis entered her bedroom with droopy eyes and a frown on his face, half asleep. The bags under his eyes and premature wrinkles made him look older than his true age.

"Good evening, my lady," he greeted her, trying to stifle a yawn and failing. He then looked around her barren room. She had a pile of folded clothes in the corner, a box of personal items she had yet to unpack next to her mirror, and two beds with thin sheets against the walls. "You requested me?"

"I did." She frowned, knowing how this looked but not planning to do what the other women did. "Lie down," she commanded, pointing at the bed she had planned to use as storage. It didn't look comfortable in her eyes but for him, it was probably the first real bed he'd slept on in his lifetime.

As he obeyed, squinting at her the entire time, she felt a blush creep up the back of her neck.

"I did not bring you here for that!" she demanded. "I just…didn't want the empty bed to go to waste." Which was true.

The man raised one eyebrow slightly, surprised but not judging her as everyone else in this place did. "Why me? There are other men who are more…agreeable than I."

The answer to that should be obvious. "Why *wouldn't* I choose you? You're the only one I know and seem the most trustworthy."

He smirked, the action annoying her even though she knew he didn't mean any harm. He must be too tired to remember his place.

"Besides," she continued, feeling she should continue defending herself so others wouldn't get the wrong idea. "There is no harm in being kind to you." Not even her mother could get angry at her for that.

"Being kind to a slave?" he asked. "I will admit it is quite unheard of, especially from someone in your position."

She clenched her fists, wondering for the third time if he had seen through her lie about being Anita. When she realized he was joking around with her, something only nobles tended to do, she became even more confused. Was he idiotically brave or was there some dubious motive behind his casual tone?

Francis looked ready to speak again when they both heard a scream in the hall outside the door, followed by the angry shouts of one of the guards. Evelyn saw Francis freeze in fear but she felt no such thing and shoved the bedroom door open to see what was going on. She hated hearing women scream, especially when it was over nothing.

In the hall was the female guard who had won the game, a woman only a little older than Evelyn, standing in bare feet with only her undergarments on and a sword in her hand. The handsome slave she had won was standing a few feet from her, completely naked and attempting to avoid the screeching woman while also hiding his body from the other concerned guards flooding the hallway.

"What's going on here?" Evelyn shouted as Francis brushed past her, carrying the sheet from his bed so he could drape it over John.

The guard turned to her, tears in her eyes, and pointed her sword at the handsome slave. "He hurt me!" she shouted, as though that answered the question.

Her level of frustration reaching its peak, Evelyn stood between the guard and the slave. "Don't do anything rash," she warned.

"It's not rash! If he can't be gentle with me, he doesn't need that!" The woman pointed at John's privates with her blade, seething.

Evelyn scrunched up her nose and willed herself to calm down. She had to be the voice of reason here. Shouting back would only agitate the woman and make her use that sword. "He is still young and probably new to this. He will learn and improve." Besides, her mother bought these slaves to mine minerals, not please women in bed.

"He's been here for years! He's had his chance to learn!"

Years? How young did they start using these men? The John boy looked younger than her. Was he even eighteen years old?

When the young woman struggled against her, Evelyn shoved her shoulder against the stone wall. She didn't want to stoop to the woman's level of violence but was reaching her limit.

"What's going on here?" One of the older guards exited her bedroom and drew Evelyn's attention away for a split second. It was long enough for the foolish guard to push past her and leap toward John. With a few swings of her blade, she managed to cut off a chunk of his thigh before reaching the part she was aiming for. The stench of blood filled the room as his flesh fell to the floor and he came tumbling down after it, gripping the wound with a silent scream and greying skin.

Enraged, Evelyn went against her previous wish and slapped the girl across the face, hitting her hard enough to send her to the floor. As Francis pressed the sheet against John's wounds, his arms becoming stained with the poor boy's blood, Evelyn kicked the girl again and clenched her fists, ready to punch her too.

"What is wrong with you? I don't care what he did or didn't do! You do not damage our men! Harming a slave for your own personal pleasure is unprofessional and unacceptable. If we killed every slave for lack of experience in bed, the mines would cease to function!"

The moronic woman just covered her head and sobbed as Evelyn raised a fist, ready to slam it into her face but hesitating as it might hurt Evelyn more than it would the woman.

"I agree."

The bystanders went silent. For a few seconds, all Evelyn could hear was her own ragged breathing, John's whimpering, the woman's sobbing, and the click of heels on stone as the commander pushed through the guards to get a closer look.

The commander was dressed in black sleeping attire and her hair had been let loose, reaching the middle of her back. She looked first at the two slaves, one bleeding to death and the other trying to save him. She then turned her attention to Evelyn and the woman she had just kicked.

"Anita is in the right," the commander said, grumpy from her interrupted sleep. "It is bad enough that you keep the slaves awake with your selfish romps but cutting them is too far. I have tried to remedy your foolishness by giving the used slaves a later shift but perhaps I was too lenient."

There was a slight gasp of fear from the other guards, as they worried their nightly games had finally come to an end.

The commander focused on Evelyn. "If something like this happens again, I will tolerate it no longer."

It was a show of responsibility, not just to Evelyn but to her mother.

"Am I understood?" The commander turned her dark eyes toward the others and was quick to receive several bows and nods. As they filtered out of the hallway, their complete silence almost humorous compared to how they acted during their game, Evelyn crossed her arms and glared at the guard lying on the floor.

"Pack your bags," the commander said to the guard, prompting even more tears. "I will inform Lady Payne that you *do* prefer a prison cell after all."

Evelyn frowned. A prison cell?

"Yes, my lady." With another dog-like whimper, the woman stumbled to her feet and nearly ran away, leaving her bloody sword behind.

Once the hall was silent once more, the commander patted Evelyn on the back.

"As expected of my mistress's heir," she told her with a smile, keeping her voice low so any eavesdroppers wouldn't hear. "I will wake the physician. No need to worry, Lady Evelyn. Everything will be taken care of. And you!" She pointed at Francis. "Return to the barracks once John is dealt with. I don't even know why you're here, Francis."

Francis bowed and didn't protest.

"He was staying with me," Evelyn explained quickly, cringing at the questioning look the commander threw her way. Let her think what she wanted. All that mattered right now was that they didn't lose that dying slave over something as foolish as this. "Once the boy's been tended to, I want both of them to stay in my room. He won't be able to heal if he sleeps in the barracks."

"How very…kind of you," the commander said, confused and intrigued. Her reaction reminded Evelyn that she was acting too soft. She couldn't and shouldn't tend to every slave she met. If she did, nothing would ever get done and people would walk all over her.

The topic wasn't brought up again as Francis carried John to the doctor's room and the commander moved to follow him.

"Does my mother know about this indecency?" Evelyn whispered before the commander could leave, gesturing to the other bedroom doors and what occurred inside them.

"I mentioned it to her once but don't know her opinion on the matter."

"I see." So, her mother had chosen to do nothing…Evelyn wouldn't be so lenient. "Thank you."

The commander bowed, reminding Evelyn that *she* was actually the one in authority here, then the woman left Evelyn alone in the hall. The blood felt sticky beneath her feet and she was glad she hadn't taken off her boots yet. They would need to be cleaned thoroughly.

After standing in her bedroom for several minutes, staring at her mirror and trying to decide how she should go about her next actions, Francis reentered the room. He had looked sleepy before but now he looked ready to drop. Despite his pale face and red eyes, though, he remained at the door, waiting for John to return from the physician.

"I'm sorry," Evelyn told him before she could stop herself. "That girl was a complete bastard."

Francis glanced at her, studying her face. She hated how invasive his gaze felt. "It isn't the first time it's happened," he whispered, turning back to stare at the wooden door.

"Noted." Determined to report all of this to her mother, she pulled an empty notebook from her suitcase and started jotting down what happened, including the names she could remember. "Francis, how many guards do you know by name?"

He hesitated. "All of them."

"All?" What an impressive memory. "Can you give me the names of every guard who participates in the night games?"

There was more hesitation and perhaps a bit of fear behind his eyes, followed by understanding. "I can." His post by the door abandoned, he stood next to her and waited for permission to speak again.

"Do not lie to me," Evelyn warned, knowing men and especially male slaves were prone to lying if it benefited them. "Doing so will only hurt you in the long run."

"I never lie," he said so confidently that she immediately believed him.

"Good. Now give me the names." He truly would be an asset. She had every intention of taking him home with her now, after all of this was over. Such a knowledgeable person should be used to his fullest extent.

After they spent a full ten minutes writing down the names, it became clear John wouldn't be returning for a while so Evelyn finally commanded Francis to at least lie down on the bed before he collapsed.

"You should go to sleep. You can't help him if you're too weak to stand," she commented.

"I don't want him to feel alone," Francis whispered, picking up one of the pillows from the empty bunk across from Evelyn and placing it on the floor. "I'll stay awake until he arrives. My work shift has been delayed anyway, with permission from the commander."

"Good. It's nice to know the commander has some humanity in her. I've always said slaves can't work hard if they're half dead."

He stared at her then, looking disappointed for reasons she couldn't fathom, before lying on the floor and closing his eyes.

"You don't want to sleep on the bed?" she asked.

"The bed is for John…Tell me about the outside world."

Very bold of him to give her an order and change the subject at the same time. Luckily, she liked him enough to ignore it. "What part of the world?"

"Anything outside the mines."

Right. He said he grew up here. "Well…what specifically do you want to know?" She couldn't imagine what men found entertaining. Besides, she didn't leave her home very often. Studying and forced socializing didn't leave room for journeys outside the capital.

"What do they do with the empyrean stones we mine?"

That was easy. "We use them to make ovens, cold boxes, weapons, and other things." She barely paid the stones any mind since they were so common in her home.

"How does it feel when you use them?"

"Well." Another thing she hadn't thought about. "It's just second nature by this point. You think about heat or cold while looking at the stone and it just happens."

"So much power," he whispered, his eyes half closed. "It must feel amazing to have such control over the elements."

"I…suppose. I must admit, I never gave it a second thought. You're right, though." Now that she was looking at it from the point of view of a male, who couldn't control the empyrean stones, it must look amazing.

"Tell me about the forest," Francis said. "And the cottages. I've heard they're beautiful."

"I grew up in the city so I don't know much about them but…I did stop at a village on my way here. It had plenty of small shops and stands. Everyone wore black and brown clothes." She had found the clothing so drab after living in such a luxurious and expensive city. "There were lots of flowers, though. That was the best part."

"Describe them to me." His pained face was finally relaxing. He looked serene, imagining something he had probably never seen since his childhood.

As Evelyn described the flowers she had seen on her way here, she started to view them the way Francis probably would, as mystical pieces of art just out of reach. There were flowers outside the mine entrance but he had probably never seen them. The slaves were only allowed to leave if they became too sick to work or were bought by someone else. Most lived and died here, never to see the sun again.

Once John knocked on the door, limping and covered in bandages, Francis was asleep. Evelyn was tempted to let John take care of himself, since it wasn't her job to care for slaves, but guilt pushed her to help him into the bed. His arms were shaking under her hands as she lowered him onto the cot.

"How long before they make you work again?" she asked, noting how the blood loss turned his skin grey.

"One week," he told her. "Shortened to five days if I recover quickly."

Such a short amount of time. If a woman had such a wound, she would have been given a month of paid leave, but men were known for recovering quickly and working under pressure. They could handle the pain better than women. That's the way it had always been, and doctors prescribed breaks accordingly. Evelyn had never questioned the rules before but seeing him like this made her reconsider them.

"You can stay in this bed for five days," she told him. "But I will not bring you food or help you walk."

He nodded, that hate-filled fire burning in his eyes again. Did he think she wanted something from him in return?

"You will sleep here and nothing else," she said, annoyed that he was looking at her the same way he did those other women in the game room. "If I wanted men in my bed, I wouldn't settle for slaves from a mine."

There was a look on his face she couldn't decipher, an expression of observation and maybe even comradery. Then it was gone and he went to sleep almost immediately, leaving her alone in the silence, thinking about flowers.

CHAPTER FOUR

Since there were no secrets between her and the commander, Evelyn felt no qualms about demanding Francis accompany her every day, under the pretense that it was under the commander's orders. If any guards put up a fuss, the commander and Evelyn's excuse was that she needed an escort and protector due to some unseen illness she possessed. In actuality, Evelyn wanted to keep Francis out of the tunnels to avoid him getting hurt. His knowledge about the mines and the people who worked it would prove valuable in the future, so she needed to bring him home intact.

The mine's ant-like tunnels sprawled from the lobby in every direction and they were too dark and narrow for comfort. Evelyn's ears would ring after a few hours listening to the constant pounding of axe against stone and the dragging of heavy carts to the surface. The air was stifling and made her feel closer to death after each five-hour shift.

Luckily, her shifts only lasted three hours in the tunnels, then she was allowed to spend the rest of it in the kitchen which, while painfully hot, was still closer to the fresh air outside.

Despite Francis being allowed to accompany her without doing any work, he was always quick to jump in and help his fellow men as they toiled away. She was confused as to why he was so eager to join them but whenever she asked him about it, he would simply say it was to lighten the load for the others. This went against her mother's teaching that men only looked out for themselves and were eager to step over each other for the slightest convenience.

On the final day of Evelyn's first week, the pair were on their way to the kitchen, passing through the central lobby as they always did, when she noticed something out of the ordinary.

The foyer was normally filled with nothing but monitored slaves carrying minerals to the furnaces, as well as the occasional group heading to the kitchen for their meal. Today, however, she saw the tallest and strongest guards in the facility standing in the corner with ancient weapons in their hands. Their red empyrean guns were pointed at a row of ten men pressed against the wall in a line.

"What's going on?" she whispered in Francis' ear, hoping this wasn't that monthly thrashing her mother implemented last year. It entailed giving the slaves lashes until they collapsed for no fault or crime of their own. Each month, a new group received the same punishment to set an example for the rest.

Her fears were confirmed when Francis gave those exact words. "It's a way of establishing order and ensuring all slaves are discouraged from escape attempts." She detected a hint of spiteful sarcasm in his voice. He was good at hiding it when he wanted to, so she was surprised he didn't keep his true feelings from her. "Even just seeing it happen to our friends is enough to discourage us from running."

She found it endearing how he always referred to the men as his friends rather than "slaves" like the guards did, herself included.

The armed guards stood at attention as a shorter woman stepped forward, armed with an empyrean whip of fire and ice. The inactive stones were straight and solid, allowing her to tap them against her hand in a show of intimidation. The men shied away as she passed, anticipating the blows to come.

"Remind me whose idea this was," she asked Francis, wondering just how much of the politics the slaves knew. Did they believe his mother was to blame for such a violent show, or did he know the truth?

"It was put into practice under the orders of Queen Ivy," he recited dully.

So he did know after all. The former queen Mirabel, a lax and scandalous woman who sold all her sons into foreign marriages and spent the kingdom's money on men, drugs, and alcohol, died in an accident that was likely intentional. She fell off the castle in a drunken stupor. Some believed it was an assassination or even the result of a shove from her own daughter. Queen Mirabel was blamed for the country's borders being overrun by pirates and the increased threat of invasion from Dalius in the east, so her death was inevitable.

With only one heir remaining, the dead queen's ten-year-old daughter Ivy came into power. Evelyn had the pleasure of meeting her in person several times a year and was even considered her friend by some, but she didn't like the woman.

Queen Ivy was ruthless, trying to make up for her mother's lack of discipline by overcompensating in every area. The militia was increased, men were treated harshly, and even the nobles were monitored closely.

Most of this didn't bother Evelyn, as she preferred order to selfish chaos, but many of her peers constantly complained about the rules and regulations regarding lavish spending and abuse of power. If any of them got caught disobeying, Ivy ensured they paid for it, sometimes with their lives.

The former queen's council walked all over her and used what wasn't wasted by *her* on their own pursuits, so the current queen arrested her own council and replaced them with people she knew would obey her. Evelyn's mother was one of the few not banished or executed.

This lashing was just another way of ensuring no one tried to stand up against the queen and her laws. Evelyn didn't approve of such measures—there must be more efficient ways of establishing order without lowering productivity—but she knew her mother wouldn't bother standing up against the queen.

Evelyn sometimes detested her mother's inaction but knew she didn't have the guts to stand up to the queen either. Ivy was too quick to execute those she disagreed with, regardless of their station. She treated the council like servants and was suspicious of almost everyone. Evelyn was one of the few she hadn't deemed untrustworthy yet, according to Evelyn's mother, so she had to continue that good favor.

"Avoid the face of the middle one!" one of the guards shouted to the one carrying out the lashes. "He's no good to us scarred."

The words caught Evelyn's attention and she studied the men, trying to figure out who was so important. The slaves' backs were turned and their bodies so filthy from soot and blood that she could barely make out any defining features. When the middle one turned, though, she recognized him.

It was John. His face was still a little clean from his five days off and some of his blond hair color showed through the grime, but his skin looked even more grey than it had been a week ago. How the guard could continue lashing him while he looked so sick was beyond Evelyn's understanding.

"This makes no sense," she said quietly to Francis, crossing her arms and debating whether she should interfere. "This only makes the slaves weaker and fuels rebellion."

"When the slaves are weak and overworked, they have no energy to rebel," Francis reminded her.

While Evelyn knew this was true and was why her mother allowed the floggings, she could see John digging his fingernails into his palms as the burning tail of the whip dug into his shoulder. Despite nearly dying less than a week ago, he still looked ready to kill if given the chance. She doubted he was the only one, too.

"I don't think I'll let this continue," she muttered, more to herself than Francis. "It's a waste."

Francis glanced at her, clearly trying to understand the hidden meaning behind her words. He didn't question her, though, which was wise. The less he knew about her identity, the better.

"I think we should continue to the kitchen," Francis finally said, turning away from the scene. She could see him sweating and knew it was from seeing his friends get hurt, rather than the heat. His spirit was beaten down, the lashings leaving him defeated. It was the exact reaction her mother hoped to see in a man.

Evelyn was about to do as he requested when they both heard a commotion from the stairs leading to the surface. As Francis pulled her away against the wall, she understood what was happening. Ten guards in golden armor and red robes marched through the tunnel, shoving people out of their way to make room for whoever was entering behind them. They bore the royal crest on their chests.

"What is the queen doing here?" Evelyn muttered as she continued backing away, not caring that Francis was tugging on her arm. She didn't mind him touching her.

After the area around the entrance was clear, the royal guards formed two lines before it and waited with their heads high. The flogging stopped as every woman and man in the foyer stopped to see what was going on. Most of the slaves looked fearful but the women were curious and even in awe. It was rare for commoners to meet the queen in person.

Evelyn noted that most of the queen's soldiers had ancient guns at their sides, armed with red empyrean bullets. A few of the finer dressed ones even had white swords too, which were expensive even inside the capital.

After a few moments, a tall and muscular woman marched forward, wearing the same uniform as the others but commanding more attention with her dark eyes and height. Evelyn recognized her as the captain of the guard, commander of the queen's armies and occasional bodyguard as well. The captain studied the room before turning back and waiting for the queen to enter.

Evelyn felt Francis grip the hem of her shirt.

"The last time she came," he explained, his voice so quiet she could barely make it out, "she forced the lashings to continue until two men died."

Evelyn wasn't surprised.

Before the queen could make her grand entrance, Evelyn's commander exited the barracks and spoke to the captain, enquiring after the reason for the queen's arrival. Evelyn was surprised not even the commander knew the queen was coming. Such things were normally planned months in advance.

"The queen is here to ensure her orders are being carried out," the captain said in a deep, raspy voice. The commander was a tall woman, so seeing the captain look down on her reminded Evelyn why she should never cross the queen. That soldier could break her neck in a heartbeat and had likely done so before.

The clicking of footsteps echoed down the long tunnel, making Evelyn realize her cover might be blown. Her and queen Ivy weren't the best of friends but they were more than acquaintances and Ivy had no idea Evelyn was trying to work undercover here. If they spoke, everyone would know Evelyn's real name.

Trying to stay inconspicuous, she stepped back ever so slightly until she was behind Francis, who was luckily a few inches taller. He didn't move the entire time. Drawing attention to himself around the queen could mean death.

Every breath in the room stopped as the queen entered. She wasn't a tall woman but there was an air about her that warned everyone to watch their tongue.

She had long black hair, which had never been cut, and it was set into three long braids, which were wrapped around her head like snakes. Her makeup was pale to accentuate her red lips and dark eyes, and her dress was a matching black. It trailed along the ground behind her, hugging her figure, and sucked the light out of the room. There were no jewels or empyrean stones on her neck and arms to make it clear she didn't care about money or status. Ivy strived to be as unlike her wild mother as possible.

Evelyn bowed her head as the queen scanned the room, studying each person intently, slave and guard alike, to ensure they were up to her standards.

"Lead on," Ivy suddenly snapped at the commander.

Evelyn's commander was quick to do so despite not being told where to lead.

As she showed queen Ivy around the foyer, the royal guard followed close behind, daring anyone to make a move and receive a blade in their gut. Despite being female, every soldier was so tall and muscular that they made the male slaves look small in comparison. These women were hired from every corner of Clostrum, chosen for their might and trained from a young age. Not even Evelyn's mother had such impressive guards.

As Ivy walked past Evelyn, the queen's eyes strayed to her. Evelyn froze, hoping she didn't look suspicious hiding behind Francis, and prayed to the gods she wouldn't be recognized.

The queen's steps faltered for a moment as she tried to place Evelyn's ashen face, then the dreaded revelation flashed through her eyes. She recognized her.

Evelyn shook her head slightly, spreading her arms out to show her guard uniform in the hopes the queen understood her intentions.

Francis glanced at her, noticing her strange movements, then he stared at the queen with wide eyes.

"Fiona," queen Ivy said, turning toward the commander.

"Yes?"

Please do not reveal my name, Evelyn thought desperately. It would be such a hassle to be found out so early.

"Tell me what is going on here." The queen gestured toward the bleeding slaves leaning against the walls, the cuts on their backs still fresh. She turned away from Evelyn and moved toward the spectacle, making the young heir slump forward in relief. Francis was the only one who noticed Evelyn's strange actions.

After the commander calmly explained the lashings and their purpose, Queen Ivy motioned for the guards to continue their torture of the young men. As the women obeyed, the blades of the whip leaving jagged marks on the skin and blisters from the ice, the slaves tried to muffle their screams but were unsuccessful. Evelyn noticed the queen's eye twitch with each swing of the whip but couldn't tell if she was enjoying the sight or disgusted by it. Regardless, she did nothing to stop it.

Evelyn studied her reaction, knowing this would need to be reported to her mother later.

The queen's observation proceeded normally until John was whipped and pressed his face against the stone wall. As soon as he turned and the queen saw his face, Evelyn noticed Ivy focus on him and she didn't look away until the lashing ended.

"I am glad you have continued following my commands." The queen pulled her attention away from the men and waved the commander on, her face a mask of disinterest. Once the pair and their guards entered the long hallway, the tension in the room eased and several of the flogged slaves collapsed, some of them hitting their heads on the floor as they fell unconscious.

"They extended the length of the punishment," Francis whispered, watching John crumble to his knees with a wince. "It was twice as long as it should be."

That was a shame. Evelyn sighed and shook her head, noting the blood pooling beneath the men's bodies. It might leave a stain on the floor. "Let's go." Grabbing Francis's clammy hands, she pulled him toward the kitchen and wiped the men's screams from her mind. If the queen commanded it, Evelyn was in no position to speak against it, regardless of how she felt. Any disobedience would be deemed traitorous in Ivy's eyes.

Once they were in the kitchen, Evelyn led Francis to the corner where she could keep an eye on the cooks but wouldn't have to talk to any of them.

As she leaned against the wall and breathed a sigh of relief at not getting caught, Francis spoke.

"The queen recognized you."

Evelyn glanced at him, then pulled a stray strand of hair behind her ear in a manner she hoped looked aloof. "You must be mistaken." When he still looked skeptical, she added, "If that were the case, she would have spoken to me."

"I knew you were to inherit the Payne business," he told her in a hushed voice. "But I did not expect you to know the queen personally."

Evelyn's eyes went wide. "How do you know I'm to inherit the business?"

He shrugged. "It was obvious from the way you carried yourself and how the commander addressed you. A noble used to work here, a murderer, and she spoke the same way you do."

"The same way? What way?"

He gave another shrug, his nonchalance annoying her. "Like you are in control, I suppose. You speak like you look down on everyone, not just slaves."

Her act hadn't been as good as she hoped. "Does anyone else know?"

"Not that I know of."

"Good. Mention this to no one."

"Yes, my lady." He paused, clearly wanting to say something else.

"What is it?"

"Well." He glanced at the slaves entering and exiting the room, some of their feet now red from the blood on the foyer's floor. "You can tell the queen to stop this," he whispered, his once dull voice now alive with excitement. "You can end the suffering of my friends."

The desperate, naïve hope in his voice filled her with guilt. She could do no such thing and if he had uttered such rebellious words to any other woman, they might have killed him for it.

She understood his reason for wanting freedom but he was ignorant of the consequences it would bring. Without the slaves, they would have no empyrean stones. Without the stones, the country would lose its power and wealth, letting Darius invade and harm not only the slaves but the women as well.

Even without the threat of foreigners, women needed the stones to protect themselves. Otherwise, men would be able to take over and chaos would rule as it had a hundred years ago. Until the gods gave women control of the stones, men were reckless and violent, creating wars that ended thousands of lives.

But Francis was a slave. He hadn't read Clostrum's history books. All he saw was the pain of his companions.

"Watch your tongue," she warned him, pressing him against the wall with one hand so the guards lighting the furnaces wouldn't hear his voice. "If you continue talking like that, you'll be killed." And she didn't want to see him die. He was a good person, unlike most she knew.

Francis shot her a look of pity, an expression a slave should never direct toward his mistress. "Do you think death frightens me?" He lowered his shirt and revealed the jagged scars covering his shoulder. The fresh ones crossed over the old, built up over years of constant beatings. He also had a few bruises, though thankfully none of them were fresh. "If not even the most powerful heiress in the kingdom can protect us from beatings, what hope is there?"

Evelyn glared at him, trying to come up with an answer or a way to scold him for holding such useless dreams. She knew what happened here was not right, but the alternative would be so much worse. She had no way of saving everyone.

The most she could do was protect this man by taking him away from this mine. The rest would have to remain.

"I'm sorry, Francis. I am just one woman." She cringed. The explanation sounded pathetic to her ears and likely insulting to his. "If you blame me for my inaction, I understand."

"I do...but you are no worse than any other woman in this country." He turned away, focusing on the slaves and their bloody hands struggling under the weight of the stones they carried. "I just wish you could see the potential I see. The homes and families these men could build. Their hands could be used for so much good."

"They are used for good now," she whispered but knew he wanted his friends to work for themselves as well as others. If only reality was less cruel.

As he moved away to help his friends, joining in the work to lessen their loads as he always did, she didn't stop him.

CHAPTER FIVE

Today marked the thirteenth night Evelyn had competed in the "nightly games". She had skipped them a few times, too tired from standing all day to keep herself awake long enough to compete.

Today, however, she was ready to call out her number. When she said "three" everyone gave her advice, telling her to pick a number that was actually possible. Some even admitted their strategy of picking the average number, assuming she didn't know how to do math. Imagine how they would feel if they knew how educated she was compared to them.

She never went above a ten, though. There was no need. Francis wasn't an option in the women's eyes so there was no competition. There were other more handsome, charismatic, muscular, or energetic slaves to take his place. Even John, who was no longer the most coveted man in the group since he was no longer useful, still had women who asked for him. They must feel an odd sense of loyalty, which only disgusted Evelyn more.

After the guesses were made, everything proceeded accordingly. Four men were sent out with the winners, then John was chosen, then five more were picked.

As John left, Evelyn marveled at how dark his eyes managed to look despite being a light blue color. Perhaps it was the many scars or dark circles around them. His gaze always made her shiver, bringing unwanted worries that he would stab her while she slept.

While the winners led their chosen men out, the young girl Cecil who had first introduced Evelyn to the games leaned toward Evelyn and whispered in her ear.

"Next time, choose twenty-five. It's my lucky number," she told her sweetly, her innocence making Evelyn hate this place's influence even more.

"Don't bother," one of the older women said with a chuckle. "She only goes after one slave and he's not much to look at."

"Oh." Cecil frowned, confused. "Then why does she choose him?"

One of the other older women laughed. "Maybe she knows something we don't."

Fear gripped Evelyn as she realized what she had done. She had singled Francis out in front of these women, making them believe he had something they wanted. All *she* cared about was his kindness and friendly conversation. All *they* cared about was what they could take from him.

"So, what's so special about this one?" one of the women prodded, winking. "Maybe I should give him a try after all. Wouldn't want to miss out."

"There is no reason," she said, which was only a partial lie. She noticed Cecil's eyes narrow as she tried to discern if Evelyn was telling the truth. "I simply don't like the competition and want to give the slave a bed for the night," she continued.

She could just send Francis to her room without competing in this game but wanted to keep an eye on these games in case something more sinister or noteworthy occurred.

Cecil smirked. "Interesting."

As the next winner walked away with her chosen escort, the hairs rose on Evelyn's back. Maybe she should choose another man tonight to throw them off Francis's scent. She didn't want to see him treated poorly by these women.

"Why should you care how a slave is treated?" her mother would have asked if she saw this. "One should never worry about a slave's well-being. If we did, we would never sleep at night."

But she did worry. She cared about him, more than she should.

She racked her brain for another name, another slave she could summon so these vultures would stop prying, but she only knew John's name and he was already taken.

As she tried to recall the men's faces, she realized just how little she cared about any of them. Only Francis had her attention. While she summoned him every night, the others were left to freeze to death on the stone floor. They were all faceless beings, not worthy of her time or thought.

"And you, Anita?" The dice roller pointed at Evelyn with a smile. They didn't seem to like her boring guesses but were glad she was participating, calling those who didn't "prudes" or "bitter virgins". This was the only social event they had besides dinner. "Who will you have tonight? Same as always?"

"…Yes."

"As expected. She is smitten with that one," the woman said to the others, prompting several whistles and laughs.

Evelyn's neck turned red from both embarrassment and anger as she got up to leave for the barracks. As she walked out, the woman added, "Perhaps we should bring him in here tomorrow and see what all the fuss is about."

"Don't you dare," Evelyn muttered as more women chuckled. They then continued the game without her and promptly forgot about Francis in favor of other men. She hoped they would remain that way for the rest of the month. In about five or six weeks, she could be rid of this place and bring Francis with her.

As she brought Francis out of the barracks again, she looked at the other men this time. Many of them were old or had broken limbs. Some even had white hair and beards. They really could use a good rest on a real bed for once. She was sure Francis wouldn't mind giving up his spot for one night either.

But that would have to wait for another time. She was too frustrated right now to inconvenience herself.

She didn't mention what the women had said about him as she led Francis to her room. There was no need to worry him. Then again, maybe it wouldn't bother him. It probably wasn't the first time he'd been treated that way.

…Just the thought of their smirks and giggles made her blood boil.

Despite her argument with Francis a few days ago when he asked her to go against the queen, he seemed in high spirits again and was making conversation as he always did when half asleep. He even cracked a few jokes, something that had become more common the longer they knew each other. Evelyn noticed he saved most of his jokes for his fellow slaves, though, which she didn't mind since they needed their spirits lifted more than she.

"You didn't see it since you were on break, but Samson managed to pile six rocks on top of each other before they fell last night. If a guard hadn't kicked the tower down, he might have gone for seven. He named it the Monument of Fools, in honor of himself, of course," Francis was saying, his eyes droopy and voice quiet as he trailed along sleepily behind her.

Evelyn chuckled, glad the men found ways to entertain themselves. Mandatory breaks had been added to the mental list of changes she would implement once she inherited the mines. She was sure Francis would have many helpful tips to add when that time came.

She also made sure to file the name 'Samson' under her memories. It might come in handy later. The name might belong to that tall man she often saw Francis working next to, or maybe it was the old man with a hunched back.

…Now that she thought about it, he had so many friends that it would be impossible to keep track of who was who.

As soon as they entered Evelyn's bedroom, Francis stood at attention beside his bed. He always waited for her to lie down first, regardless of how tired he was.

The room was currently well-lit with candles, but they always blew them out before resting since Francis wasn't used to sleeping in the light.

"What do your friends think we do in here every night?" she asked him as she locked the door behind them. The guards' comments were still weighing on her mind.

"We never discuss it and pretend it doesn't happen."

"Oh? I thought the men would wear their summoning like a badge of honor."

He looked ready to judge her for her statement but thankfully noted the sarcasm in her voice. She was simply quoting what the others had said and didn't believe the words herself.

"We are beaten down and broken all day, then some of us are used at night. If the men are too tired to make the women happy, they are beaten or cut as John was. There are very few men who brag about the summoning and those who do stop after a few nights. The women's treatment of my friends at night is humiliating, not a matter of pride."

"Interesting. Are you ashamed to be summoned by *me* every night?"

He blinked twice and looked away. "...Not necessarily."

She crossed her arms and wanted to smile, caught off guard by his shyness and enjoying it.

Before she could tease him, he spoke. "I could turn the question back on you. What do the guards think about you continually summoning the same ugly slave every night?"

"You're not ugly, Francis. You're just..."

"Just...?" He sounded hurt but was smiling now, clearly having fun seeing her struggle.

"You have nice eyes and sharp facial features. Your sense of humor is attractive." She had always believed complimenting a specific feature was better than putting a label on the person's appearance. "And to answer your question, they don't say anything about you," she lied. "They are glad to have one less person competing against them."

"Oh. About that." His cheerful expression disappeared and he fiddled with one of the candles before putting it out with his palm. "I meant to speak with you about John. His mental health has been deteriorating. He's not getting enough sleep and I..." He gulped. "I think he's considering killing himself."

"I see." She nodded. This wasn't out of the ordinary for a man in Clostrum, slave or not.

"I was hoping you could...summon him next time. Even one restful night will do him good. I would prefer you take him home with you but I know you won't."

How little faith he had in her, and rightfully so. She was a coward, caring more about the queen's opinion than the life of an innocent man.

"I'll do my best," she muttered, motioning for him to lie down.

The worst part of this job was not the stifling air, the ash covered skin, or the crude language of the guards. It was the look of hopelessness Francis gave her, the spark within his eyes that told her she *could* help these men and chose not to.

If she took Francis home with her, he would bring those eyes with him. Her teenage self would have hated the mere thought of employing such a slave, one who made her feel guilty with his honesty, but she had come to like that part of him now. It made him feel more real and less like an emotionless doll. Her mother had always taught her growing up to treat men like they did not exist, but Evelyn enjoyed talking to Francis. He made her days feel a little more meaningful, even if he spent the entire day discussing how to stack rocks.

If protecting John for one day put Francis at ease, she would do it, but that's where she drew the line. She would not put an end to an entire country's practice of slavery just to make him happy.

CHAPTER SIX

Evelyn's job was easy today, monitoring the distribution of rations in the kitchen. This was one of the most coveted shifts, as it entailed overseeing the cooks and ensuring the food was distributed fairly to the incoming slaves, even though the meals consisted of meager leftover stew from the guards' dinner and some hardened loaves of bread.

It was fascinating to watch the empyrean stones being used so productively. Living in a mansion with endless servants meant Evelyn rarely entered the kitchen back home, especially in the midst of meal preparation.

The slaves had to wear thick gloves to open the white empyrean stone box used for keeping food cold because the stones could freeze one's fingers. Similarly, the red empyrean stone pots would make whatever was dropped inside cook or boil within seconds, so one's hand could suffer a similar fate if they touched it without protection.

Evelyn's mother had always discouraged her from using empyrean stones, as they could be very useful in cooking or freezing food but were also exceedingly dangerous. It was a cruel gift from the gods to send down such a volatile gift.

The slave handing out the rations to the rows of slaves entering and exiting the kitchen was the old cripple she had noticed on her first day. He had several scars across his face, as most of the workers did, but he was also confined to his wooden chair. His legs were twisted under his torso in a position that made her cringe. She was tempted to ask why he sat like that, despite it looking so uncomfortable, but the voice of her mother reminded her she should not speak to slaves unless giving orders or gathering information.

The kitchen quieted as the latest group of slaves left the room. The shuffling of feet ended and all that remained was the occasional word from the women monitoring the cooks or the hissing sound of an empyrean stone being activated.

It would be a few minutes until the next group arrived, so Evelyn watched the cripple shift his feet underneath him now that his hands were empty. Her curiosity ate away at her as she studied him, his face scrunching up from the pain. Why was he brought to the mines if he had so little he could do?

The young heiress stepped closer, her mother's voice in her head reminding her to ignore the slave. He was here for a reason. It wasn't her job to question her mother's decision.

But her mother wasn't here right now and Evelyn could do what she wanted.

"Aren't you uncomfortable?" she whispered, glancing at the guards and cooks several feet away to ensure they weren't paying her any mind.

The man looked up at her with bulging eyes, afraid he'd done something wrong.

"It doesn't hurt your legs?" she gestured to his crossed feet, which were thinner than the rest of his body.

The man shook his head furiously.

"Are they broken?"

"Yes, of course. Many times." He added the last part like it was obvious but she didn't understand what he meant.

"I didn't know breaking your legs was so common in the mines." Far more people died from malnutrition and lung diseases.

"Not in the mines." He pointed through the kitchen door toward the foyer exit, which led up to the surface. "They were broken outside."

"That makes more sense." She nodded, relieved that the world was logical again, but that still didn't explain why he was brought here to work. "How did you break them?"

"I tried to escape. I won't do it again."

That didn't answer her question, yet he acted like it should. "You tried to escape and they broke your legs?"

Another nod. "As punishment. Once they heal the wrong way, the guards break them again. Four times so far."

Evelyn's eyes went wide. They broke his legs four times in a row? For *one* escape attempt?

Her heart raced as she stepped away from her post. "I see." Without bothering to let the other guards know why she was leaving, she headed to the commander's office.

This was unacceptable. Not only did that punishment go against her mother's wish for constant productivity, it was…excessive. That man would be in pain forever because of one mistake.

Her blood was boiling by the time she barged into the stuffy office.

The walls were lined with ancient weapons of various shapes, encased in locked glass, and the bookshelf was covered in dusty books with titles like *The Lineage of the Royal Family*, *Ensuring Discipline and Obedience*, and *The History of Clostrum*. The name plate on the front of the desk was also covered in soot and dust. It read *Fiona Drestana*.

The commander was seated at her long desk, reading a book which she didn't lower until she realized Evelyn was the one who entered. "To what do I owe the pleasure, my lady?"

"How long have you been breaking slaves' legs?" Evelyn asked immediately. "And does my mother know about it?"

"How long? Eight years, if I recall correctly. Your mother implemented it. There was a band of slaves who made six separate escape attempts. They grew bolder each time. So, after the fifth one, your mother decided making an example of their leader was an appropriate response. The cripple now stands as an example to the rest."

A wave of cold washed over her. "I don't agree with this."

"It is necessary," the commander said with a sigh. "I thought you, of all people, would understand that."

"There must be other ways to keep them in line."

The woman dropped her book and stared Evelyn down, making it clear she was just following orders. "I am open to suggestions, my lady."

Evelyn furrowed her brow. In the heat of the moment, her mind had gone blank, which infuriated her even more.

"We tried several methods during the earlier escapes. First, we gave warnings and increased our patrols, then we tried rational discussion and negotiation. Neither worked. The men kept finding new ways to flee. In the end, after observing them for several years, I made the call to increase the number of ancient weapons, lower the number of rations, and break their legs. The queen's ordered beatings were also beneficial in that regard.

"Despite the myth noblewomen tell themselves that men and women are equal in terms of physical strength, it isn't true. Even with our empyrean stones, the males can overpower us, especially in such great numbers. If well fed and rested, they can and will revolt against us at any opportunity. The only efficient way of controlling them was beating them into submission with constant exhaustion. If one cannot fully function, they cannot fight back."

"And you don't feel bad for treating them this way? For breaking their bodies and spirits?" Evelyn shouted, glad the door was shut behind her so no one could hear.

"Of course I feel bad!" The commander rose from her desk so quickly that it made Evelyn jump. "Do not deceive yourself into believing you are special for bearing a conscience, my lady. I have been tempted on several occasions to purchase the cripple's life and set him free. I sometimes dream about it every day." She sighed. "But in the end, the mines must continue. The state of our economy, foreign relations, and even religion are at stake."

"What do slaves have to do with the sky gods?" The gods didn't get involved with humanity. They existed only in books and in the mouths of priestesses. The empyrean stones were the only evidence they existed at all.

"That is a question you must ask your mother." The commander sat back down and rested her chin on her hands. "And I suggest you bring this issue of lashings up with her as well, if you feel so strongly about it."

"What if we paid the men in return for risking their lives every day? Would that give them an incentive?"

"You could...but with that comes the illusion of choice and once they decide they do not want to work here anymore, they will try to leave and we will be right back where we started, albeit poorer than before. Mining is a miserable job. No one does it by choice. Why do you think the only female guards we manage to employ are former convicts?"

Evelyn bit the inside of her cheek and tasted blood. She knew all of this, though the convict part hadn't been clear to her until now. Her emotions were merely on high alert from seeing the miserable cripple, overpowering her logic. Now she was calming down and her mind clearing.

"Are you a convict as well?" she asked the commander, wondering if her mother should trust such criminals with her life's work.

"…Yes. I was part of the royal guard until I committed a crime that should have resulted in execution."

Evelyn raised an eyebrow, doubting the woman would reveal what it was. Assassination was the first thing that sprang to mind, as before queen Ivy's rule it was one of the few crimes that justified female execution.

"The great queen Ivy and your mother agreed to spare me for my crimes by letting me work here."

"It must have been a very important crime if my mother was willing to defend you." Now she was curious. "What did you do? Who did you kill?"

The commander's eyes glazed over, as though reliving the murder. "I swore to tell no one and have already said too much. If you wish to know, you may ask your mother or the queen."

"Very well." Evelyn crossed her arms and leaned against the wall, frustrated by how little she had accomplished. She didn't much care about the convicts or their past crimes. She cared about the present and what she could do now. Just as Francis said, she had so much power yet could do nothing to help anyone.

The commander came a step closer and patted Evelyn's shoulder. She had the same look of pity and disappointment Francis often wore when looking at her. "We can discuss more lenient punishments in the future when you are in charge. For now, I answer to your mother."

There was a knock at the door and one of the guards peeked inside, telling them the queen's carriage had arrived for another inspection.

The commander glanced at Evelyn with a raised eyebrow. "Her next inspection is not scheduled for three weeks. I wonder what I did wrong this time." She left with the nervous guard in tow.

Evelyn still had no answer for what punishment the slaves should face instead of broken bones. Maybe she should ask Francis...but he would probably tell her to free them all. She hoped he would gain more realistic expectations by the time she took him home with her. His dangerous talk of rebellion would enrage her mother and get him killed.

As she reentered the hallway—her mind elsewhere as she thought about Francis—she noticed the captain and Queen Ivy enter one of the tunnels leading into the deepest parts of the mine. She knew both Francis and John were working down there today.

Despite her gut telling her to return to her post, the commander's comment on the strangeness of the queen's quick return prompted her to follow them. If something was wrong, she had a right to know and report it to her mother.

The inspection proceeded normally. The commander led the queen down the slave filled tunnels, pointing out their progress and how the tools they used were more advanced than the previous models. Evelyn spotted Francis halfway down the tunnel, pounding away with a pickaxe, and stopped him once the queen had passed.

"Are you okay?" she whispered. "If you need a break, I can demand you accompany me like you used to."

"No. I'm fine. I'm used to the work." He looked exhausted but when he smiled, she felt bad for asking and continued stalking the queen.

The end of the tunnel was the darkest. They hadn't set out torches and lanterns yet, so the slaves working the area were nearly blind. The loud hammering rang down the tunnel so Evelyn couldn't hear the queen's voice, but Ivy looked calm and composed as always, arms crossed in front of her and chin held high. She looked upon the slaves like they were insects beneath her feet.

"Bring torches!" the commander called. Once they did, Evelyn saw the slaves standing at attention in the far end of the tunnel and bowing to their leader. She recognized John standing among them. His appearance was the same as when they first met but his face looked worse. He was ragged, like he had grown new wrinkles overnight.

The queen either failed to notice his deterioration or didn't care. She was staring at him with a slight smile, something she rarely wore. Now Evelyn knew why the queen had returned so soon for an unnecessary inspection. She was here to see John.

Despite the queen's upturned red lips forming an eerie grin, her eyes had an innocent shine to them, like a girl experiencing her first love. Evelyn had seen that same look in the mirror a few times growing up when her childhood mind had latched onto one of her more handsome male tutors.

The queen had taken a liking to this slave.

"I suppose that makes sense," she muttered to herself. "Her childhood was stolen from her so perhaps she can relive it now." Due to her mother's sudden death, Ivy became queen at the age of ten. She didn't have time for love while trying to upend a corrupt council and bring Clostrum back to its former glory, so now that she'd reached twenty-three years of age, she could finally pursue the joys she missed in her young age. That included young love and infatuation.

As Evelyn kept an eye on the queen, she tried to recall if there were any rules against a noble marrying a slave. As far as she knew, it was frowned upon in high society but not legally forbidden. After all, Evelyn's mother had married a slave. The rules for royalty might be different, though. There was more at stake politically. The country of Dalius, for example, would never allow their rulers to do such a thing.

Her heart sank as she wondered how Francis would feel about this. Everyone knew Ivy was cruel toward every person she encountered, including what few friends she had left, but perhaps she would treat her husband differently. If the queen took John for herself, as Evelyn suspected she would, his life would either drastically improve or become a nightmare.

Evelyn glanced over her shoulder at Francis, who was dutifully working without acknowledging her at all.

He had requested she bring John to her room so he could rest during the night and she had been ready to do it if she won the game, but now the situation had changed. If she summoned John to her room now, even if they were to sleep separately and do nothing of consequence, the queen would be enraged. She didn't like sharing.

Evelyn bit her lip as she considered how Francis would react if she summoned him again tonight instead of fulfilling his request. She hoped he would understand after she explained the situation but doubted it. He would have that look on his face again, of disappointment and pity because she wasn't brave enough to do what was right. She hated that look. Yet she kept wanting to see him regardless.

CHAPTER SEVEN

"And Anita? What ridiculous number are you choosing today?" the dice roller asked that night.

The bedroom was a little less crowded today, since there was a flu going around, but Evelyn still felt uncomfortable with their eyes on her. The women she had worked with for a month and a half still felt like strangers to her and she hated letting them believe she was here for the same, foul reason they were.

"Today...I choose twenty," she answered coldly.

There was a multitude of raised eyebrows and playful gasps. Evelyn crossed her legs, ignoring them.

"She's actually competing today," one of them whispered with a laugh. "What caused this change?"

Evelyn didn't acknowledge her.

"Interesting." The woman holding the cup of dice gave her a bow. "I wish you the best of luck. And Cecil?"

"Twenty-five."

The roller continued around the room, collecting and memorizing the numbers to prevent cheating.

The men were lined up against the wall as always, like cattle being perused. John was at the far end of the line now, no longer the center of the women's attention. The fact he was still in the room concerned Evelyn, though. Someone might still pick him before she could.

Part of her hoped he would be picked first so she could use it as an excuse to choose Francis again. The poor sap who chose John could face the queen's wrath and Evelyn would be safe.

She bit her lip as the guesses came to an end. She didn't want to choose between John and Francis. Part of her feared Francis's disappointment more than the queen's anger.

There was more suspense than usual as the game mistress rolled the dice and many women leaned forward to see the result. Everyone was patting Evelyn on the back, rooting for her since this was her first true attempt. Every touch from their filthy, blood-stained hands disgusted her.

"And the winning number is..."

The room went silent as every breath was held, excluding that of the exhausted slaves.

"Twenty-five. Cecil! Congratulations."

Evelyn clapped mindlessly as the young winner, the little girl who had introduced her to the games in the first place, got to her feet and gave a pretend bow. She was grinning from ear to ear, giggling as the women cheered her on.

"So, which lucky man will be spending the night with our youngest member?" the old lady asked, gesturing toward the pick of the litter with a dramatic flair.

The girl fiddled with the bronze rings on her fingers, biting her bottom lip. "I will have..." She glanced at Evelyn, giving her an impish look like they shared a secret of some kind. "I will have Francis, the one Evelyn keeps summoning every night."

The rounds of "oohs" blurred together as Evelyn's mind went numb. Francis? Why?

"You thought you could keep him hidden from us forever?" one of the women called with a snicker. "Cecil, be sure to tell us the details tomorrow. I want to know why that one's so special to our Anita."

Their Anita? Who did these convicts think they were?

Evelyn snapped out of her daze and rose, glaring at the laughing old crones. Her reaction only prompted more amusement and even the little girl joined in, finding the drama exciting.

"Sorry, Anita. The slaves belong to all of us, after all," the child told her.

"Is that so?" Evelyn sneered, making the girl's smile disappear. "They belong to you, do they? You have no idea who you're talking to."

A few women snickered but some of them noticed Evelyn's shift in tone and shut their mouths.

"I have tolerated your cockiness long enough. You!" Evelyn pointed at John, then at the door. "Wait for me in my room. The rest of you, return to the barracks."

"What?" Several of the women leapt to their feet. "What do you think you're doing? Know your place, Anita!"

"My name is not Anita." She pulled a small, empyrean knife from her jacket and the women backed away with hands raised as she held it high.

"Where did you get that? It's forbidden to carry one of those!" Only the royal guard and high society members owned anything empyrean.

"It's forbidden for *convicts* to carry these, but I am not one of you." She felt a pathetic thrill from their confusion and bewilderment. The women were glancing at each other and a few looked ready to call for the guards on duty to help them.

"Get the commander," the game mistress ordered but no one was brave enough to move past Evelyn.

"Go ahead. Call the commander. It will do you no good...She answers to me."

There were more furrowed brows and whispers, then glares were eventually directed toward her. Only the older ones were willing to continue arguing. "You cannot do what you please in here. The rules exist for a reason."

"I make the rules around here." She lowered her weapon and gestured for the tired males to exit. "My real name is Evelyn Payne, and you will obey me from this day forward. No one is to lay a hand on Francis...and I would suggest you keep your hands off John too if you know what's good for you."

The mention of her family name was met with gasps. If they didn't recognize *her* name, they at least knew her mother's.

As she led John toward her room, three women ran down the hall toward the commander's office for confirmation. The commander would not be happy about the late-night interruption.

"I'm taking you out of the tunnels," Evelyn told John as they entered her bedroom together. He didn't react. "I'll have a bath drawn for you tomorrow. The queen will want to see you in a proper state when she arrives...unless she likes this kind of thing." She gestured toward his soot and blood covered skin.

Still no response.

"Do I need to force you to talk?" she asked after a long pause. She knew John wasn't a mute—he spoke to Francis often—but she wanted to hear his response.

"I don't talk to people like you," he answered, no part of his face moving besides his mouth. It was almost creepy how still he could be.

"People like me?"

"Women."

Understandable. She didn't care if he spoke to her. She'd heard enough today anyway. "Stay here while I fetch Francis. Actually, on second thought just go to sleep." He looked ready to faint.

She was expecting Francis to be furious when she summoned him, as it meant she had chosen him over John again, but to her great surprise he had a huge smile on his face.

"What happened?" he whispered with glee once they were alone in the empty foyer between the guard and slave barracks. "The others said you sent them back." He was referring to the men she had dismissed from the night games ten minutes ago.

"I told everyone who I was," she said. "And insisted on having both of you."

"How scandalous," he joked.

He stopped walking and, when she turned toward him to ask why, he gave her a hug. It was brief and cautious, but it felt so warm and comforting that she forgot how forbidden it was.

"I'm proud of you," he told her. "This will be the beginning of great things."

Her heart dropped as he ran ahead of her. He thought she had plans to do more than this, that she would use her power to set all the men free, but she wasn't going to. She would take *him* with her when she left, of course, and forbid the night games and punishments from continuing, but there would be nothing more.

She was relieved when Francis focused all his attention on John once they reached her bedroom. While the handsome slave had been cold towards her, his somber expression lessened once Francis entered and started raving about how great a full night's sleep would be for John.

As the two chatted quietly and took a seat on the floor, Evelyn looked John over. His hair was dirty and black with soot but once she returned its golden shine, he would look quite appealing. His toned body would also look nice once she got rid of the dirt.

After a thorough cleaning, he might even look like a prince, which meant she could charge the queen more for him or at least list a high price before offering him as a gift. It would improve the queen's attitude toward her since their sparse conversations had done little to foster a friendship.

She smiled as the plans formed in her mind and she barely noticed when Francis bid her goodnight and blew out the lanterns.

CHAPTER EIGHT

Sleep eluded Evelyn that night. Her mind was awhirl, going over what she should and shouldn't do once she was given control of this place. She tried to imagine the consequences of her decisions so she could prepare for them ahead of time. By the time morning came, she had a headache but also an alternative for breaking men's legs if they fled.

Francis and John sleeping on the bed and stone floor beside her didn't stir as she lit one of the lanterns. They didn't wake as she washed her face and arms in the basin of water by her bed either. Once she felt clean enough, she opened one of the large cases her servants had carried in on her first day. At the top of the case's contents, mainly clothes and documents, sat a uniform that was completely different from the poorly sewn one she had worn during her stay. This new jacket was sewn from black silk, the buttons were encased in gold, and the boots were made of the finest leather in Clostrum. The shoulders bore the blue and purple crest of the Payne family—a peacock with the claws of a lion.

She heard one of the slaves finally awaken as she removed her sleep wear and changed into the new outfit. "Do not turn this way," she told whoever it was, buttoning the jacket and smoothing it with clammy hands. Once the pants, stockings, and boots were on and secured, she turned to see who she had awoken. It was Francis and he was obediently looking in the opposite direction.

"You are free to move," she told him, pulling a pair of golden cuff links from a velvet pouch in her case.

His eyes widened when he laid eyes on her face and his gaze followed her every move as she did her hair. The plain bun all the guards wore was replaced by a braided crown woven around her forehead. It was a style only noblewomen wore.

The longer she worked, the taller Francis stood and the more she saw him fiddling with his hands. His nonchalant tilt of the head and slumped shoulders were gone, replaced by the stoic face and stance of a servant. As she adorned her ears with gold lined diamonds, he started folding the blankets and hiding them under the bed to keep himself busy. By the time she had finished, he was standing by the door with his hands at his side. She had never seen him look so proper before. He would almost fit in with the servants back home.

"Is there anything I can do to help?" he whispered, muttering "my lady" at the end. He had rarely done so when addressing her before. Her new appearance must have finally made him realize how affluent she was.

His fidgeting made Evelyn uncomfortable. She preferred his casual stance and tone. "Go to the commander's office and give her a message for me. She should be awake by this hour."

"What should I tell her, my lady?"

"Inform her I have decided to take control of the mines ahead of schedule," she told him. Her mother had not expected this day to come for several months or even years, but she would be pleased by the quick turnaround.

Francis nodded and exited, closing the door especially quietly behind him.

Once he was gone, Evelyn finally studied herself in the dirty mirror on the wall. The woman who looked back was barely recognizable.

The guard Anita had been plain with dirt-streaked cheeks and no expression. The lady Evelyn Payne on the other hand had rosy cheeks, a gold trimmed neck, and a practiced smile. The reflection reminded her of the way Queen Ivy carried herself. Maybe they were not as different as she liked to think. She didn't blame Francis for feeling apprehensive around her.

As she finished applying her makeup—a skill she used to consider frivolous but now appreciated compared to the dirt and soot—she noticed John stir in his bed and sit up.

"Good morning," she told him, returning her powders to their case and turning to him with crossed arms. "You won't be working in the mines today."

There was no response, as expected, and not even a curtesy glance toward her.

"I can tell the queen has plans to buy you from me since she has no concubines and you are the first man she has paid attention to." Again, no response. She did see his eyes shift this time but couldn't decipher them. "I will summon a servant to clean you and change you into a proper outfit." There was a small reserve of male uniforms in storage, prepared for slaves being shipped to the city. It wasn't up to the queen's standard but would do for now.

She hesitated, not sure if she should speak freely with him about what would happen to him in the castle. "I do not know how well the queen will treat you, but you will be free from this place. I view that as a mercy."

She gave him an opportunity to speak as she rubbed perfume on her arms and neck. He didn't make a sound but when she looked back, he was standing at attention by the door. She would take that as a confirmation.

"If Queen Ivy grows tired of you, I will send you to work in my mansion. Rest assured, you will not be tossed aside." Her mother was in the habit of dismissing slaves but Evelyn refused to do the same. She wanted to inspire loyalty in her servants and that only came out from treating them well.

"I have heard rumors," John said.

She froze, his deep voice catching her off guard. It was even lower than it had been yesterday.

"It is said the queen kills those who displease her."

"Yes." That was indisputable.

"If she comes to dislike me, I will share the same fate."

"Well..." Her voice trailed off as she considered something.

If the queen hurt him and he fought back, what would be the repercussions if he killed her? He would be executed, of course, but if the queen had no heir, Evelyn could become the next leader. She was a distant relative of Ivy and the council approved of her mother. If John did her dirty work, no one would have to be cautious around the bloodthirsty queen again.

"If she attacks you, I am sure you are capable of defending yourself," she told him carefully.

The slave bored holes into her, studying her intent. It was clear he understood what she was hinting at.

"Yes. I suppose I am capable," he whispered, nodding and standing at attention. Something shifted in him then. While Francis had become uncomfortable around her noble persona, John seemed to loosen up around it.

"I am under your command, my lady," the man said with a bow, the beginning of a smile creeping onto his face. She didn't like it, but he wouldn't be her problem much longer so it didn't matter.

After she heard the guards exit their rooms and head down the hall, she opened her door and stepped out too, her boots clicking on the stone floor as she walked toward the commander's office. John stayed in the room, as ordered, and shut the door behind her.

The guards running past slowed to study her new outfit, the younger ones awed by its splendor and the older ones shrinking away, trying to look as small as possible. The only ones who didn't look afraid of her were those who hadn't participated in the games. They knew they were in her favor.

The barracks were empty by the time she reached the office. Francis and the commander were inside, waiting for her. Francis looked stiff, standing against the wall, but the commander was the opposite. She stood up from her desk with a slight smile. If this takeover bothered the woman, she refused to reveal it.

"I am under your command, Lady Payne," the woman told her, bowing and stepping away from the desk so Evelyn could take her seat if she wished. "I shall remove my items from the office so you may move in."

"Don't bother. I still need someone in charge when I'm gone."

"My lady?" Finally, a surprised reaction.

"I trust you to follow my orders and offer critiques when necessary. We will find ways to avoid rebellion without beating our slaves senseless."

"Very well. I appreciate your mercy, my lady."

Evelyn cringed at the formal tone. Yesterday marked what was probably the last honest word she would have with this woman. "I have a list of rules I want implemented immediately and more will be added over time."

"Understood."

"The nightly games are to be abolished. No male is to enter a guard's room unless he is her husband. The slaves are already overworked. We don't need to add rape to their list of humiliations."

Francis shifted slightly at her words but she didn't let it distract her.

"The beatings are to be discontinued unless the queen is in attendance. Rations are to be increased. I trust the added productivity from the slaves will be enough to cover the cost of the food. And finally." She pointed out the door and down the hall in the general direction of the kitchen. "Give the cripple a cushion to sit on."

Francis moved to obey that final order, an excited glint in his eye. He must have waited years for someone to help that cripple.

"Summon my family doctor and instruct her to heal his legs if she can, or at least lessen his suffering," Evelyn added.

"I admire your kindness toward these slaves," the commander whispered as she wrote the new orders in a notebook. "But when these men regain their strength, what will you do when they try to fight against you?"

"This is a mine with one exit. If the worst occurs, we can cause a cave-in and place red empyrean stone in front of and around the exit so they cannot escape. I think these other solutions will help us avoid that last resort, though."

The tall woman frowned, then jotted it down. Perhaps she doubted Evelyn's words but wasn't willing to counter her yet. "Is there anything else?"

"That's enough for now."

"Very well. I will begin immediately." As the commander closed the book and hid it in her jacket, she studied Evelyn's new outfit. "You look like your mother now. I am eager to serve under you, Lady Payne."

Evelyn resisted the urge to cringe. She partly admired her mother, but had never wanted to fully be like her.

Evelyn was confident the commander would keep everyone in line regardless of the rules set in place. She had been in charge for ten years, after all, and showed zero motivation to disobey.

For a moment, Evelyn felt a shred of doubt about her actions. This might lead to chaos and bloodshed as her mother feared.

However, as she entered the kitchen and found Francis showing off the pillow he'd found to the cripple, her fears faded away. The old man's face lit up and it filled her chest with warmth. She felt like a child again.

This was the right decision. She was going down the correct path and if she ever strayed, Francis would undoubtedly lead her back to it.

CHAPTER NINE

Evelyn spent the next five hours overseeing the changes in the mines and redistribution of rations, as well as asking the other guards what new rules they wanted to see implemented. Everything had to be thoroughly inspected today, as tomorrow she would return to the city to ensure an additional shipment of rations could be sent. Her mother would be upset about the changes but could be convinced if Evelyn discussed it with her in person.

Once her work for the day was done, she summoned Francis from the tunnels and escorted him to her room, which was empty now that John was being bathed.

"Meriel and Alida were angry about your night game ban," Francis informed her as they walked, referring to the guards he worked under that day. "They might try to harm you." His voice wavered from concern, making her heart stir.

"I knew they would react that way." She waved it away with a twist of her wrist. "I'm not concerned. If they are that desperate, they can wed one of the slaves." It would not be considered shameful for women of such low stations to marry a slave. Plus, they could always find a second husband once they left. She personally didn't approve of such practices, since she saw it tear apart both her fathers and her mother, but she acknowledged it as an option.

"Yes." He didn't sound pleased but cleared his throat and followed along silently. He was still treating her cautiously.

"I hope you're mentally prepared for a bath," she told him. "Once John is finished, you're next."

"Me?"

"Of course. You can't stand before my mother covered in soot."

Francis froze and his eyes clouded over. She gave him a few seconds to realize he was coming with her to the capital and once he did, he seemed even more shaken but his eyes brightened and his smile returned for the rest of their walk. He must be relieved to finally leave this wretched place.

A few minutes later, the woman in charge of cleaning John knocked on Evelyn's bedroom door to inform her the slave's cleaning was complete. "Do you wish to see him now, my lady?" she asked

"I am admittedly curious," Evelyn confessed, speaking more to Francis than the woman.

Bowing, the woman led both her and Francis to the bathing room and Evelyn opened the door herself.

The man waiting inside was unrecognizable from the slave she met a month ago. His blond hair—which used to be so caked in dirt it became straight—was now curly and framing his face. His muscles and scars were even more visible but it gave him a rugged look and the new uniform helped hide his underfed frame.

What stood out most, though, was his face. The servant had trimmed his eyebrows and washed the caked blood from his cheeks. The filthy boy the guards had fought over would only be considered handsome down here, but this new John looked striking. Every woman in the capital would be clamoring for him now.

She was tempted to ask John how he felt about his appearance but knew it was improper to do so and he wouldn't answer regardless, so she simply looked him up and down pointedly and nodded.

"Rest in my room for now," she told him. "We leave tomorrow morning for the capital."

She felt Francis stiffen beside her, but John's expression never faltered.

"You have one more person to clean," Evelyn told the washing woman, who looked thrilled to be addressed directly. Evelyn gestured toward Francis. "Just wash him with soap and give him the same uniform as John. Don't worry about primping him too much." She didn't care how he looked so long as he was clean.

She was still excited to see the changes, though. More than John.

CHAPTER TEN

Evelyn had planned to continue working while she waited for Francis to be cleaned but everything was done. All that was left was for her case of clothes to be brought to the entrance, which would happen tomorrow.

So after John returned to her room, she waited outside the bathing room door and practiced what she would say to her mother. She had to give the impression that all these changes would improve the mines and not hinder their progress. She also had to ensure Francis became valuable in her mother's eyes, otherwise he'd be sent back here.

She was so lost in her own mind that she jumped when Francis opened the door behind her.

"Are you all right?" he asked. "My lady?"

"Yes, I'm fine." She frowned and took an extra second to compose herself, then turned to examine him.

When she laid eyes on the man, she couldn't help but smile. His black hair was clean, his skin finally visible and clear with the exception of his red scars, and his black uniform looked quite dashing on him. Now that she could see him without all the grime, she could also tell he had a bit of Dalian blood in him, resulting in a slightly darker skin tone than hers. Even after knowing him for months, there were still things she was discovering about him.

She couldn't resist leaning forward and whispering, "How do you feel?"

"Fresh." He grinned, showing off his surprisingly straight teeth. "I'm starting to understand why the nobles are so obsessed with cleanliness."

"You look good." She patted his arm and grinned back, then pulled her hair behind her ears and frowned, refocusing. "Anyway, we need to get a good night's sleep. Everything changes tomorrow."

Francis nodded several times, still smiling. "Lead the way, my lady. I'll follow you anywhere." His tone was playful again, like it was before she changed back into a noble.

He stayed by her side as she ate a quick dinner, washed the makeup off her face, and went to bed. When they went to bed, he slept by the door, probably still paranoid about the angry guards making good on their threats. Even though she knew he was just trying to protect the benefactor who would finally free him from this prison, a small part of her wished it was because he cared about her.

CHAPTER ELEVEN

None of the guards came to bid Evelyn farewell as she left, not even little Cecil whose bright personality had been dimmed by Evelyn's new rules. The commander was the only one who escorted her out.

"I look forward to seeing you again, my lady," she told her as they ascended the steps. "Truly. I believe you will become a great leader and am thrilled to see what kind of improvements you bring. I also hope to see Francis again." She nodded at him. He looked like a noble's servant now in his uniform, no longer a mere slave from the lowliest location in Clostrum. Francis bowed to the commander with a smile but didn't speak.

"I'll return in a month or two," Evelyn informed her as they moved up the steps toward the light. "Decide which guards you trust and which ones you can release, because I plan to return many of your employees to the prisons where they belong and replace them with more responsible ones."

"I look forward to it." The commander lowered her chin and simpered, stopping at the entrance so Evelyn could continue forward without her. Neither of them waved goodbye to each other. They would see each other again soon.

The guards in the towers above the mine entrance kept an eye on Evelyn, as did the servants standing before the purple carriage that had arrived from the city to pick her up. Every male and female servant bowed to Evelyn as she approached with Francis and John at her back.

Being out in the fresh air with the welcoming shades of green pine filled Evelyn with relief but she was too distracted by Francis's whispers to relish it.

"I haven't seen flowers since I was six," Francis whispered to John, who didn't answer. "Did you know they could be red? I've only seen yellow ones."

"Who cares," John muttered, and Evelyn shot both of them a silencing glare.

"Remember your place," she hissed, just out of earshot of the servants ahead. "You may be dressed like servants, but you are still slaves. You will only speak when spoken to."

"Yes, my lady," Francis said with a bow of the chin while John stared ahead with empty eyes.

Once they were in the carriage and the family servants were seated atop it to lead the horses, Francis opened the curtain covering the carriage's window so he could see outside. His eyes were like those of a child as he scanned each stone on the road and every butterfly flittering past.

Seeing his childish wonder reminded Evelyn to appreciate what she took for granted.

During their three-day journey to the capital city, Francis gazed at the forests and fields they passed with love-filled eyes, but when the dirt roads changed to smooth stone and the trees were replaced with massive buildings of wood and brick, his cheerful countenance disappeared. Evelyn noticed his hands shake and his eyes dart to and fro in a panic. John, however, looked unmoved by everything, including the people on the street staring at the carriage as it passed.

The walled capital city housed nearly a million people, the majority of them the pale natives of Clostrum with only a small mix of dark skinned Dalians and white-haired Antalians. The real diversity came from the different classes. Everyone lived within the walls, from the lowest slaves and commoners to the richest nobles in the entire country. The city was designed for classes to avoid each other, hence the main road only housing the wealthier shops and the smaller mansions. The castle and highest families lived in the center of the city, where Evelyn was headed. The edges of the walls were where the poor districts resided and Evelyn rarely ventured into them.

The women walking on the streets were dressed in robes of all colors, their hair tied up in endless braids and strung with jewels or pearls. The servants who followed wore plain shirts and tight pants bearing the family colors, though the men often wore a more subdued shade. Francis looked desperate to comment on the clothes, as he kept staring at them. This was probably his first time seeing so many colors at once.

"Just wait until we reach the center of the city," she told him, beaming. "I know women who wear dresses of pure gold, just to show off."

Francis glanced at her, opening his mouth to speak but hesitating.

"You can speak freely when there is no one to hear," she said. "But only in front of me."

John rolled his eyes but Francis's lit up. "What do slaves eat in the city?" he asked eagerly.

She didn't have the heart to tell him that slaves were treated just as poorly in the city as they were in the mines. They might eat slightly better, though. "You'll have to wait to find out."

He looked satisfied but John kept glaring at Evelyn, then out the window at the buildings. He didn't seem interested in any of them until they passed the castle. It's tall black walls of stone and red flags were imposing and he kept his eye on the structure until it was out of sight.

Unlike the castle's dark exterior, the Payne family's mansion was smaller, second only in size to the queen's castle. It had white marble walls with silver windows and purple flags of the peacock atop them. There were many female and a few male guards lined up before every door, dressed in silver armor and purple robes. White empyrean stone swords hung from their waists, kept visible for any intruders brave enough to venture near.

Twenty of the household servants were waiting outside to greet Evelyn but she didn't see her mother among them. Did she not know about Evelyn's arrival, or had she not considered it a priority?

"Follow me," she instructed Francis and John as the carriage ground to a halt. "Do as you're told once you're inside and remember that in everything you do, my name is tied to it. Embarrass my family, and my mother will take your life."

She then stepped out of the carriage. The maid in charge of the household, a white-haired woman who had worked here longer than Evelyn was alive, greeted her at the door and led her down the great entrance hall without giving Evelyn time to greet the other servants.

"Where is my mother?" Evelyn asked as they entered the empty hall, its floors and walls a matching white marble.

"She's in the dining room. Shall I announce your arrival?"

"No. I can greet her myself." Evelyn handed the maid her coat and pointed at John. "Take the blond slave to a room and clean him up. Dress him in the finest uniform we have, something fit for the ball tonight."

"Forgive me for questioning but…you are referring to the queen's ball?" the maid asked, studying John with narrowed eyes.

"Yes. Make his appearance fit for a queen," she added with a sly smile.

"Shall I prepare a gift for you to present to the queen?" the maid added, since it was the queen's birthday.

"No. I already have one." Evelyn glanced at John once more, then turned toward Francis. "And prepare a room for this one. He will serve under you from now on."

As she said it, Francis stood straighter and gulped, eyes focused on the floor. She'd never seen him so nervous. While the mines were uncomfortable, they were familiar to him, so this clean and stately place must be far more intimidating.

With a low bow, the maid gripped John's arm roughly and led him down a different hall. Evelyn felt tempted to warn her to treat him gently but thought better of it. The servants would not intentionally harm him unless they deemed it necessary.

The marble halls quieted as the maid led John away and Evelyn was left alone with Francis and a few guards standing a few feet away by the front door. The entrance hall was so long that Evelyn could whisper and no one would hear.

"What do you think so far?" Evelyn asked Francis quietly, eager to know his perspective. It was always refreshing.

"The slaves look well fed," he replied with a smile, though the eagerness was subdued by his wobbly voice. "And well rested."

"I'm not surprised that's the first thing you noticed." Evelyn smiled at him, then frowned at the end of the hall where she knew her mother was waiting in the dining room. "Remember to watch your tongue, Francis. I know you have a habit of speaking out of turn and being too friendly. That may be tolerated in the mines with slaves and convicts but here, even the servants obey proper etiquette under pain of death."

He nodded, his smile fading. "If I may be frank, my lady, I only speak that way with you and my friends. I am well aware of my station, or the lack thereof."

Only with her? "And why is that? Do I give off a friendly air that I'm not aware of?"

"No." He laughed before catching himself and covering his mouth with one hand. "No. Not at all, my lady. Do not concern yourself. I will do as I'm told."

She had to admit it felt odd having him address her so formally after speaking freely during the last month. This was the way things had to be, though. She couldn't risk him being returned to the mines because of a slip of the tongue. "Stay quiet and follow me."

Taking a deep breath and ensuring her purple dress had no wrinkles, she walked to the dining hall door and waited for the guard standing nearby to open it. She then stepped inside with her head high and hands at her side.

Despite only two people residing in this mansion—herself and her mother—the dining table was long enough to seat fifty. Paintings of her ancestors stared down at her from the walls, their eyes judging her from beyond the grave for bringing in a slave like one would a companion.

The far end of the table to her right was covered in food, ranging from an entire untouched chicken to spiced vegetables and cakes. She was expecting Francis to stare at the food like a dog but when she glanced at him, he was focusing on the marble floor, only occasionally looking up at her mother seated at the head of the table. Lady Cassandra Payne's golden hair was tied up in a military style and she had several documents open before her beside a plate stacked high with meats and pastries she hadn't eaten.

"You may enter," her mother said without making eye contact. "Though it seems you have already done so."

"Mother." Evelyn moved toward her, unsurprised that she received no greeting. Her mother didn't care about pleasantries or other pointless affairs. She only bothered to make eye contact when Evelyn stopped beside her chair and looked down on her.

"Fiona tells me you've decided to take over the Valhander mines," her mother continued, turning the page of one of her books. "It's a bit premature but I hope there was a good reason for it. Did the decision spring from a place of duty or a wish to escape the uncomfortable environment?"

"I'm ready to lead and continue the family legacy," she answered, avoiding the other reasons.

"And who is this?" There was a brief acknowledgement of Francis, who hadn't moved beyond the door. He did so now, shaking under her mother's scrutiny. He seemed to be mimicking the guards at the front door, placing his hands behind his back as the soldiers did.

"This is a slave from the mines. I brought him here because he grew up there and has a strong memory of names, practices, and—"

"And the other slave?" her mother cut in. "I was told there would be two."

"Yes. The other I will bring to the queen's ball tonight and give him to her as a gift. She took a liking to him during her inspections."

Francis shifted uncomfortable, shooting Evelyn a concerned look that she ignored. He had to understand that John's fate was out of her control. If Evelyn didn't give him to the queen, Ivy would take him on her own eventually.

"Word of our generosity should spread quickly and she may come to view me as a friend," Evelyn added, as her mother looked unconvinced. Her stoic expression had not changed during the entire exchange. "I have never seen the queen study a man as she did this one. I know this will change her opinion of us."

"The queen hates everyone, including her dead mother. I doubt a mere man will change that." Her mother shook her head and leaned back in the chair, focusing on Francis again. "So, you brought him here because of his knowledge? That's all?"

"Yes. The commander informed me he was the most trustworthy slave in her acquaintance. He will give you accurate information that the women may try to hide from us."

"An informant? Nothing more?"

"Nothing more," Evelyn lied confidently.

"Will you send him back to the mines once he has told me all he knows?"

"Oh, well, I...I was hoping to train him to become a bodyguard. The last one I had was, as you know, a liability." Her former bodyguard had been a woman who was overpowered by a male thief trying to break into the mansion for their empyrean stones. "I think a male, especially one as trustworthy as this, would be more capable of protecting me."

Her mother raised an eyebrow doubtfully but didn't comment. "I trust your judgement."

"Thank you, Mother." She rose from her seat and gave a quick bow. "I must prepare for the ball so I will leave him with you to answer all your questions."

Her mother's invasive gaze drifted from Evelyn to Francis, who looked unsure how to react. Evelyn motioned for him to join her mother, then she left to fetch John. As she walked away, her thoughts tried to stray to Francis and how her mother would treat him, but she couldn't afford to waste time on such worries. This party tonight would be her reintroduction into Clostrum society, so she had to leave a good impression. She couldn't afford to be concerned over a slave when much bigger things were at stake.

CHAPTER TWELVE

"Remember what I told you," Evelyn reminded John as the carriage drove through the castle gates behind twenty other carriages. "Do not speak or act out of turn. If you say something wrong, the queen will have you killed and possibly my household as well. That means any slaves owned by my family will face the same treatment."

John, who was now dressed in a black suit with a red robe to fit in with the party they were attending, looked away from the window. He had been watching the wealthy women exit their carriages, dressed in empyrean dresses and holding numerous handsome men by the arm. He turned to Evelyn with zero expression, just as he had in the mines. The change of environment had not affected him.

"You assume I care about the other slaves as Francis does," he told her in a monotone voice. "I do not. Nor do I fear death. I have come close to it enough times for it to lose its hold over me."

"Well, at least you have the vocabulary of a noble," she commented, ignoring what he'd said. "You'll fit in with the other slaves in the castle."

"So, I'm to be a concubine?" he changed the subject as the carriage lurched forward again, following the line.

"It's a step up from being passed around," Evelyn told him coldly. "And you won't be worked to death in the mines."

"And if I decide to kill myself?"

That was sudden but Evelyn recalled Francis mentioning his suicidal tendencies before. "I understand why you feel that way," she began, removing her emotions from the conversation. This was different from dealing with Francis. "As the queen's lover, you will be one of the most powerful slaves in the world, so there is little reason to feel discouraged."

"A slave is still a slave, regardless of how powerful his mistress is."

"But you will be able to sway her and, if necessary, dispose of her if she becomes too volatile."

His eyes, which had strayed toward the window again, shot toward her. It was clear he recalled their previous conversation about killing the queen. "And if I do as you say and kill her, what am I to receive in return?"

"Besides feeding that blood lust I see in your eyes?" she asked. "You will protect Francis and other men like him. I know you don't think much of others but Francis considers you a friend so I hope you feel the same." She tilted her head, studying his reaction. As expected, he didn't seem to disagree.

His jaw became pronounced as he clenched his teeth. "What is to be my price for the queen?"

"Nothing. I am giving you as a gift."

"Am I worth so little?"

"No. You are worth quite a lot, actually. There are few things that catch the queen's eye. You're the first person I've seen her care about."

"Women do not care about men."

She raised her hand to silence him. "Do not speak that way in front of other women. You never know who will take offense."

"You don't disagree."

She grimaced. "Certain women do not care about men but not *everyone* is set on harming you. I understand your prejudice—you've been abused your entire life—but there are women whose consciences are still intact. Some will cherish you and treat you well."

"I have yet to meet such a woman."

His words stung and she could tell he meant them, which meant he didn't consider her kind either. What made it worse was he was right. She did nothing to help others and was therefore no different from the other women in these carriages.

"Not everyone is allowed to obey their conscience," she grumbled. "And rest assured, if your wife does not love you, you can father a daughter. Your child will love you regardless of your gender."

He gave her a long stare, reminding her that he couldn't actually father a child now, thanks to the abuse he suffered. Then, when her guilt became clear on her face, he addressed a different part of her statement. "My child would love me? As you loved your father?" he mocked.

"I..." Her chest clenched as she tried to recall the face of her father, a man she had not seen past the age of nine. Her mother had dismissed him and her two other husbands after they stole or became too demanding. "I barely knew him."

John chuckled. "As I said, all women are the same."

Feeling defeated before the ball even began, she chose to stare out the window as the carriage pulled up to the front door. The castle steps were crowded with female officials and tall bodyguards, so Evelyn wasn't noticed as she climbed out of her carriage, helped down by the two female soldiers her mother had prepared for her.

John stepped down after her, his eyes darting around their surroundings. A blatant twist of his lips showed how disgusted he was by the wealth and glamor around him, from the gold and crystal statues to the empyrean dresses the women wore. He had seen countless men die just so these women could adorn their necks. Evelyn ignored the pang of sympathy as she led him up the stairs and into the crowded foyer.

The party contained various sweet and sour alcohols, as well as broiled chicken wings, fruity pastries, fried pig, and small cakes that could fit in your hands. The drinks and snacks littered every table in the foyer yet it was, according to Evelyn's mother, nothing compared to how it used to be ten years ago. The current queen banned drugs, unmonitored alcohol consumption, and sex slaves from all social events as a response to the former queen's over consumption.

Noblewomen walked about, conversing and laughing as they tried to climb their way up the social ladder. Their heels clicked on the floor as they fritted amongst social groups. Handsome male slaves, some of them dressed in little more than pants, hung on the ladies' arms and never spoke a word.

A few of the nobles greeted Evelyn as she entered, recognizing her due to her family name, but she didn't bother with small talk. There would be plenty of time for that after she accomplished her goal.

As John trailed along behind her, she noticed him focusing on a pair of young boys holding the arm of an old woman dressed in silver. The boys looked twelve but might be even younger. They must be the women's husbands or concubines, as Queen Ivy hadn't outlawed such low legal ages yet.

"So," John whispered in her ear as they walked, "You ban the rape of children in the mine but when it occurs here, you turn a blind eye."

"It doesn't mean I approve," Evelyn hissed. "And when I'm in charge of the Payne business and become a council member, I'll put a stop to it."

"The commander said the same thing when I was younger," he scoffed. "And we saw how that turned out."

Evelyn hadn't heard about that. "Well, I'm not the commander."

"But you are no different."

She paused her walk through the crowded foyer to glare at him. If he kept talking that way in front of the queen, it would be the death of her. Several women were already looking their way, studying this handsome young man. If they heard what he said and Evelyn didn't make a show of stopping his blasphemous words, her mother would hear about it.

"Do not forget what is at stake here," she reminded him, mouthing Francis's name. She hated using Francis for her own gain but there were few other options at the moment.

The castle was a large building but the majority of its rooms were inaccessible during the event. The main hall they entered through the door was where the food and dance floor were located. It connected to two winding staircases, which led to the throne room and smaller bedrooms above, which were obviously off-limits for the attendees. Due to this, the entrance hall was filled to the brim with perfume-soaked women and food laden servants.

Standing at the top of the stairs was the queen herself with two female bodyguards by her side and the captain of the guard a few feet behind her. Ivy wore a long, black gown that wrapped around her body like a raven. Her hair was tied up and decorated with black empyrean stones, one of the rarest and most valuable adornments in the world. She was currently studying everyone on the main floor, looking both bored and angry at them despite this party being held to celebrate her own birthday.

"Before I go up there," John said, staring up at the woman who would soon be his new owner. She hadn't noticed him yet. "You must promise that no harm will come to Francis."

That was easy. "I promise." She had no intention of hurting Francis anyway. He was one of the few slaves she cared about.

"Then I will do what you ask." John's face was taunt, preparing himself for what she was about to do to him.

"Good." Evelyn watched as his hateful demeanor shifted into that of a mindless statue, expressionless and without the bloodthirsty look he never bothered to hide.

She paused to practice her smile, then slowly ascended the empty stairs. The guards let her pass once they recognized her but moved to stop John, only letting him follow after she said he was with her.

The queen acknowledged Evelyn when she reached the top step. Evelyn wasn't sure if the late greeting was because Ivy didn't see her beforehand or she was simply ignoring her as some type of intimidation tactic.

"Did you tire of the mines, Evelyn?" Ivy asked, her voice as empty as John's. She still looked down at the masses, avoiding eye contact.

"No." Surprised she didn't have to initiate the conversation herself, Evelyn stepped forward and felt John at her back. "I am set to inherit the mines and have plans to run them more efficiently than my mother."

Ivy studied her for a moment to see if she was telling the truth or just spouting lies as many nobles did. "Just ensure no rebellions happen under your command. The last time that happened, thirty soldiers and two thousand slaves died."

"Yes, my queen." Most of the slaves had been killed to set an example, rather than out of necessity. They weren't casualties of war, though few knew the truth about the massacre.

"I assume you came to negotiate." The queen cut straight to the point. "Despite being distantly related, your mother and I have never gotten along, which is unfortunate considering how much we could benefit each other."

Evelyn reminded herself to watch her words. The queen could snap at any moment. There was a reason few people dared speak to her nowadays. "What about my mother's practices displease you?"

"Her hoarding of black empyrean stones."

"I see."

The *colored* empyrean stones were valuable and useful. They were essential to controlling the slaves and building a strong military, as well as forging new weapons. The Payne family had tens of researchers discovering new ways to utilize the empyrean stones efficiently.

The *black* ones, however, served no purpose. No one knew how they worked so they were merely used as art pieces or jewelry and were only valued for their rarity. "Is there something I should know about the black stones that my mother hasn't told me?"

Ivy raised an eyebrow. "You don't know about their connections to the gods?"

"I've heard rumors but nothing substantial." Some said the stones could tell the future, others said they cursed those who held them. The commander had mentioned something about them too, vague as she was.

"The priests have studied them for generations but recently, they began to hear a voice from the stones. After decades of silence, the gods are finally communicating, though only to specific individuals. I am one of those individuals."

"And what do the stones say?" Evelyn was growing intrigued and nearly forgot her reason for coming.

Ivy opened her mouth, then shut it and narrowed her eyes. "I have no reason to tell you. We barely know each other. Just because we grew up together doesn't mean I trust you."

"Fair enough." They *were* distant cousins and similar ages, but Evelyn avoided social interactions for most of her childhood and Ivy did the same, so they never fostered a friendship. "What would you say if I promised to give you more empyrean stones, as long as you give me a high position on the council?"

"I would need more than your word to be convinced."

"Well then, as a token of our potential friendship." Evelyn stepped aside so John could finally gain the queen's attention.

The queen had spent their entire conversation building up obvious walls between herself and Evelyn, but as soon as she focused on the slave and his clean appearance, her eyes widened and her pale cheeks turned pink.

She had the look of a young girl laying eyes on a boy she was attracted to. Perhaps, due to inheriting the throne at such a young age, the queen had never experienced this emotion.

Evelyn knew the queen would give whatever she asked for now.

"This is John, one of my slaves," Evelyn explained, knowing her words barley registered as the queen stared at him. "I noticed your interest in him during your visits to the mine and thought you would like to take him for yourself. Consider it a gift, as a way of extending my friendship."

A flicker of victory entered her heart as she saw the queen falter, trying to keep a stoic expression but so focused on John that she didn't react. She wasn't in shock but her nerves were taking over.

"Do you wish to have him?" Evelyn prodded calmly. "I have no use for him."

For a brief moment, Evelyn saw John's eyes flicker toward her. During their entire acquaintance, the only emotion she had seen out of them was anger as hot as the red empyrean stones, but now she saw fear, a silent cry for help. He wanted her to take him back, away from the queen. He must have heard the rumors about Ivy and her temper and was having second thoughts.

But it was a request she couldn't afford to answer.

"Yes." Ivy hesitated, then wrapped her arms around John's in a possessive manner, like she feared Evelyn would change her mind. "I'll take him." She shot a glare at Evelyn and the guards around them, like a child holding its favorite toy.

It was the first time Evelyn had seen her queen act possessive of anyone. It felt uncanny. "I hope this is enough to prove my loyalty to you," she continued, ignoring the prick of guilt John had lit in her. They both knew her words about the queen treating him well were a lie. She had just given this young man to a known murderer in return for a few favors. Francis would have been ashamed of her. "In exchange for my future loyalty, I would like a seat on the council."

Ivy strained to move her gaze away from John just long enough to give Evelyn a curt nod. "You may leave," she said without a farewell.

By the time Evelyn took one step back, the queen was leading her new slave into the throne room, away from the splendor and prying eyes of the ballroom below. The captain of the guard walked after the queen to ensure her safety, leaving Evelyn alone above the crowd.

Her breath caught in her throat as she steadied herself on the balcony and looked down on the people below. No one was looking at her. All she saw were faceless pawns, selfish women who annoyed her and viewed her as nothing more than her family name.

But what would Francis see?

She tried to look through his eyes and for maybe the first time in her life, she noticed the male servants and slaves instead of the pretty women. Figures who would normally blend into the wall became known to her, standing guard over their mistresses or acting as romantic companions. She saw love in some eyes, annoyance or envy in others, and even hatred toward their mistresses.

She also noticed some women returning kind looks to their male captives. Some might even view these men as their equals. But there were also those who viewed their men as trinkets, trophies to be held and tossed when they lost their shine.

Now she understood why Francis couldn't hate everyone as John did. He saw the complexity behind every person. Not everyone was kind, as she wished they were, but they were not all evil savages either.

It was overwhelming. She didn't like this. It was easier to view every individual as simply one or the other.

Her moment of clarity vanished as she realized she would need to spend the next three to five hours socializing with these women, forming bonds she had avoided making when she was a child. If she were to inherit the Payne mines and businesses, she had to become friends with the wealthiest and most influential females in this room. There was no space for empathy when she would have to flatter women she knew were brutes or murderers.

Evelyn just wanted to go home and see Francis again. He made her feel like a good person. She wished she could spend time with him and no one else.

Clenching her fists and inhaling a deep breath, she practiced her smile, then descended the stairs. A few eyes turned to focus on her and she headed toward those women, recalling their names and businesses so she could begin a conversation with ease. Her mother had trained her for this but that didn't mean it would be easy…especially after everything she'd seen.

CHAPTER THIRTEEN

The moon was full when Evelyn finally returned home. Her clothes stank of alcohol—though she barely drank any herself—as well as the nauseating mix of different perfumes and incenses from all the women she had to smile at and please with meaningless words.

The noblewomen had been quite relieved to see her return from the mines, though they also claimed they hadn't noticed her absence, which made their real feelings toward her—or lack thereof—clear.

Now, she was finally free and couldn't wait to be with Francis, who would speak his mind regardless of the consequences. There would be no flowery words and empty flattery from him.

There were only two guards in front of the mansion to meet her, a vast difference from the greeting earlier today when she first arrived in the city. Evelyn couldn't help feeling a little disappointed as she stepped from her carriage onto the mansion grounds. This place felt so lonely despite it being her home from infancy. Without her fathers or retired tutors, she had no one.

That feeling only changed when she spotted Francis standing in the mansion's doorway. All disappointment vanished. He didn't smile at her until they were both under the protective shadow of the building, but seeing his eyes brighten was enough to light a fire inside her chest.

"Welcome back, my lady," he said once they were in a hallway out of earshot from the other servants. "How was the party?"

She smiled but couldn't help stating the obvious. "You're asking about John, aren't you?" Not about her.

"I'm enquiring after both of you," he said quietly as they turned down a different hall toward her bedroom.

She chided herself for being jealous of a slave, especially one she sent away herself. "I gave him to the queen, as I said I would during our journey here." She clenched her teeth, feeling guilty already. She wanted to be angry at Francis for making her feel this way but knew he'd done nothing wrong.

"Do you think he'll be treated well?" Francis whispered.

"Perhaps." She genuinely didn't know. "The queen has never been in love until now, so perhaps she will treat him well because of it."

"She might." Francis stopped in front of Evelyn's bedroom door, hands behind his back and eyes focused behind her instead of at her face. "But what if she doesn't? I don't want to hear news of him…ending his life."

She knew John wouldn't do it. He had promised to please the queen in return for Francis's safety. Ending his own life would break that promise.

She couldn't tell Francis about their agreement, though. It would fill him with guilt he didn't deserve. "He's not as weak as you think," she said, wanting to end this conversation. "Have you been given a bed?" She harshly changed the subject as she gripped the handle of her bedroom door, agitated from the party and cruel treatment of John..

"Yes, and a room of my own as well." He smiled and she regretted speaking so roughly. "They say I'm to become your bodyguard after I receive some training," he continued.

"Good. Make it quick. I don't like hired soldiers watching over me." They didn't feel as trustworthy as those who served in the household regularly.

But to be honest, she cared less about her protection and more about keeping Francis safe. If he was by her side with a true job and purpose, she could ensure he didn't endanger himself or make her mother suspicious. It would also be nice to spend more time with him. His loyalty and honestly eased her mind, which would become a necessity as she gained more responsibilities and agitation in the coming years.

"I'll do my best to become worthy of standing by your side." He bowed with a tired smile and waited for her to enter her bedroom.

She cringed slightly as she realized she wanted to keep the conversation going even though he was exhausted. His presence had such a hold over hers.

"Don't get too comfortable in your room," she warned him as she stepped inside and prepared to shut the door behind her. "Once you become my official bodyguard, you'll have to sleep in my room to prevent any attempts on my life."

He tensed, his expression unreadable again, and she shut the door with a chuckle before he became even more nervous. Her good mood had returned thanks to his presence. She hoped his training ended quickly so she could see him regularly again.

CHAPTER FOURTEEN

"You want to reduce the lashings," her mother repeated, the unimpressed look on her face standing out among the shocked expressions of the other ladies in the room.

Evelyn was currently seated in her mother's office beside three of their mine commanders, none of whom Evelyn was familiar with. The office's violet carpet was soft beneath her boots but the musty books covering the walls made the large room claustrophobic, just like her mother's condescending tone. Evelyn had just brought up the new rules she wanted to implement in the mines of Valhander and it wasn't sitting well with anyone here.

"Just to be clear," her mother continued, crossing both hands over her desk and staring her daughter down. "You want to be rid of a punishment the queen implemented."

"Yes." Evelyn put her hands on her lap to imitate her mother's stance. She was currently dressed in a black suit similar to what the commander wore in the mines, in the hopes that it would help her be taken seriously. Dresses were only worn by higher class women wealthy enough to waste time and avoid manual work. Military and working class wore pants. "The lashings increase the risk of weakness and infection among the slaves. It's a risky practice when we rely on them to such a great extent."

"While the empyrean stone mining is important, you need to bear in mind that slaves are useless if they don't respect their mistress," her mother countered. "If the men get it into their heads they can overpower us, they'll do so and it will create a ripple of rebellion that will spread through all of Clostrum. If that happens, the military will be forced to fight its own people, becoming so weakened that Dalius can finally invade and take over."

"Yes. The commander said something similar. That's why I think we need to find other ways to hold the slaves back, without reducing their productivity."

"And what do you suggest?" Now her mother was crossing her arms and the other commanders hadn't bothered to say anything yet. They were lucky this office was so large and airy, with tall windows looking out on the city. Otherwise their chairs would have been crowded together and they might have been forced to participate.

Her mother continued. "Fiona said you discussed cave-ins and empyrean stone walls to keep the rebels from digging their way out, but I have destroyed mines before. It ends the lives of thousands and destroys years of progress. Remember, we aren't just digging for empyrean stones. We're looking for ancient technology, buried by previous civilizations."

Did her mother really believe she didn't know this? Evelyn had spent her entire life learning such things.

Luckily, Evelyn had given this answer some thought already, since the commander asked the same thing. "The cave-ins are a last resort. Why not use red empyrean stones to create collars and shackles for the slaves? If they rebel, the women can activate them and wound their wrists. If the men persist, the guards can burn their throats as a last resort."

The idea made the corner of her mother's mouth rise. "A good suggestion and one I've considered myself. Perhaps I should have my researchers find a way to use as little stone as possible. Empyrean stones are expensive, after all, and shackling every slave in the mines will cost us."

"But if the slaves are strong and healthy, they'll be able to bring us more stones than before. That should cover the cost."

"Perhaps." Now her mother was smiling completely. "Good. I'm glad you haven't gone soft, as I feared."

"Soft?"

"I was beginning to worry you might start prioritizing sympathy over the safety of the country. The commander mentioned your affinity for that slave you brought here, so I feared his presence might affect your judgement."

"No." Evelyn stared her down, knowing her mother wouldn't want Evelyn to sacrifice the lives of the many for the needs of a few. She agreed with it in most regards. "I simply want us to keep our humanity. We can own slaves without treating them poorly."

"Yes. Indeed." Her mother lowered her chin, still studying her, but the conversation moved on.

CHAPTER FIFTEEN

Unfortunately, after working all week, Evelyn wasn't able to see Francis at all.

He was often away in training during the day and by the time Evelyn finished her work, he was likely asleep. The head maid assured Evelyn that Francis was working hard and being cared for. Evelyn had never known the woman to lie before, so she believed her and used the free time to focus on her own improvement instead of checking on him. She didn't dare enter the servants' quarters just to check on a slave, so it was better to remain apart. The maids would spread rumors if she asked after him and everyone would assume she was becoming "soft" as her mother feared.

She missed him, though. He had a calming presence—one she desperately needed right now.

During the week, Evelyn worked alongside her mother to implement the new mining rules. She also continued her studies of finances and Clostrum law, as well as attended social events to find potential allies in political and business circles.

"I don't know what happened to you in those mines," her mother said on the fifth day after catching her daughter reading through documents during dinner. "But I'm glad you've finally matured."

"It was bound to happen one day." Evelyn dodged the unspoken question about what caused the change, putting down the book she'd been reading so her mother wouldn't grow more suspicious. Sadly, it didn't work.

"Is there a specific reason for this?" her mother continued, not to be deterred. "Or perhaps the empyrean stones began speaking to you while you were in the mines?" Her voice was monotone, probing, and her makeup perfect even in the privacy of their home.

"Do the empyrean stones actually speak? You've heard them?" Evelyn asked, curiosity rising.

"No. They don't speak to me, thank the gods. I am convinced they speak to the queen, though, and whatever they're saying leaves her more agitated every time I see her."

That was strange. Perhaps Evelyn would see it in person the next time she visited the castle. Her first council meeting would be a week from now if she received an invitation to attend.

"But you avoided my question," her mother continued, taking a delicate bite of her skinless chicken. "What caused this change? A few weeks of living in rot should not be enough to turn you into such a motivated lady."

"Why not?" Evelyn shrugged, heat riding up the back of her neck as Francis's face came to mind. "I saw the state of the mines and knew they could be run more efficiently."

"I'll pretend that wasn't an insult." Her mother raised an eyebrow, evaluating her. "I see something new in you that I didn't see before…and I don't like it."

"Oh?"

"It's the same way I acted when I was young…when a slave caught my eye."

Her mother was more perceptive than Evelyn had hoped. "My standards are not so low as to fall for a filthy slave," Evelyn said, ensuring shock and disgust filled her voice. "Besides, I learned from *your* marriages that lowly men make for poor partners."

"That they do," her mother said, "Which is why I want to ensure you don't follow that path. It's better to marry a man of similar standing so you know he isn't using you."

"A nobleman can be just as desperate for wealth as a slave," Evelyn pointed out. "And I don't recall Father being money hungry, at least not to the extent you propose."

Her mother shot her a warning look. During Evelyn's life, her mother had three husbands. The first, Evelyn's father, was a slave who was later banished from Clostrum after he tried to steal empyrean stones from the family. The next two husbands were of slightly higher standing but weren't much better and were eventually dismissed as well. That was years ago. The mansion had been empty ever since.

"I am merely warning you," her mother said with a shrug Evelyn could tell was forced. "And I will keep an eye on that man you brought in, just in case you fall into the same bad habits."

"You *know* why I brought him in."

"Yes, and he has given me all the information I need. Now there is no reason to keep him."

Evelyn had picked up a piece of raspberry pastry as her mother spoke but the mention of sending Francis away made her squeeze the baked good between her fingers. "Mother, I find it insulting that you think I cannot own a male without falling for him."

There was another shrug from her mother. "I'm sorry, my dear. I shouldn't have thought so poorly of you—"

Halfway through her mother's hasty apology, Evelyn heard a footstep from the dining hall door and turned to see Francis standing a few feet away. The look on his face made it clear he had been listening but she didn't know the extent of what he'd heard or how he felt about it. Had he heard her call slaves filthy?

He looked much better than he had the last time they saw each other. His gaunt cheeks were filled out and his skin was regaining its natural color. His arms also looked more capable of holding a sword. He had been strong before but was so malnourished he looked ready to collapse every night.

His eyes remained the same, though. Still friendly and hopeful but sad and disappointed whenever directed toward her.

He had been changed into yet another uniform—one that befit his future station as a bodyguard. The fabric was a light blue—only a little darker than the sky—and his buttons were a mix of copper and silver. His boots were black and metal tipped, better than anything he had worn in the mines, and the gloves were white, a staple in the Payne household. His dark hair had also been styled with a gel to frame his face better. He could not be considered handsome by any standard, but it was enough to catch *her* eye.

When their eyes met, he gave a polite bow and stood at attention by the wall, already mastering the stance the rest of the maids used. It took everything in Evelyn to turn away and hide her joy at seeing him again. She had started to worry he was being mistreated or shipped off without her permission.

"Just bear my warnings in mind," her mother repeated as she dropped her fork and rose to exit. "And if *you* aren't willing to listen, at least the men are required to."

"Mother!" Evelyn was ready to give the woman a lecture of her own, but the woman was out the door before the young lady could even think of a retort.

Now Evelyn was alone with Francis and etiquette demanded he not speak until she addressed him.

"I was starting to think my mother returned you to the mines," she admitted, turning in her chair to face him with a practiced smile.

He shook his head and relaxed his stance. "She said I could serve as your protector for now, as well as a spy in her household in case one of your servants turns against you."

"That sounds like her." Evelyn shook her head. "Always paranoid of men stabbing her in the back."

"Have you heard any news from John?" Francis asked, his faster speech making it obvious he'd wanted to ask this all week.

"I assume things are going well," she said. "There hasn't been any word of the queen acting brash or violent in my social circles, which is a rarity."

"Or perhaps she is taking out her anger on him instead of your friends." Francis's eyes darkened and her smiled vanished. She felt bad for worrying him.

"He'll be fine. I ensured his entrance was public so if he disappears now, people will ask questions. A queen's concubine won't be as easily forgotten as a noblewoman's." John hadn't been announced as a concubine yet, but it would likely happen in the next council meeting. Even those as lowly as royal concubines still had to set an example for the people.

"He was bound to be bought eventually," Francis muttered, easing her conscience slightly. "If the queen didn't take him, one of the guards would have."

"Most likely." Time would tell which of the two evils would be greater. Tired of feeling guilty, she changed the subject. "When will your training be complete?"

"In a few months," he said. "But I've been given permission to escort you whenever you leave the mansion."

"Good." She nodded, pleased. "Once your training is complete, even if I die, you can still serve under my mother." He would never have to return to the mines again.

"You don't trust me to protect you?"

"No more than I would any other guard. Besides, I brought you here for your knowledge, not your muscle." And she needed his moral support too, though she couldn't admit that to him or anyone else.

"I have already told your mother everything I know."

"And how did that go?"

"She had a servant scribe it, then sent me away to be cleaned. I haven't spoken to her since my arrival."

"And she didn't ask about anything else?" Particularly about what they just discussed: the dangers of marrying slaves.

"She gave me a lecture on concubines and how my station is too low to become one of yours."

So she *had* mentioned it. What an embarrassing misunderstanding he'd been brought into.

"But she said she might tolerate me as a concubine because I'm the first man you have paid attention to," he finished.

Her heart leapt—she wasn't sure if it was from excitement or horror—and she forced a laugh. "This is the first time she's misread a situation," she told him, hoping he would believe her. She could already feel the blush creeping up her neck.

"Misread?"

"Of course! Why would I..." Her voice trailed off as she saw the look on his face. His eyes were wide and the cheerful expression that had started to emerge vanished. "Francis, you didn't think I brought you here for *that* kind of thing, did you?"

There was a long pause as he drew his attention to the ceiling, thinking it over. "I assumed my 'knowledge' as you called it was not extensive enough to take me out of the mines, but I have no other skills to offer. Your lack of concubines and suitors led me to believe you needed someone to father an heir."

Why did everyone assume she was so eager to give birth? She had yet to reach twenty-one years of age. The Payne family had several distant cousins. If she died, there were others to inherit the family wealth.

"I apologize for the misunderstanding," he said, overly formal again. This servant tone was beginning to sound like a defense mechanism. He only acted formal with her during intense topics of conversation now. "I am perfectly happy to serve as your bodyguard."

"Good, because that's all I had planned for you." She turned away, her cheeks painfully hot. She had not summoned Francis with those intentions. The thought had crossed her mind a few times, but she had brushed it away as the remnants of an immature teenage mentality.

"As long as you don't send me away," he told her with a smile, making her feel even worse. Had she led him on and gotten his hopes up without realizing?

She shook her head. She shouldn't care how he felt about it. A man's only priority was to obey his mistress without question, which is exactly what he was doing. She should follow his lead.

"Does your duty as a bodyguard begin today?" she asked, rising from the table so quickly he jumped in surprise.

"Yes, my lady. That's why I'm here."

"Then you must know that entails following me everywhere." She led him down the long hallway, moving past a few maids and pretending they weren't there. Her position above all the servants, including Francis, had to be clear. "I'll be showing you to my room now."

There was a moment of hesitation on his face, likely recalling what she told him a week ago about sleeping next to her bed, but he followed along as commanded.

Her bedroom felt far too big for one person now. It was nearly the size of the entire barracks in the mines. Most of the bedding and carpets were a deep red and purple, giving the room a gloomy atmosphere, but there were gold curtains and yellow flowers to brighten up the space. She knew some of the servants had heard her mention how similar this room was to the dark mines and had tried to change it for her while she was out working.

The very same maids she had snubbed a few minutes ago had tried so hard to help her feel better…

She stopped in the doorway, pressing two fingers against her forehead in frustration. Having Francis with her always reminded her of how cruel she was toward the people around her, even if it was her duty to do so. Maybe she shouldn't keep him around after all.

No, the thought of that made her unbearably lonely.

As she stepped inside the room, she started removing the outer layers of her suit. She was so used to having female servants attend her that one of her shoulders was bare before she recalled Francis was standing right behind her. By the time she snapped her head toward him, he was already pointedly turning his face to the window.

"Just move over there," she muttered, self-conscious.

"As you wish, my lady." He did as commanded, but his voice held a sarcastic tone and when she looked at him, she could see his lips upturned in amusement as he walked away. She should be upset that he found her embarrassment so funny but instead, it felt comfortable, and her heartbeat returned to normal.

"I have one more order," she told him as she finished changing and prepared to remove her makeup.

"Yes, my lady?"

"...Don't be too formal when we're alone. It makes me uncomfortable."

"Understood." He started pacing the room as she doused her face in cool water from the covered bowl the servants had left on her dresser. "I do have one question, then."

"What is it?" she asked.

"Where do I sleep during the night?" He jokingly pointed a finger at the bed and received the expected eye roll in response.

"Unless you request a cot, you'll be on the floor. You prefer that anyway, right? You always complained about my bed being too soft in the mines."

"You know me too well." He smiled and took a seat on the windowsill, keeping an eye on the door as she finished her washing.

When she went to bed that night and heard him lie down a few feet away, resting on a blanket above the hard wood floor, she felt more comfortable than she had in years. Her fear of the dark, something she never revealed to her mother, vanished as his slowed breathing reminded her he was nearby.

She would never send him away, regardless of her mother's commands or the guilt he unintentionally made her feel. She enjoyed having him around. The world felt dull without him.

CHAPTER SIXTEEN

As Evelyn had hoped, less than a week later her mother informed her she had been invited to the council's biweekly meeting. The pleasure was evident on her mother's face as they rode the carriage toward the castle.

Francis and two other bodyguards were riding atop the transport alongside the driver. Her mother didn't comment on Francis's presence. She was too impressed by the queen's invitation to care about a mere man. In less than two weeks, Evelyn had managed to impress Ivy, something most people took years to achieve. This was something to relish.

"Be wary of what you say," the older woman warned as Evelyn fiddled with the ends of her purple sleeves. She wore the family colors today, as was customary during council meetings, and the thicker fabrics of her dress were adorned with diamonds and white empyrean stones. The dress colors helped the queen know who was from which family. If there were familial alliances in the council, the colors would make it obvious and harder to hide.

"I managed to impress her more in a few weeks than you have in years," Evelyn reminded her with a teasing smile. "I think you can trust me to handle myself."

"I'm aware." Her mother smiled back, softening. They'd always had a tug-of-war growing up, with her mother trying to raise Evelyn well while also being a responsible mother. It was rare to hear praise, so receiving such a compliment made her forget her mother's sternness for a moment.

The castle looked like a new building without the streamers and pretty dresses from the party two weeks ago. The entrance hall looked empty now, with only a few armored guards standing against the walls, and the only color inside the black building came from the empyrean stones on the ceiling. The red, white, green, and yellow stones formed artistic portraits of the previous queens. There were only five and Ivy's mother was not among them.

As Evelyn followed her mother inside the building, moving alongside other entering ambassadors and councilors, she paused to look up at the blackened statue of queen Ivy guarding the front door. It was made entirely of black and white empyrean stones and must have cost a fortune. The black was used for her dress and hair, and the white for her pale face and arms.

Evelyn stopped beside the statue for a moment, listening for the illusive voice said to emit from the empyrean stone, but she heard nothing. She leaned her ear toward it, listening for anything, then glanced at Francis. After he saw what he was doing, he leaned toward the statue too, curious what she was listening for.

He wasn't allowed to know about the empyrean stones—not even *she* was supposed to know what they did—so she said nothing and followed her mother up the stairs toward the throne room.

Like the entry hall, the throne room felt immensely empty as well. This one was better lit, with tall windows on every wall except the entering one, and the light reflected off the golden walls and floor, but the only thing inside was the tall, black throne at the end of the room and the long table leading toward it. There were matching black chairs lining the table with gold cushions on the seats, but it felt too clean and lifeless.

"The throne room used to be filled with pinks and reds," her mother had told her when describing the former queen's decorations. "Her mother used to hold less than savory parties in there. When she died, Ivy forbade the use of colors unless they had a purpose. I think they overwhelm her, like her mother did."

Evelyn had always been glad she never met the former queen, since her mother described her as a hassle at her best and dangerous at her worst, but the stifling state of the current castle didn't feel like an improvement.

"Take a seat," her mother hissed as Evelyn continued staring at the room. She was quick to obey, coming to rest beside her mother near the front of the table.

Ivy herself was seated on her throne a few feet away, wearing her typical feminine black attire and studying each council member with slanted eyes. John was seated on a cushion by her feet. He wore black, as she did, and it made his pale skin and light hair stand out. His blue eyes were empty as always and only brightened slightly when he saw Francis.

Evelyn wished she could let Francis and John greet each other. The concubine needed at least one kind word in this horrid place. Unfortunately, Francis couldn't leave his position behind her chair, just like the ten other bodyguards and corresponding councilors.

The meeting proceeded immediately but didn't interest Evelyn. She was still too young to comment and none of the topics felt relevant anyway.

The ambassadors from Antalius to the west—short women with white hair, pupil-less white eyes, and tan skin from their outdoor lifestyle—were discussing outlawing slavery again to no one's surprise. Antalius was a country of forest-dwelling farmers who rarely traded but were formidable enough in combat to grant them a seat on the Clostrum council. Their opinions were always ignored and they were only tolerated because if Clostrum was invaded, Antalius would defend them, and if Clostrum fell to Dalius, Antalius would as well.

Next, the topic of Dalius dominated the conversation. The eastern neighbor across the sea was increasing their military numbers again, which also wasn't a surprise. They had always coveted Clostrum's empyrean stones and if they were finally powerful enough to invade, they would. Unfortunately, the dark-skinned ambassador from Dalius didn't offer much information when prodded, even when the queen asked questions directly, so the discussion ended quicker than everyone would have liked. If these were dire times, the queen would have raged at the ambassador for being vague, but as long as Evelyn's family continued arming Clostrum's armies with empyrean weapons, the queen didn't need to fear an invasion. Not yet at least.

Once the room was stuffy with tension and the queen started tapping her nails on her throne's arm rest, they discussed some barbarian pirates from the northern sea being captured and executed. Then the priestess at the table mentioned erecting another shrine to the empyrean gods.

Nothing new was brought up. There was no mention of the black empyrean stone voices or the queen's new concubine. It was clear Ivy wasn't hiding him, but no one had asked about her intentions yet.

Evelyn almost wished she hadn't come. She was beginning to think her presence had zero purpose until the queen commanded everyone leave the room except her.

"I wish to have a private discussion with my cousin," Ivy said when Evelyn's mother gave her a confused look. Of course, no one questioned the ruler, not even her mother, but Evelyn felt a chill as every woman exited the room with hushed conversation and questions amongst each other. She bristled as her mother forced Francis to exit too, abandoning her to deal with the queen alone.

Only after the door closed and it was just Evelyn, the queen resting her cheek on her fist, and John staring at the wall, Ivy finally spoke.

"I plan to make John my prince," Ivy stated.

"That's good news," Evelyn lied, shocked this was how Ivy wanted to start the conversation. The queen and John had barely been together a month. "But it will cause quite a stir in the capital."

"I am aware." Ivy said. "The council won't approve of royalty marrying a slave, especially after my mother had so many."

"I agree." She was stating the obvious.

"I'm planning to announce my intentions in the next meeting. I don't care what any of them think but I don't want to deal with their nagging," Ivy continued. "So I require your help."

Evelyn noticed John jerk upright and wondered what he thought of this…not that she cared, of course.

"Evelyn." Ivy's voice was sharp, no doubt assuming she wasn't listening. "I want you to defend me when I make this announcement so they don't believe I'm intentionally going against their wishes. Again, I don't care what they think of me, but I don't want to risk someone trying to assassinate John. Make it clear that if someone lays their hands on him, I will have them and their extended family publicly executed."

"I don't think anyone will try to kill him," Evelyn began cautiously. The glare she received made her regret countering the woman.

"I thought you wanted us to be friends," Ivy mimicked her earlier words with a sneer.

"I do. I am simply ensuring we go about this cautiously. I *am* pleased you are so happy with him." She was honestly surprised he had left such a good impression. Part of her had assumed he would lash out or try to kill the queen the first chance he got.

The woman leaned back in her seat and ran a hand through her raven black hair, the show of anxiety so rare that Evelyn wondered if it was an act of some kind. "Now there is the matter of...conceiving an heir."

That must be the cause of her worries. John couldn't produce a future queen, not after what happened to him in the mines. Evelyn was surprised the queen hadn't already thrown him away after she discovered his condition.

Should she hide the fact she knew he couldn't father children? The queen might become angry if she found out Evelyn intentionally gave her an infertile man.

"I need an heir but don't wish to have a second husband. It's a practice I have always detested." Likely from being raised around her scandalous mother. "I want you, and perhaps your mother, to find me a suitable heir—a baby that will look similar enough to me or John that no one will suspect it isn't ours. This must be kept a secret from everyone in the capital, even your servants."

"I understand." She couldn't help feeling a hint of respect for the queen staying loyal to one man. John didn't look as touched by this— he was staring at the ceiling again—but he would be grateful for it in the long run. Having to compete against other husbands was mentally exhausting, especially if the wife was the type to dispose of those she didn't like. Her own fathers had clearly become taxed by it.

"I will inform my mother and no one else." The Payne family had thousands of soldiers and researchers under their care. Evelyn was sure at least one of them would mother a bastard they didn't want.

Plus, an illegitimate child would serve as excellent blackmail against the queen.

"No. Keep it to yourself for now. The less people know about this, the better."

Evelyn hesitated, not sure if she could carry out such an important task on her own. Her mother would want to know about this.

Ivy studied her. "You don't think you're capable?"

This was a test, to see if Evelyn was trustworthy and dependable enough to handle more responsibility in the future. Acquiring an heir was child's play compared to running the numerous businesses under her mother's care. "No. I can do this. How soon do you want the child?"

"After the marriage, obviously." Ivy frowned. "Perhaps after a year has passed so the timeline makes sense. I don't want the people to believe I was forced into marriage due to an unexpected pregnancy."

"Of course." Evelyn bowed.

"I trust you the most in this council," Ivy admitted quietly, her honesty catching Evelyn off guard. "There are few people my age and so many have proved irresponsible."

"I am here to serve, my queen."

Ivy looked desperate to trust Evelyn. It must be hard to have so few allies, especially after Ivy witnessed so many councilors take advantage of her mother. "Thank you."

Evelyn knew this was the right time to leave but as she moved away, she caught a glimpse of John's face. He was glaring at her, clearly unhappy with the situation. Evelyn had made it clear during the party, by ignoring his silent plea for help, that she was just like every other woman in his life. She didn't care about his feelings. The queen's opinion was her priority. She was sure he wouldn't glare like that if the queen was treating him right. She must be hurting him behind closed doors.

Another pang of guilt hit her as she exited the throne room and locked eyes with Francis, who was waiting in the hall. She would have to lie to him tonight, assuring him John was happy and safe inside the palace.

Perhaps it would become true in the future. Raising a child could distract John from his misery—though with his personality, it might make things worse.

CHAPTER SEVENTEEN

Francis had gotten used to the blanket and pillow under his head. Sometimes the unfamiliar softness and scratchiness agitated him, but the sound of Evelyn's soft breathing always lulled him to sleep regardless. Knowing she was so close at night used to be a distraction, but it quickly turned into a comfort.

He expected tonight to go as any other but when he heard something hitting the wall right next to his head, he sat up and reached for the knife under his pillow. It was his job to protect Evelyn, even if the fear of death screamed at him.

His bare feet made no sound as he pressed his body against the wall and listened. When the noise stopped, he moved toward the window to see what had caused it.

To his surprise, there was someone atop the blossoming tree outside the window, looking down at him. It was a man, draped in a black cloak and hood, but the face was visible in the moonlight.

It was John.

Eyes wide, Francis opened the window. "Why are you not at the castle?" he hissed, glancing at Evelyn's sleeping body to make sure she hadn't moved. "What are you doing here?"

John smirked, that same evil grin he always wore when doing something he shouldn't, and pushed the window open fully. "The castle is easy to escape. There are unused tunnels beneath it that lead into the streets. They're in such poor condition that not even the castle guards use them."

"Isn't the queen worried someone will sneak into her castle through them?"

The young man shrugged. "There are enough soldiers stationed inside the building so they don't care about the exterior."

"Won't the queen notice your absence?"

"When she has trouble sleeping, she takes medicine that makes her impossible to wake." He motioned for Francis to join him outside. "I'm here to help you escape."

"Escape?" Francis frowned.

John had looked excited a moment ago, like a blissful child, but he returned to his familiar dark glare when he didn't get the reaction he expected. "We're finally free to leave, just like we talked about when we were young. I stole enough gold to keep us fed for two months. We can avoid the main road patrols and by the time the queen sends a search party, we'll have reached Antalius's borders."

Francis glanced at Evelyn again. "We could do some good here, John," he ventured. "There are thousands of slaves in this city. We could use those resources to help them escape."

"If they want to leave, they can do it on their own. We need to worry about ourselves. If we don't leave in another week, the queen will announce my engagement and everyone in this city will know my face."

"Marriage? I haven't heard anything about that." Evelyn had promised him John was being treated well as a concubine. Marriage was a much bigger deal and might cause an uproar.

John's frown deepened. "It doesn't matter. Regardless, we need to leave. We can hide in Antalius and live freely forever. You can build a cottage like you always dreamed of and father children."

While that was Francis's dream growing up, he had always imagined doing so with a woman he loved. There was no point building a home if he had no one to share it with.

And right now, the woman he dreamed of marrying was sleeping behind him.

John noticed his hesitation and hissed under his breath. "You really won't come with me?"

"I'm sorry, John. I couldn't live with myself if I abandoned everything here. There are several slaves working in the stables across the street who want to leave. I've passed a few men in your castle who do as well. We could help them. Just look at your clothes. Your shoes could feed a man for a month." He pointed at the silver buttons and gold-trimmed laces.

The concubine's nose scrunched up, though he did pause to study his boots and their golden threads. He knew Francis was right. "How many people must we save before your conscience allows you to leave?" he groaned in frustration.

Francis knew he could never put a number on that. Besides, helping people wasn't the only reason he wanted to stay. "Let's just focus on the ones I mentioned for now. Then we can decide later."

"Fine." John turned away, ready to leap off the windowsill into the bushes below, but Francis stopped him.

"Does the queen treat you well?" he whispered, hoping Evelyn hadn't lied to him.

To answer, John lowered the hood so Francis could see a fresh, red bruise on the side of his face. "She threw a vase at me this morning," he said. "If I so much as look at another woman, she rages."

Seeing the wound almost made Francis reconsider his decision. "If you leave on your own, I won't hold it against you."

The concubine sighed. "There would be no point in going alone. I can tolerate the beatings…for a while. I'm more afraid of my own temper than her weak punches."

"Do you fear hurting her?" Francis felt a spark of hope that perhaps John might come to care about his mistress, as Francis did for Evelyn. Perhaps she had some redeeming qualities and potential to become a better person, as Evelyn did. It wasn't the best way to think of one's abuser but it was preferable to nothing.

John bit the insides of his cheeks, making the veins stick out on his neck, then shook his head. "I only fear the consequences of harming her."

Clearly tiring of the conversation, John jumped from the tree and disappeared into the shadows.

After he was gone, Francis closed the window and began forming plans to secure money and safe passage for any men who wished to escape. He had to ensure it couldn't be traced back to him and especially to Evelyn, so he might need to coordinate with John to free slaves from other sections in the city.

The thought of creating an entire system of escape routes thrilled him. For the first time in his life, he could have an impact on this world.

But if he was discovered, Evelyn would take the fall for it, since she vouched for him.

He would have to be exceedingly careful. She was one of the few women he knew who had the potential to make real positive change in this country. He had to protect her, even if it meant sacrificing his own happiness, and he couldn't help her change if he ran away.

Sleep felt elusive as he returned to his spot on the floor, but her presence helped him drift off again and he dreamed of a wood cottage surrounded by purple flowers and laughing children.

CHAPTER EIGHTEEN

By the time the next council meeting began two weeks later, Evelyn's confidence had risen.

Her mother had fully implemented all of Evelyn's suggestions in the mines and this morning they received reports that more empyrean stones had been excavated this month than in the last year combined. "It appears I was wrong to discourage your new ideas," her mother had said, filling Evelyn with ecstasy.

Now Evelyn was ready to tell the entire council—a group of women who had essentially controlled the kingdom for nearly ten years—that she believed a slave should become a prince. When she was writing the speech in secret, she almost felt like she was trying to convince herself as well. If their queen could marry a slave, why couldn't *she*?

Evelyn had planned to bring up the marriage gradually when the ladies' discussion dragged, but before she could even sit at the table with the others, the queen gave her announcement.

"I plan to marry John," the young woman said, not flinching at the women's gasps. "My mother was married at twenty-three so I shall as well."

Evelyn noticed her mother's jaw clench and knew she was itching to respond. Other women had already risen from their chairs and were explaining why it was a bad idea.

"Your children should have noble blood."

"The prince represents the queen's rule. If he is a man with no etiquette, the people will be insulted."

"What if we allow him to remain a concubine, rather than become a prince? There is no need to put him on such a high pedestal."

Ivy gave the speaker of the last suggestion a warning look. "I refuse to become like my mother. Concubines are for people who give in to their animalistic urges. I need only one partner."

"*My* queen would never allow herself to stoop this low," the ambassador of Dalius said, pointing at dead-eyed John.

Evelyn glanced at Francis, trying to read his thoughts. He looked sorry for his friend.

"The child will bear my blood and that's all that matters." Her jaw twitching, the queen tapped her finger on the empyrean gun resting on her arm rest. It was filled with red empyrean bullets that could be launched across the entire room and burn the skin of any woman here. Their noble blood wouldn't protect them from fire.

"The queen of Dalius will be insulted if you refuse to marry one of her sons," the Dalius ambassador warned.

Evelyn could tell the queen was struggling to find a comeback so, gulping, Evelyn stood from her chair as well, drawing the eyes of everyone in the room.

"The public does not need to know the man's heritage," she said, her script forgotten. "The people know very little of his background. If we claim he is part of a noble family, they will believe it."

There were a few nods but also scowls and harsh whispers.

"The Rygiel family is a fine line to adopt him into. No one remains alive to protest the lie." The Rygiels were wealthy merchants who hired an assassin to kill the current queen and had been executed for it. "Make him wear noble clothes, train him in etiquette, and he will be forgotten within a month." He would become another snooty nobleman raised with a silver spoon in his mouth. They blended into the woodwork like every other male.

Evelyn noted a slight upturn in the queen's mouth. Either Ivy approved or she viewed Evelyn as a weak-minded pawn.

"Will this suffice?" Ivy looked each woman in the face, staring them down until they consented. The meeting adjourned ten minutes later without any productive discussions and when the women dispersed to leave Evelyn alone with the queen like last time, Evelyn's mother paused to squeeze her shoulder painfully.

"I hope you are doing this to gain the queen's favor," her mother whispered in her ear, keeping a firm grip as she leaned down. "And for no other reason."

Her words made Evelyn increasingly aware of Francis's presence behind her.

Blinking slowly, she nodded at her mother and smiled. "Of course, Mother."

Lady Payne nodded, then scowled at Francis until he followed her out of the room. This time, John exited too, and she saw him join Francis before the door closed behind them.

"Well done, Evelyn." Ivy grinned at her like a cat and pointed at the seat closest to her. "You will be sitting here from now on, next to me." Evelyn did so, then waited for the queen to continue. "I assume this means you will help me explain to the Dalius queen why I am choosing a slave over her sons."

"I can…if I know *why* you chose John over them."

Evelyn saw the queen's normally white face turn a light shade of pink and smiled smugly. The cold-hearted queen truly had fallen.

"It's no concern of yours." Ivy fiddled with the black empyrean necklace around her throat and Evelyn decided now was the best time to bring up the real question she had.

"Tell me what the empyrean stones say," she said, knowing the queen would welcome the diversion. "If I am to offer counsel, I need to know if these voices offer any useful insights into the future."

Ivy's fiddling hands stopped and rested on her lap. "They only warn me of the present—the politics in Dalius and Antalius."

So, it was true. They *could* speak.

"And they warn of spies in our midst," she added, then leaned back in her chair. "Among other things," she added dismissively, making Evelyn more interested but afraid to pry.

"What do the voices sound like?"

"A woman."

"Do you recognize the voice?"

"No." Ivy's answers made it clear Evelyn was venturing into unwelcome territory, so she stopped.

"On the subject of Antalius," she ventured, "and their laws against slavery, I was wondering if we might take these propositions into serious consideration." Abolishing slavery was unheard of for now but it wouldn't hurt to place the idea in Ivy's head.

The queen scoffed. "The majority of Antalius is too poor and sparsely populated to control their own men. They couldn't own slaves if they tried so their opinion hardly matters."

"I only ask because I want to prevent another rebellion."

"Preventing rebellion in the mines is *your* job, not mine," Ivy reminded her.

"Yes, but if the men are treated fairly, they have no reason to rebel in the first place."

"So, you're implying we free our men because they *might* rebel? If that is your reasoning, it's all the safer to keep them locked up. Men are violent, Evelyn. You of all people should know that after living in the mines."

"Well…" She wasn't so sure anymore.

"Look at our history. Until the gods gave sole control of the empyrean stones to us, women were the slaves. We treat the males far better than they treated us hundreds of years ago. You've read the books."

She was right. Evelyn knew every known detail regarding the wars that ravaged Clostrum a century ago and the thousands of deaths that had occurred. The mines used to be cities, until warring men turned them into tombs. Most of the empyrean stones they found now were the remains of a lost society that doomed itself.

"Besides," Ivy added. "The gods have instructed me to continue searching the land for more stones." She hesitated. "They also say there is a great weapon hidden beneath the land that can grant unlimited power to whoever wields it."

"Does my mother know of this?"

"Partially. It's why I instructed her to increase the workload in the mines. However, I don't trust her enough to mention the weapon. You, on the other hand…"

"I'm honored." Such a weapon didn't seem unheard of. Many of the empyrean stones they found had already been welded into guns and spears, though the rocks were no bigger than one's hand and had no power beyond their own element.

"Perhaps if we find this weapon, we will no longer need the slaves," Ivy concluded. "But until then, you will continue in your mother's footsteps."

Francis would be disappointed but Evelyn knew the queen was right. If they found something that made slaves obsolete, his dream would come true.

As Evelyn exited the throne room, Ivy shouted one more word of thanks.

"Tell your mother to bring her finest tailors to the castle," Ivy added. "If they make John look like a prince, perhaps the people will view him as such, just as you said."

Just as she said.

Would people be so easily swayed by his appearance?

As she stepped out and saw Francis waiting outside the door for her, a stone-faced John by his side, she wondered if the same could be said for her mother. If Francis looked like a nobleman instead of a slave, would her mother accept him?

CHAPTER NINETEEN

Francis paid more attention during the council meeting than some of the women seated at the table. He always listened for each name, memorizing who was in attendance and their role. Knowing who owned which slaves and where they lived might prove useful for future escape attempts.

His attention would often waver when looking at Evelyn, though. She sometimes became so focused on the meeting that she'd end up staring at a single person for too long. There were other times he'd catch her scribbling flowers on the sides of her book instead. He found both extremes exceedingly cute and always smiled unintentionally until she caught him staring.

He had always found Evelyn pretty while they worked together in the mines. Even without makeup and empyrean jewelry, she still had a charming face and adorable expressions. After working together for months, he had finally become immune to her looks and his heart wouldn't race as much, but then she started wearing makeup, accentuating what was already beautiful and making him nervous around her all over again.

While Francis enjoyed staring at his mistress, he knew doing so attracted the attention of Lady Payne, who would always glower whenever she caught him staring too long at her daughter.

Francis hadn't mentioned it to Evelyn, but her mother often lectured him to stay as far away from Evelyn as possible. She must have noticed his feelings during their first meeting and didn't want him taking advantage of her daughter. He understood her concern, as he'd known men in the mines who manipulated the departing guards into taking them with them, but he'd always assured the older woman he had no intention of using her daughter.

It was only partially true, but he was a good liar…most of the time.

Once the meeting was over and he was forced to exit the throne room with everyone else, he stationed himself next to the door and waited patiently for Evelyn to finish her private discussion with the queen.

"I will have the carriage sent back to pick up my daughter," Lady Payne informed Francis as she prepared to leave. She raised her chin at him and didn't stop glaring until he bowed low to the ground. "See to it she makes it home safely," she added, her words sharp to imply she was more worried about *him* hurting her than anyone else.

"I understand, my lady." He bowed again and kept his eyes forward until the mother was gone.

Once the hallway was empty aside from him, John, and two tall men standing guard on the stairs, Francis finally relaxed and turned to his friend.

John was dressed in a black suit with a long trail and golden collar. His hair was growing and tied up now, giving him a regal look. If Francis didn't know him personally, he might have assumed John was noble born. The only thing that gave away his true upbringing was how easily John sneered at everyone he passed.

"She has you on a leash," John hissed, nodding at the throne room's door.

They both knew what he meant. Francis had no reason to stay in this capital for a mere noblewoman when freedom was so close at hand, especially one with a mother who looked ready to murder him.

"Evelyn is not like her mother," Francis whispered, making John scoff.

"They all are. You just can't see it yet."

Francis forgave his friend for being so jaded. John had never met a woman who truly treated him kindly. Francis hoped Evelyn would prove John wrong with time, but it might take years for the changes to occur.

His mistress's discussion with the queen was muffled through the door but he could make out a few words about slavery. John clearly heard them too, but he didn't comment. Evelyn's actions gave Francis a spark of hope, though, that both Evelyn and John still had the potential to become the good people Francis knew they could be.

Francis had planned to say goodbye to John before escorting Evelyn out when her discussion with the queen ended, but his mistress marched out of the throne room so quickly that he had to hurry to keep up, unable to even wave to John as they descended the stairwell to the castle door.

The Payne family guards bowed to Evelyn as she passed through the castle gates and the carriage had also been prepared, as Evelyn's mother said it would, but it was ignored as Evelyn headed right into the street.

Not a word was exchanged but Francis could tell from his mistress's hurried steps and clenched fists that she was either angry or determined to get somewhere quickly. He waited until the guards following them had fallen back before questioning her in a low voice.

"Did something happen during the meeting, my lady?" He nearly forgot to add the title but caught himself at the last second.

"No. Nothing happened."

She was headed for the shopping district, a trio of long streets near the castle gates. The buildings were formed from deep red bricks and purple wood with white empyrean signs hanging from their windows. Shopkeepers waited outside the glass windows to welcome customers into their abode and send away any who didn't look wealthy enough, shouting to passing patrons about the fine garments or spices they offered. However, the more expensive the wares, the quieter the keepers. They knew if a woman had money, she needed no prodding or advertisements. This held true for Evelyn. The light blue dress covered in white empyrean and pearls commanded attention as she passed through the crowd with her row of armed soldiers at her heels.

Seeing everyone shoot shy glances at his lady made Francis remember just how different she was from him.

Evelyn's determined steps only slowed once she reached a clothing boutique and she took a moment to peer inside the windows. Francis did the same and was surprised to see male suits of brown and blue hanging from doll's bodies inside. He had never seen male clothing sold before. Most were hand sewn or inherited from their predecessors. A common man needed no more than two outfits to survive—one for work and another for special occasions—and slaves had only the former. Women were the ones who required variety.

"Are we purchasing a wedding gift for Jo—for the queen's fiancé?" he ventured as she entered, much to the excitement of the two women working inside. The ladies were quick to greet Evelyn by name and welcome her in, telling a third woman in the back to grab some measuring strips.

"Have him fitted," Evelyn commanded, pointing at Francis with a raised chin. "And prepare ten outfits of varying colors."

The girls looked him over. "And what is his station?" the eldest of the two employees asked as the third ran in with a sewing kit, measuring tapes, and fabrics hanging from her arms.

"He is a nobleman," Evelyn lied. "And he requires a suit befitting his station."

The seamstresses nodded, juggling their tools in a panic and whispering numbers to each other as they studied Francis's figure. After a few minutes of measuring strips being held across his shoulders and colored papers dangled next to his hair, the women sat the pair down in a separate room with a curtain for privacy and began assembling the clothes for the fitting. Evelyn's guards remained outside the building, preventing others from entering. The shop wouldn't need any more customers today. Evelyn Payne would spend more in a day than most could in a month.

"My lady," Francis whispered once they were alone. The only sound beyond the private room's curtain was the muffled excitement of the seamstresses. "Why are you doing this?"

She avoided eye contact. "I realized how strange it looked to have a servant by my side all the time. You'll fit in more if you're dressed like a noble."

That didn't make any sense. Plenty of nobles and even royalty had stewards by their side. *They* never wore expensive clothes, at least none that suited a higher station.

"Are you ashamed to be seen with me?" he ventured, relieved by the shocked expression on her face. He recalled how insecure she looked when she asked him the same question in the mines, in regards to summoning him to her room. Did his face mirror how hers looked back then?

"Of course not," she hissed, gripping the top of her skirt with white fists.

"I don't think it wise for me to dress as a noble when I am not one."

"It's not illegal."

"But it is frowned upon. Would your mother approve?"

"My mother spends her days in business meetings with her friends. She doesn't remember you or any other slave in our household."

He knew that was wrong. Perhaps she hadn't noticed how much his mother watched him, waiting for him to slip up.

"Besides," she continued, "The queen isn't embarrassed to be seen with John, so why should I be with you?"

He couldn't ignore the parallel, but Ivy and John were lovers. He and Evelyn were not. Did she…want them to be?

He wanted to hope she was doing this because she planned to eventually make him her partner. Perhaps she was subconsciously trying to convince herself it was acceptable to pursue a relationship with him.

He wanted to confront her about it, to hear her admit it aloud, but knew if he pushed her too far from her comfort zone, she might send him away. She might even return him to the mines if she realized he had developed an attachment to her.

"It's not your job to ask questions," Evelyn reminded him. "What I do is my own business. Just obey."

"Yes, my lady."

As Francis peered through the curtain, he saw the women walk by holding an expensive white suit with gold threads and red empyrean stone buttons. It took less than a second to calculate how much gold the suit was worth. It was enough to fund twenty slave escapes. Running away was dangerous but if one had the money, people in smaller villages outside the capital were willing to house a fugitive. If what the servants in the Payne mansion told him were true, the common folk outside the city cared less about slavery laws than the nobles of the capital. Most of them couldn't afford a slave so why should they care?

Francis wanted to protect Evelyn, but he also knew a few slaves working in her mansion were looking for an escape and merely needed the funds to purchase food and water for the trip. The buttons on this suit would grant them that opportunity, and he wouldn't even have to steal like John did to help them. The only issue was the buttons' disappearance would be easily discovered.

"I can accept the outfits," he told Evelyn, forcing sincerity into his voice. "But if you truly wish to make me appear noble, jewelry would be more appropriate, my lady." And would be easier to smuggle out without notice.

"Very well. I'll buy both. Will rings suffice?" she asked.

"Yes, my lady."

"Summon them," she commanded. "But I still want at least three suits." As he obeyed, rising from the wooden chair he'd been placed in and informing the women of the changes, he looked back and finally caught a glimpse of Evelyn's face. What he saw filled him with guilt. She was smiling at his back.

He hated taking advantage of her kindness…though she didn't *need* the money.

The next three hours were spent with his arms out as the women pinned and poked him until they had the fabrics just where they wanted them. Evelyn spent the entire time seated in front of him with her legs crossed. She remained stoic at first, but once the first outfit was complete, he caught her grinning at his reflection in the mirror.

As much as he wanted to detest her for living in luxury while men like him died in the mines, he couldn't resist feeling excited by her proud smiles. She was like a child dressing up a doll and when his back was turned and she assumed he couldn't see her, he caught her staring at him in the mirror. She had an expression of longing in her eyes, something he only recognized because it was the same way he looked at her.

"Don't do that," he muttered under his breath. *Don't give me hope.*

When he arrived in the Payne mansion wearing a high-collared blue shirt and silver-buttoned coat, Evelyn's mother gave him a second look when she came to greet her daughter.

The older woman didn't comment on his state, but she looked between him and Evelyn several times, searching for more changes in their relationship. He made sure to stand straight and at attention while keeping his eyes low, appearing as meek as possible. He didn't want her to misread the situation again.

There was nothing between them.

Though he wished there was.

CHAPTER TWENTY

The next time John showed up outside Evelyn's bedroom window in the middle of the night, Francis was ready. He had one of the rings Evelyn bought on his finger and prepared a black cloak to hide his identity.

"There is a young man working in the stables across the street," he told John as they crept through the mansion gardens. "While I was speaking to him last week, I noticed some bruises on his arms. His mistress beats him and when I suggested escape, he said he was ready and willing to leave if we gave him enough money."

"This won't make your own mistress suspicious?" John asked.

"No. The boy's owner is considered a rival of the Payne family, so it's unlikely the families will discuss *one* runaway slave. Besides, the boy is barely ten. He won't draw attention."

Francis saw John's jaw clench at the mention of someone so young being abused. "And he's ready to run by himself? I won't escort him beyond the city."

"He just needs the money," Francis confirmed. "And someone to unlock the door."

John smirked and pulled a strange metal tool from his pocket that Francis didn't recognize. "I stole this from one of the guards. It can unlock any door if used correctly."

Francis didn't like how reckless John was to steal it but knew his friend didn't care. If he was caught, John didn't fear death or torture. He'd experienced it enough to be desensitized.

"While you've been training to guard your mistress, I've been learning how to escape mine. This can open the door, hopefully, unless the castle locks are different from those in the mansions." The future prince's eyes lit up as he showed off the tool. It was rare for him to show any emotion so Francis took this as a good sign. "Let's go."

Sneaking into the mansion was easy since Francis had asked the boy where the guards were stationed and how they patrolled. The slaves slept in the basement and there was a tall female guarding the door leading to it, so Francis and John had to wait near the stairs for the woman to leave, hiding in an empty nearby room until she did so.

"Have you reconsidered my offer to leave?" John asked as they waited, his voice so quiet not even Francis could hear it well.

"No." He kept his head forward and didn't give his friend the satisfaction of a reaction. "We've been over this."

"Look." John pulled back the sleeve of his black outfit and revealed a large bandage wrapped around his wrist.

Francis grimaced. "How did you get that?"

"Ivy broke a bottle and cut my arm with it."

"Why?"

"It's those black stones of hers. She'll go into a private room to talk to them like some lunatic, then when she exits, she accuses me of sneaking out in the night to sell my body."

Francis didn't want to say this but, "*Have* you been doing that?"

"Of course not." The young man hissed in disgust. "I only sneak out to do this." He pointed at the stairs. "She's just insane and never believes me."

"Perhaps she doesn't sleep as soundly as you assumed," Francis suggested, not believing magical stones could be the true cause. "You should be more careful. Maybe I should do this alone."

"No. I've tried waking her and she never moves. She's just a maniac looking for a fight. I'm sure your precious Evelyn will do the same eventually."

"Evelyn's not like that. She has potential to do great things. She needs only the means and motivation."

"That's what women make you think. If she truly wanted to make a change, she would have done it by now. Bear in mind, Ivy acted sweet and kind to me today until she spoke to the stones, then she was ready to kill me. No matter what you do, Francis, they'll turn on you eventually. They're just waiting for an excuse to take their anger out on you." He pulled the sleeve back over his wound and peeked down the hall. "She's leaving her post. Now's our chance. I'll unlock the door, then stand guard while you free the boy."

Francis wanted to console his friend but knew it would only annoy him. To distract himself, he thought about the black empyrean stones John had mentioned. Evelyn had acted suspicious around them, reacting like they could make noise or even speak.

He tried to refocus as the guard walked past. She looked into the room where they hid but they were concealed in the shadows so a second later, she continued on. Once her footsteps were far enough to be muffled, John crept into the now empty hallway and led Francis to the basement, his footsteps so silent Francis knew he'd been practicing.

John was determined to succeed in these escape attempts. It was commendable and the first time he seemed to actually care about something.

The basement of this mansion was more like a dungeon, with cages full of male slaves. Lucky for them, these slaves had pillows and blankets to sleep on, as well as candles, a far greater arrangement than Francis had growing up. Most of the men were asleep, other than a few older ones, and they only stared at the intruders as they entered. Not a sound was made to alert the guards down the hall.

It took less than a minute for Francis to find the boy he had mentioned. He had first encountered the child while training with a sword on the street and the boy had been nearby, mucking the stables. They struck up a conversation to pass the time and the child had seemed sweet but shied away from any woman who walked past. It had reminded Francis of John when he was younger and was the reason he became so determined to save him.

The boy was now sleeping on his blanket in the corner of the room, the walls of his cage offering plenty of room to spread his legs. The child awoke quickly when John started unlocking the door, though, as it wasn't a quiet task.

"Make it quick," John hissed once he had the door open and returned to the stairs. "If the guard comes, I'll shut the door and you'll have to hide."

"Understood. Hello, Erik." Francis smiled at the boy and coaxed him out. "We spoke a few days ago in the stables. Do you remember me?" He kept his voice low but soft so as to not scare the child.

The boy looked at him with narrow eyes, then rubbed them as they adjusted to the light. "I remember you! Are you here to get me out, like we talked about?"

The sheer glee on the child's face melted his heart. "Yes. Come with me and we'll escort you to the edge of the city." He pushed the ring Evelyn had bought him into the boy's hand and led him down the row of cages. As he went, his joy from saving this one boy was lessened as he saw how many others were locked away down here, unable to leave without risking death. How many others wanted to be saved?

John barely acknowledged Erik as they reached the stairs and rushed back to the room they'd hidden in previously. There was a window there. It was easy enough to pry open and climb down without getting noticed by the guards, most of whom were stationed at the front and back doors.

Surprisingly, while they were inside the mansion, Francis hadn't felt like they were in any danger. He had planned this escape for several days, watched the guard patrols from Evelyn's bedroom window, so he'd prepared some lies in case they got caught.

But he still felt like this escape had been easy—too easy.

He could tell John's new lockpicking skills and Francis's own combat training were contributing to their success but as they reached the street and snuck the child away, a strong sense of being watched made Francis's hair rise. It persisted down the dark alleys and roads. Were they being followed? He couldn't see anyone behind them but the dread persisted.

"You did good, boy," John told the child once they finally left the tall mansions and brick streets behind. Now that they were surrounded by the small wooden homes and dirty roads of the capital's poor district, the child could blend in and continue on his own. "Remember to avoid the main roads and if anyone tries to stop you, hit them with this."

Francis gasped as John pulled a knife from his pocket and handed it to the boy. "John, he doesn't need to kill anyone. He just needs to hide. A child doesn't need blood on his hands." His conscience had always told him to avoid killing unless it was absolutely necessary.

"Ignore this man," John said with a dark chuckle. "He isn't realistic." He patted the boy on the head and pointed to the west. "Trade that ring for some better clothes and food once you reach the country. The towns near the capital are wealthy enough to accept such an expensive piece of jewelry."

Francis gulped but didn't counter his friend anymore. Maybe what he said about Francis being unrealistic was true.

The boy looked terrified as Francis hugged him but he was also hopeful for his future, which was all Francis wished to see in a child. It was better than the soulless gaze worn by the young ones toiling underground.

Once the boy was on his way and it was just John and Francis again, they avoided any talk of their living situations or the women in their lives. Doing so only made John irritable and Francis worried, so they instead discussed the new foods they'd tried, the games other slaves played in their free time, and the geography of Clostrum. By the time they returned to the Payne mansion, that eerie sense of being stalked was gone. It only returned when he entered the garden behind the Payne mansion.

This time, the feeling originated from the top of the mansion, its vast windows peering at him like a many-eyed monster of folklore. However, one of the windows was lit by candles despite how late it was. He gulped as he realized it was the office window of Evelyn's mother and her shadow stood in the window, looking down at him.

He'd been caught.

Was she going to kill him for sneaking out at night? Or banish him to the mines?

…Would Evelyn defend him?

The thought of seeing her protect him almost made him wish for Evelyn's mother to dismiss him. It would be interesting to see what excuse Evelyn could come up with to make him stay. It might also confirm her feelings for him.

No. He didn't want to risk it. In the mines, he could do nothing. Here, he could help people.

He had to be more careful in the future to protect his position.

And he couldn't leave Evelyn's side.

He was shaking as he went to sleep by his mistress's bed, already feeling the incoming lashes on his back and maybe even breaking of his legs. He'd never been good at tolerating pain. Too much of it might turn him into John—violent and out for revenge. He feared *that* more than the pain, since it meant hurting the woman sleeping beside him.

CHAPTER TWENTY-ONE

Evelyn was glad she had started dressing Francis up as a nobleman, just as Ivy did with her fiancé. Now when people saw her entering shops or parties with Francis by her side, they didn't look down on him as much or give him orders of their own. Some even mistook him as her lover. The thought of it gave her a juvenile thrill.

Even now as he stood behind her in this tea party, he looked regal in his white and purple suit. It matched the lilac-covered dress she had chosen.

They were currently seated at a round table in a mansion belonging to a former Antalius weapon designer, surrounded by women Evelyn's age. This event was considered a tea and cake party, though some were sampling wine instead. The women around Evelyn's table included herself, the queen, and four other ladies of high stations. Many were young heirs to large businesses or the daughters of Antalius ambassadors.

These types of parties allowed Evelyn to plant roots in high society—something she avoided as a young teenager due to shyness—and it helped her determine what type of difficulties she would face in the future if she tried to abolish slavery. The Antalians had already experienced this since their country had abolished it only a few years ago. They had a significantly smaller population, though, compared to Clostrum and Dalius, so enacting extreme laws seemed easier.

The conversation eventually strayed to the queen's wedding plans, though the other girls at the table seemed far more excited about it than Ivy. Based on the queen's occasional glances at her lover, who was standing a few feet away staring at a wall, she was more interested in the marriage than the ceremony itself. Ivy never struck Evelyn as the type to care about pretty flowers or elaborate decorations. Then again, she rarely cared about anything besides order and obedience. John was the rare exception. It still felt odd that she fell for him so quickly and easily.

"And he's to be your only husband?" one of the Antalius girls asked, her empty eyes crinkling with a smile. "Wasn't your mother well known for having close to thirty?"

Evelyn felt a fearful jolt. This newcomer must not know Ivy well.

"My mother had zero restraint," the queen answered with a tight smile. "She spent a year's worth of taxes meant for the military on a single wedding. It was the reason barbarians were able to invade from the northern isles and massacre two thousand citizens. If it weren't for my orders, they would have killed more."

Evelyn recalled hearing about that. The barbarian attacks began a month before the former queen's sudden death. It was yet another thing that motivated whoever had killed her.

The young woman shifted uncomfortably under the queen's gaze. "I apologize. It was foolish of me to insinuate. I only have one husband myself."

There was an awkward silence, the tension building as the queen stared down this bright young woman in a flowery dress, then Evelyn's mother stepped up to the table and interrupted.

"Girls, I would like to introduce you to the prince who just arrived from Dalius. He's the eighth son of Queen Triana Theron, so please try to leave a good impression on him." She patted Evelyn's shoulder as she said this, squeezing a little too hard to match her pinched smile. It was a clear indicator that this warning was directed at Evelyn specifically.

The young man she was referring to was standing a few feet away, waiting to be introduced. He was of average height but had a strong build, as expected of a Dalius prince. Both male and female Dalians were known for their strength and militant discipline. His skin was dark—a common trait in the east—and his long curly hair was pulled back in a refined ponytail. His face was the most striking thing and made several female eyes focus on him. His nose and jawline were sharp, as were his dark eyes, but he had high cheekbones and full lips to add a softer look.

Even Evelyn had to admit this was one of the most handsome men in her acquaintance. He made even John look plain.

If she were a teenager, Evelyn's heart might have raced at the sight of such a person, but now that she was older and had other priorities, her heart only pounded when Francis got a little too close. The feeling made her feel vulnerable and weak, which she hated, so she was glad her heart didn't respond to this other man as well.

"A pleasure to meet you, my ladies." The prince's words flowed off the tongue in a practiced manner, his sweet smile and deep voice making up for his rehearsed manner. "This is my first time visiting Clostrum so I hope I don't break any etiquette. Do warn me if I've said or done anything out of turn."

He bowed as he spoke and when he stood straight again, he locked eyes with Evelyn. She wondered if it was accidental.

"You may pull up a chair next to my daughter and our lovely queen Ivy," Evelyn's mother said cordially before walking away. Her intention was clear. She wanted Evelyn to suck up to this prince and leave a good impression. Dalius had a lot of military might, more than Clostrum, and if it weren't for all the empyrean stones in Queen Ivy's possession, Dalius might have tried to invade a decade ago.

As the prince came closer, Evelyn heard Francis shift behind her chair and turned to see him bristling.

"So, Lady Evelyn." The prince focused on her as the other ladies chatted amongst themselves. "Your mother's told me a lot about you."

"Oh. Do tell."

"She says you're smart, beautiful, which I can see, and very sweet." He smirked, as though his own words amused him. It was clear he knew how bewitching his looks were, as he completely ignored all the female gazes from nearby tables. "I hear you're to inherit your mother's duties. I take it that means we'll see each other in my home country, as your mother often comes to meet with mine."

"I suppose. I haven't been to Dalius in over a year. Has it changed much?" Was it still as suffocating as before, with its black obsidian homes, constant military presence, and cannons on every wall?

"Not that I know of. I admittedly didn't step outside the castle for months until I came here. My mother's been training me to become a general since it's clear I won't inherit the throne."

"If that's the case, why are you here?"

"To be honest, I've never much liked the thought of commanding an army. I'm embarrassed to admit it, but I've never been comfortable on a battlefield. My brothers are far more skilled in that regard." He scratched his head and gave a nervous laugh, but Evelyn was confident it was fake to make her feel sorry for him. When she glanced at Francis, the look on his face told her he felt the same. "I've always preferred talking to fighting. Meeting with people of every class and country interests me."

"Really? Why is that?" Was this a trap set by her mother to see how she felt about slaves?

"I find when you're at the top of the hierarchy, everyone treats you the same regardless of rank. Everyone's beneath you." He studied her as he spoke. "So, I strive to view everyone as my equals and act accordingly. Don't you feel the same?"

Evelyn shrugged, not liking this man very much. He was clearly prying about her opinions on slaves. "I'm sure your tongue will be a valuable asset in Dalius." Her words prompted giggles from some nearby women but she ignored them. The prince knew what she meant.

She rose from her seat, clearly surprising the prince since their conversation had barely begun. It was rude to end it so quickly, but she didn't like being tested. "I'm afraid this cake is not agreeing with me so I will take my leave. I hope you enjoy your stay."

"I hope to see you again," the prince said, grabbing her hand and kissing it before she could escape. "Your mother hopes we will become great friends."

"How kind of her," she said, gritting her teeth in a pretend smile. "Until then."

She was tempted to grab Francis's hand and drag him behind her so they could escape faster. She had come to this party to discuss slavery with the Antalius nobles. Now that her mother had placed a potential spy beside her, there was no point in staying.

"Where are we going, my lady?" Francis asked.

She didn't answer. Glancing over her shoulder, she saw the prince shifting his attention to the queen, since his first target was clearly not willing to cooperate. Good. The queen would make for an even worse conversation partner. She would see through that man's fake smile too.

When she turned back to Francis, she saw concern in his eyes and for a moment, her heart starting racing. "Which prince did he say he was again?" she asked, covering her pink cheeks with a handkerchief as she attempted to distract him.

"The eighth," he answered quietly.

"So, his name is Antonio," she grumbled. She knew the name of every prince and ambassador in Clostrum, Antalius, and Dalius, though it wasn't by any will of her own. "He looked like a child the last time I saw him. He can't be older than nineteen." Close to her own age.

The hallway they used to exit the mansion was empty. Instead of guards, there were massive pots of flowers and vines growing along the ceiling, as expected of a descendant from Antalius.

"Does this place make you happy?" she asked Francis, recalling the time he asked her about flowers.

"It is beautiful," he said, smiling wistfully at the ivy. "But I prefer flowers in the wild, growing without the walls to hold them back."

His words made her ache to leave this city and all its fake, flowery words concealing dark intentions.

"What do you think of the prince now that you've met him?" Francis asked, catching her off guard. When she looked at him to understand why he had asked, there was a hint of red on the tips of his ears. Could he be jealous?

"I don't know much about him," she skirted around the question. "What do *you* think of him, Francis?"

The slave turned away, building a wall between them. "Men aren't allowed to judge others."

"I don't care about that. I want to hear what you think. You're a better judge of character than most."

"I appreciate your compliments, my lady." He chuckled, his laugh so much nicer than the prince's. "But I also don't know him well enough to form an opinion. All I know is that he came to the mansion yesterday while you were away and visited your mother."

"As I suspected!" she said a little too loudly, her voice echoing in the hall. "I knew she brought him here on purpose to spy on me!"

"Spy on you?"

Evelyn paused, regained her composure, then cleared her throat. "Don't tell anyone I said that. Spy is a strong word."

"You think he's a spy for Dalius?" Francis asked.

"No. I shouldn't have brought it up. I meant he might be a spy for my mother, not Dalius." Accusing anyone of such treachery against Clostrum was too harsh and this conversation was getting too serious for her liking. She shouldn't bring Francis into this. She had only asked what he thought because she wanted to see if he was jealous. Seeing him blush excited her. Instead, they were discussing politics and betrayal. "I'm sure it's nothing. He's just a young man with a pretty face. I doubt he's a threat."

Francis's eye twitched when she called Antonio pretty but Evelyn warned herself to ignore his reaction. Even if he was jealous, she couldn't do anything about it. Her feelings for him couldn't be allowed to grow. He was beneath her, after all, and no woman in the Payne family could marry a slave again.

CHAPTER TWENTY-TWO

The queen's council meeting ended five minutes ago but Evelyn had gone to relieve herself so Francis was left alone in the castle's foyer, awaiting her return.

The meeting had gone well, from his point of view. Evelyn had been more forward in her manner of speaking and he could tell the elder members of the council were beginning to respect her, despite her age and mother's shadow. If this continued and he started suggesting more freedoms regarding the slaves, perhaps she could sway the country's leaders. She hadn't asked for his advice on such things yet, but he always hoped she would.

The castle was silent as he waited for his mistress, so Francis was surprised when he heard a shout from the second floor. It was a female voice. The other councilors had left already so it must be the queen.

He hesitated, curious but afraid. It wasn't his place to interfere. Evelyn might return at any moment too.

But then he heard a cry that was undeniably John's and all fears disappeared. He ran up the stairs and stopped in front of the tall, dark door where the sounds emanated from.

"I haven't done the things you accuse me of," John was saying from inside the room.

"Stop lying to me!"

There was a crash and Francis opened the door a crack to see inside. The interior of the room looked like a dining area with plates and cups set on a table. The queen was standing on the right, a plate in her hand and the remains of a broken one at her feet.

"I know you've been sneaking out at night!" She raised the plate to throw it at John, who was standing on the other side of the room with his hands over his face to defend himself. "You've been meeting with other women! Am I not good enough for you?"

"I've done no such thing! What evidence do you have?"

"I don't need evidence! The gods know! They've seen you leave my side and hear you lie to my face the next day!"

The queen's face, normally so empty and doll-like, was now scrunched up and her eyes burned with rage. John looked the same, though Francis could tell he was holding himself back.

"Then the gods are lying to you. I don't want to be with other women. This is ridiculous."

The queen dropped the plate and grabbed the necklace around her throat, holding up the black empyrean stone on the chain so John could see it. The stone was shaped like an eye. "You may be able to hide from *me* while I sleep but the gods are always watching! They told me! They saw you leave! You've done it five times now!"

She was right. That was the exact amount of times John had come to visit him and help their fellow slaves escape. Was she telling the truth?

"Fine. I'll admit it! I have been leaving," John admitted, "to escape the confines of this prison." He waved his hands at her, stepping closer and sneering. "But I would never go to another woman. I hate all of them." He looked ready to wring her neck. "Why would I flee those mines where I was raped every night, only to repeat such treatments here?"

Ivy's eyes were filled with fear now as she gripped the empyrean stone. John stepped closer and she backed away. It dawned on Francis that he may need to save the queen instead of John.

He was tempted to step in to prevent John from killing a monarch, but John did it himself before Francis could move. The future prince lowered his hands and when he glanced at the door, spotting Francis's movement, he had an expression of remorse on his face.

Perhaps John didn't hate the queen as much as Francis had assumed.

The future prince's defensive stance changed to a submissive one and he stepped away from his future wife. "Francis. What are you doing here?"

Francis glanced at the queen, who had calmed down. John was using casual speech in front of her and she wasn't reacting, but Francis feared she might be offended if he did the same. "I heard shouting," he said, bowing. "I apologize for getting in the way."

"Evelyn's slave." Queen Ivy acknowledged him, then motioned for him to go. "You should attend to your mistress."

"Yes, my queen." He bowed again but felt bad about leaving them alone. They might murder each other if these fights continued.

"Where *were* you going every night?" he heard the queen ask John as Francis stepped away from the door.

John looked at Francis once more, then turned back to his mistress. "To the gardens," John said, the lie rolling off his tongue as easily as Prince Antonio's flattery. "To look at the flowers."

The queen's eyes softened and she gave him a rare smile, tracing John's cheek with her finger before Francis turned away and stopped watching. He had never seen the woman act so kind toward someone before and she always ignored John during the council meetings. He hadn't expected them to be so close.

Evelyn was pacing by the front door when he returned, and she grabbed his arm as soon as he joined her. "Where were you? I was worried!"

His heart melted at her touch and he wished he could do to her what the queen had done to John. "I heard something break and was making sure nothing was wrong," he said, which was mostly true.

"What was it?"

"Someone dropped a plate."

"Ah." She released him, looking self conscious. "Are you ready to go?"

"Yes."

As the young noblewoman walked ahead of him, the urge to touch her overcame him, as it often had in the past weeks. They had gotten closer with time and the longer he lived by her side in this capital, the harder it became to leave her alone.

He knew he shouldn't get close to her but if this continued, his self-control might reach its limit. It might be better to make his feelings clear now, before they overflowed.

CHAPTER TWENTY-THREE

Before the mines happened, Evelyn spent most of her days at home, reading in her bedroom or studying with tutors. She hated fraternizing with other women because they always felt too wild, foolish, or fake. Adult Evelyn still agreed for the most part, though some of the girls weren't as bad as she originally presumed. She still envied the girl who could avoid those responsibilities, as she now had to spend nearly every day either talking to her mother, scientists, nobles, or the council for hours on end.

Now she appreciated the moments of peace and privacy in her bedroom even more, even though Francis was usually with her. She was currently lying in her bed, reading a history book in the candlelight and enjoying the silence. Her mind was finally free of anxiety.

Francis was standing by the window, keeping an eye out, but she caught him glancing her way every few minutes and sensed he had something to say.

"The queen's wedding is in a few weeks," she told him, shutting her book. "Are there any updates on John and how he feels about it? I know you sometimes speak to him when we're in the castle."

"She still beats him." He kept his eyes trained on the outside, probably looking beyond the buildings to the faraway forest beyond the city walls. "And I saw them at each other's throats after the last council meeting."

"They seem too similar at times," she said and he nodded. "I must admit, I was worried they wouldn't get along."

"Evelyn." Francis turned his dark eyes toward her, the veins popping out on his neck. "Can you help him escape before he gets hurt?"

"Escape?" She laughed. "Why would I do that?"

He broke eye contact. "I was hoping you, of all people, would be willing to protect him from abuse. I thought that's why you were changing the mines…to help people."

So, he was still clinging to dreams of freedom and equality. She had hoped the reality of the capital would rid him of those dangerous thoughts. "I know it hurts to watch your friend get hurt but there isn't anything I can do about it, Francis. I can't buy him back. You know the queen would never allow it."

"Hence, the escape." Francis was getting irritated.

"If we help him run away, the queen will place the blame on me and if I die, you'll die with me," Evelyn reminded him.

"I am aware."

"So you know why we can't do that."

She leaned back as he sat on the edge of the bed, his closeness making her more nervous and guilty. "What if we ran away together, the three of us?"

"What?"

"If we reach Antalius, no one can reclaim us. We can accompany John across that border and live as we please, forever."

What a foolish idea. "Are you really explaining your escape plan to your mistress?"

"No. I want you to come with me."

She gulped, brushing the temptation aside. "Why would I do that?"

There he was, hesitating again. He had something he refused to say, the sole motivation behind this foolish plan. "In Antalius, we could be together, not as a mistress and slave but as equals. I could take care of you."

"You already take care of me, as my bodyguard."

"Not like that." He fiddled with the blanket, avoiding her eyes. "In Clostrum, no matter how close we become, you will always be the heir to the wealthiest family in the country and I will always be a nameless slave from an empyrean stone mine."

She failed to see what was wrong with that. She had no reason to leave. So much depended on her presence here. "I don't understand what you want, Francis." Not that it mattered what a slave wanted, she reminded herself for the tenth time.

"I promised myself I would never say this, but I cannot hold myself back any longer." He pressed both hands on the blanket and leaned toward her so they were a mere breath away from each other. "Evelyn, I want to be together with you...as your equal."

This conversation felt like a council debate. They were going in circles and not getting anywhere. She blinked several times, giving him a chance to continue so she wouldn't have to dissect his confusing web of thoughts.

"May I speak frankly, my lady?"

"Of course."

"Despite our brief acquaintance, in the months we have known each other, I have come to care for you a great deal."

Her heart leapt, hopefully from anxiety and not joy.

"To be frank, if I were a nobleman, I would have already asked for your hand in marriage."

Now there was no denying that she was happy about this, numbingly so. She had always wanted him to admit it, since she never could on her own.

Her heart pounded noticeably hard and she knew her cheeks would turn pink at any moment, a weakness she thought she had overcome in the past weeks. "Your feelings are likely a result of our close contact, rather than compatibility," she insisted, convincing herself more than him.

"I have known many women in the mines. I've never felt this way before." He was staring at her with eyes full of want and tenderness.

The romantic voice in her mind tried to dominate her inner dialogue but she pushed it away. "You know my mother would never allow such a thing, Francis. You need to rid yourself of these feelings." And the same went for her.

"Your mother cannot stop me if we move to Antalius."

"Again, Francis, I—"

"I am happy to serve you, Evelyn, but I would rather do so in a place where it is of my own free will."

"We will not speak of this again, Francis."

"Am I mistaken in thinking you feel the same way?"

"Yes," she lied. "You are very mistaken. I have no intention of disobeying my mother and betraying my country, especially for a slave."

She knew her words hurt him. They were supposed to, but it tore her apart to see his heartbreak written all over his face.

What made it even worse was the smile he forced. She would rather he frown like John did.

"Very well, my lady." He reverted back to his slave stature, losing his beautiful smile. "I apologize for causing you distress. I will not speak of this again."

"See that you do." She hurried to blow out the candle before her cheeks became heated.

"If you need me, I'll be outside the door," he whispered as the room went dark. She remained still in the bed as he exited, softly shutting the door behind him.

As soon as he was gone, she released the breath she had been holding and touched her burning face. For months she had told herself his jokes, smiles, and laughs were just him being polite or kind rather than a symptom of any feelings he harbored toward her. It had helped her push down her own feelings, to kill the butterflies threatening her stomach. Now her worst fears had been confirmed.

She could never be with him. She had a thousand reasons to stay here and only one reason to go...even if it was a very enticing reason.

She would have trouble sleeping tonight and, just as she feared, her dreams showed her what would have happened if she said yes. She saw a small cottage with a garden and two children, one with raven black hair and another with golden hair. She could see him lifting the children into his arms and making them laugh. It made reality feel like torture when she woke the next morning.

CHAPTER TWENTY-FOUR

The next morning was awkward, as Evelyn had to face Francis immediately after rejecting him.

As she stepped out into the hall and saw him standing at attention, his face devoid of expression and his posture perfectly straight, she wished he would show anger or sadness. Anything was preferable to seeing him so hollow.

There were no events today, so she planned to spend all her waking hours studying her family finances, but as she entered the dining hall where her mother was already eating, she found not an empty table but the commander of the Valhander mines, Fiona Drestana, sitting there with a fork in her hand. She looked the same as she had before, though her stern countenance was absent.

"Lady Evelyn." The commander stood to attention and bowed as Evelyn entered the room. Fiona then smiled at Francis, who bowed back. "I am glad to see you in good health."

"Leave us," Evelyn's mother said to Francis. She hadn't moved from her seat despite her daughter's arrival. "And shut the door. We are to have a private discussion."

As Francis obeyed and exited the room, Evelyn felt her tense body relax. "Commander. It's good to see you again."

"You will address her as Lady Drestana," her mother reminded her as both Evelyn and the commander took a seat, then she took a bite out of the peach and strawberry pastry in front of her. "She is no longer your commander and as of today, she takes orders from you."

Evelyn's eyes went wide. She was placing Evelyn in charge after only a few months?

"Which is why I'm here," the commander said to Evelyn. "It's been several months since you established the new rules and the slaves have grown stronger, as you wished." The commander glanced nervously at her mother. "However, there is a matter we must discuss."

Oh no.

"As expected, some men have tried to take advantage of the new rules. So far, five have tried to either kill their guards or escape. Because you ordered us to stop breaking their legs, one of them tried again a week later."

Evelyn raised her chin. She was afraid this would happen. "Mother, how long will it take for the empyrean stone collars and shackles to be produced and sent to the mines?"

"Not for a few weeks, at least," her mother answered quietly. "You'll need to find a way to keep the men in check until then."

Evelyn frowned and stared at the food on the table, knowing she would have to fix her own mess. "Are the men who rebelled still working? Or have you detained them?"

"They've been locked in cages for now but we only have so many. If the others see rebellion go unpunished, they'll be encouraged to follow their lead."

"Indeed." She started tapping her foot nervously and knew her mother noticed. She didn't want to stoop to the barbaric means her mother had but couldn't be docile either.

"I can tell she's struggling," her mother cut in, voice smooth as butter. "Fiona, until we can shackle every slave, continue with the original punishments. Break the legs of that repeat offender and lower the rations of those who tried to escape. It's too late to reduce the rations for everyone, as that will anger those who still obeyed, but show that we will not tolerate violence and disorder."

The commander looked ready to comply, but Evelyn cut in. "There must a better solution. We need their respect, not their fear."

"Respect is hard to obtain and easy to lose," her mother said, turning steel eyes on her. "Men are fickle. When they see an opening, they take it, regardless of how kind you've been in the past."

"Unless you have another idea, Lady Evelyn, we should proceed with this plan," The commander said sympathetically. Evelyn still got the feeling the woman didn't like harming others. "Once we receive the collars, the more brutal means of keeping the slaves in line can finally be abolished."

Evelyn struggled to think of another option but all she could visualize was an army of angry men charging on the capital, ready to kill every woman in range for revenge. She was sure John fantasized about it every day. Evelyn couldn't allow such hatred to be released on Clostrum.

"Very well. Do as you've said." She sighed. "A few weeks isn't long when compared to a decade, right?"

The conversation continued without Evelyn so she let herself eat, shoving food into her mouth to distract herself from Francis's voice in her head. After seeing what happened to that poor cripple in the kitchen, after feeling disgust at the person who had allowed it, she was now doing it to someone else. She had become the thing she hated.

The food had no taste in her mouth so she started biting her lip. The pain distracted her from the frustration.

"Evelyn." Her mother called her name, concerned wrinkles forming. "If you're struggling with this, you can talk to me. I understand what you're going through. I had similar thoughts when I was younger, remember? When I married your father."

"I know."

"I want to help you avoid my mistakes."

"I know."

"I don't think you do. You remember the rebellion that happened eleven years ago and the cave-in that followed? That was my fault."

Why was she admitting this? Her Mother didn't like appearing weak or foolish.

"Because of your father's influence, I tried to treat all slaves the way you're trying to now. It worked for a little while, until my husband went behind my back and helped his fellow slaves coordinate an attack on the mine guards. They raped and killed every woman there and moved on to the nearby villages. They were only stopped when the queen sent her military in. Every single slave who fought back was slaughtered and the rest were sent back to their mine and left die, including your father."

She had always been told her father was sent away for stealing. She had no idea he turned against her mother like this.

"Now do you understand why I'm so protective of you?" her mother prodded, her voice genuine and soft. "I need to defend you from dangerous ideals that will get you killed. Not only are there are innocent women and children out there who need your protection, but the slaves themselves need to understand that demanding freedom will only result in their own deaths. Males are too stubborn, too focused on their own goals, to realize this. Only we, women who view the world as it truly is and learn from history, can do the right thing."

Evelyn glanced at the door, knowing Francis was on the other side. He was the embodiment of what her mother feared. If she let him run amuck, crawling toward freedom, he would wound himself and everyone he tainted with his ideals.

She had to protect him from this, to ensure he never ran.

"I understand, Mother." She met her mother's eyes, hardening her eyes and resolve. "I won't disappoint you." Her attention then moved to the commander. "Lady Drestana, do as my mother says and keep me updated. If the attacks and escape attempts continue, do what you think is right." She trusted the commander's judgment. "I will ensure you receive the slaves' restraints as soon as possible."

The proud smile on her mother's face made Evelyn feel conflicted, but she didn't let it sway her. Her mind was made up.

"And Fiona," she added. "Don't tell Francis about this."

She had to do this for her family, her country, and for him. He would understand with time. The longer she kept him with her, the more likely he was to give up his idea of freedom. He would be much happier here anyway, with food and a home, rather than in a land where he knew nothing and no one.

This was the right thing to do.

She would tell herself that until it felt true.

CHAPTER TWENTY-FIVE

Over the coming weeks, Francis and John managed to free five more slaves using the skills they gained from Francis's training and John's secret practice. There were a few times when they almost got caught but they survived by either hiding or talking their way out. However, the longer they did this, the more nervous Francis felt despite each slave reaching the edge of the capital safely and leaving with one of Francis's rings.

Everything felt too easy and convenient. Despite that constant sense of being watched, nothing ever happened to interfere with their work.

That was, until they freed a slave from the castle.

A few weeks ago, Evelyn stopped letting Francis follow her into meetings or parties, even though it was his job to protect her. He had to wait outside the door obediently and as he did so, he would strike up conversations with the other guards or servants nearby. They were always happy to chat, even if it was about the weather.

Francis had met the man they were currently freeing while waiting outside the council meeting. The man was an elder who served as a maid in the castle for fifty years and told Francis his dream was to see a green empyrean stone, something that was only common in Antalius.

Touched, Francis had prioritized helping the man escape. If Francis couldn't fulfil his own dream, he wanted to at least help this elder do it.

The old man named Estar followed Francis and John through the small tunnels under the castle. The tunnels used to serve as an escape for royals during an invasion but now only the occasional slave used it to stay out of the queen's sight as they went about their business. The exit from the tunnels to the city street was locked but John had learned to unlock it two weeks after moving in. This was the door he practiced lockpicking on every night.

"Always liked flowers," the old man said as he followed Francis down the dark tunnel. John was ahead of them with a torch, rushing too fast for the seventy-year-old man's legs. "Did you know green empyrean bowls can make any seed sprout in an hour? Meanwhile I have to spend years growing trees in the garden." He was in charge of the castle landscaping and on the day they met, was walking past with a potted tree in his wrinkled hands.

"I'm sure it's a beautiful sight," Francis said with a wistful smile. "What will you grow in your Antalian garden, Estar?"

The man took a few moments to consider as they reached the end of the tunnel. The exit was blocked by a steel door with a matching padlock. The grin on John's face as he picked the lock matched that of the old man's.

"I think I'd start with some tulips. They're too colorful for queen's Ivy's taste so I haven't grown them since I was a boy," Estar said as they waited. "What would *you* grow, Francis?"

"I haven't thought about it."

"You two can worry about flowers once you're in Antalius," John interrupted as the padlock fell from the door. "Right now, focus on getting out alive. You're not safe until you cross the border."

The sun hurt their eyes as they stepped into the street, the orange light beginning its descent over the buildings. But as soon as they breathed fresh air, Francis was once again struck by the ominous feeling of eyes on them. It was so bad this time that he grabbed John's shoulder and yanked him back into the tunnel, away from the open road before them. Someone was out there!

John shouted, swearing at Francis for tossing him to the ground.

Not a second later, an arrow flew from one of the building windows in front of them and struck the old man in the chest.

"No!" Francis grabbed Estar's limp body and dragged him into the darkness. He scanned the buildings before him. Where had the arrow come from? Who shot it? All he could make out was dark glass and shadows. If the killer was there, he or she had already hidden.

"Get back!" John pulled a stunned Francis further back into the tunnel. He then kicked the old man's body onto the street so he could push the door fully closed.

"What are you doing? We can't leave him out there!" Francis shouted.

"He's already dead and we will be too if we don't run!" John shot him a glare and nodded at the dropped torch on the ground. "Go back the way we came! I won't have you dying too!"

Francis hesitated. Maybe Estar was still alive. They couldn't abandon him. Would John do the same to Francis if he was the one who got hit?

"Francis, I won't tell you again!" John shouted as he closed the padlock over the doorknob again. "Whoever it is won't be satisfied with just the old man's blood."

To prove his point, there came a pounding on the door. Whoever it was wanted in.

Convinced but still feeling guilty, Francis grabbed the torch and dashed down the tunnel with John on his heels.

"Who do you think it was?" Francis asked as they ran.

"Who knows. Could be any slaver. Doesn't matter. Let's just lay off the escape attempts until after my wedding. Let them think we gave up," John answered.

"*Are* we giving up?"

"No. Not unless you want to."

John wasn't willing to back down. Good. Francis wasn't either. He didn't fear those who used their power to hurt others.

"The one thing I do know is they were waiting for us," John growled. "They must have been watching for a while, learning our patterns. We need to change things up. Act unpredictably."

Francis was surprised by John's determination. In the beginning, Francis had to talk him into helping people. Now, *he* was making the plans and strategizing.

The future prince almost looked like a different person when they did this. The young man Francis met in the mines had no passion or drive to do anything, not even to eat or drink. This new John, on the other hand, was serious and wise about his actions.

Seeing these changes in him almost motivated Francis more than helping his fellow man. He hoped they could do this again soon, even if there was risk.

After he snuck home, though, Francis once again saw Evelyn's mother standing in the window of her office, overlooking the city streets. The fear of getting caught returned. He wasn't sure if she saw him but when he encountered her later that morning while escorting Evelyn outside, her eyes burned into the side of his head.

The woman still commented on his closeness to Evelyn on occasion. He knew she was looking for any excuse to be rid of him without going against Evelyn's wishes. If his escapades were discovered, it would be the perfect opportunity to dispose of him.

Why hadn't she confronted him about his nightly escapades?

He agreed with John. They had to be more careful, but he still had three buttons and four rings to give away. He could still help six men gain their freedom and have one left for himself.

He only planned to keep the one ring in case something went horribly wrong, but he hoped he'd never have to use it. The mere thought of abandoning Evelyn pained him. However, John's reminders to be cautious and never trust any woman made him keep the ring anyway. After all, it wasn't Evelyn he was worried about. It was her mother.

CHAPTER TWENTY-SIX

Evelyn knew the queen was expecting her to attend the wedding rehearsal as one of her friends, since the queen had few, but Evelyn had other priorities. She received word yesterday that the Payne family's researchers had finished work on the prototype collars and wrist bands. They only needed permission from her or her mother, then the restraints could finally be sent to the mines. Evelyn wanted to end the slaves' torment as soon as possible, so she chose to head to the lab instead of the wedding.

She hoped the queen would forgive her late entrance.

Francis was the only one who joined her for the carriage ride and he spent most of the time discussing the wedding, asking questions about the ceremony and what was said during the vows. She found it fascinating just how little he knew about such traditions.

"We aren't going to the rehearsal," she finally told him when she realized he was excited about attending. "I'm going to the Payne labs to see the new empyrean restraints for the mines."

"Restraints?" His smile evaporated.

"They're for the slaves," she explained, wanting to reassure him. She was doing all of this for him, after all. "It's so I can feed the slaves more and end the lashings without fearing escape."

"Oh." He looked away, clearly thinking it through. "Will the restraints hurt?"

"Only if they try to run. We'll use red empyrean stones so the guards can burn anyone who flees."

He was trying to hide his reaction but his pallid skin betrayed him. He was frightened. Why? Wasn't this what he wanted? Why was he looking at her like that?

"This way, they won't have to starve or lose their legs," she added, raising her voice. "They won't be in pain or exhausted anymore."

"What good is energy if it's to be wasted in the mines?" he whispered. "Without a family or future to build towards?"

"…The stones they mine protect this country from invaders. Their sacrifices aren't in vain."

"For you, perhaps." He turned away and didn't speak again, leaving her to question every decision she'd made during these months. Had it all been for naught? Would it never be enough for him?

She wanted to counter this, to defend her actions, but the arrival of the carriage at the labs prevented more argument.

The lab was a large stone building, each door and wall reinforced with steel and guarded by the strongest women under her family's employ. Each soldier bore a sword and gun of empyrean to guard the secrets inside. The armored women before the entrance wouldn't even let Evelyn enter until they saw her face. Normally, her name was enough to grant her entry anywhere.

"These collars are just the first step," Evelyn told Francis weakly as she stepped from the stopped carriage. "Trust me." Freedom would come eventually, especially if they found this powerful weapon the gods described. For now, he'd have to settle for this.

The woman who came out to greet Evelyn was her mother's age, with an ugly face and hair chopped as short as a man's. Her hands were calloused from working with steel and empyrean stones. Evelyn could even see a few scars on her arms, likely from touching the stones by accident while they were active. It was a wonder she hadn't lost a limb.

"Welcome, my lady. I was worried we wouldn't see a member of your family for months, due to the royal wedding." The woman bowed to her but had a constant smirk on her face. "Please come inside. I won't keep you long."

Evelyn nodded and followed her. The walls they passed through were as thick as she was wide, and every table inside was colorless stone. The lighting was excellent from lanterns and torches hanging along the ceiling, but the only color came from the empyrean stones.

Each wall was draped with diagrams and empyrean architecture blueprints. Next to them were a variety of weapons ranging from familiar whips and guns to new technology like explosive balls, rockets, cannons, and saws. She had learned about these devices in the past, but they were so rare in the kingdom that she had yet to view one in person.

The building housed one giant room with only two doors at the back—one bearing the label *waste disposal* and the other marking an exit. Standing in front of these doors were five guards, each woman dressed in heavy silver armor and wearing helmets to hide their faces. They were so tall that even Francis looked small beside them.

"Come this way." The woman led her to a table in the far corner of the room. Atop the slab of stone were thin rings of red and white empyrean. Some were the size of a fist, others large enough to fit around the neck.

"They look like they could break easily," Evelyn commented.

"Oh, no. Nothing can break empyrean other than an opposing element," the researcher assured her, calm and composed. Evelyn could feel the woman's eyes on her, awaiting a positive reaction. "What do you think?"

"If only an opposing empyrean stone can change their shape, how will you put them on the slaves without harming them?" she asked.

"We weld them onto the slaves with the opposing cold element. It will hurt for a moment but will not do any permanent damage. It is prolonged exposure to the heat or cold that wounds someone. This is why they will serve as such an excellent deterrent, albeit an expensive one." The woman smiled proudly as she picked up one of the wrist bands. "Allow me to demonstrate."

Evelyn was so focused on the collars, trying to imagine what they would look like on a slave, that she didn't realize what the woman was doing until she heard a sharp grunt from Francis.

Turning, she beheld the researcher holding Francis's arm and using an activated white empyrean stone to meld a red shackle around his wrist. She used a mold to reform its circular shape, creating a perfectly round bracelet. The part of the red stone being touched by the white stone melted in the woman's hand, making it malleable enough to wrap around his wrist before it hardened into the mold once more.

As the researcher stepped away, showing off the band of red securely wrapped around his wrist, Evelyn spotted a burn on Francis's skin where he'd been touched by the white stone. His flesh had turned red and was now changing to a swollen pink, blistering from the briefest touch of ice. Even now, the man was cringing from the pain.

"This is how we place the restraints on them," the woman continued, her cheerful tone grating on Evelyn's ears. "And they cannot be removed unless we wish them to be. Now." She clapped her hands and one of the guards standing nearby stepped forward. "Allow me to demonstrate what will happen if one of the slaves disobeys."

"Wait. I've seen enough." Evelyn reached for Francis's wrist. She wanted to command the woman to remove the bracelet but knew doing so would look suspicious. "I don't want you testing these weapons on my servants."

"Oh, don't worry," the woman assured her as she focused on the shackles, using her mind to control the device's temperature. "It has already been tested numerous times. This is merely a demonstration."

"Unshackle him!" she shouted, no longer caring how much emotion she showed.

It was too late.

The runes around the bracelet glowed a bright orange and Francis started screaming in pain, falling to his knees in anguish. By the time Evelyn turned on the researcher, raising a hand to slap her, the demonstration was over. She could hear Francis panting and moaning and when she glanced at him again, the skin around his wrist was completely red and swelling against the restraint.

Anger overtaking logic, Evelyn let her slap land. The resounding hit elicited a cry of shock and pain from the woman. The guard standing nearby moved to defend the researcher but stopped herself when Evelyn glared at her. As the heir to the Payne family, she had authority over both the researcher and the guards. They couldn't disobey or raise a hand to her.

"I commanded you to release him!" Evelyn shouted, blood rushing to her head. "You did not have permission to touch what is mine!"

"My lady, I was merely—" The woman shut her mouth as she saw the fury in Evelyn's eyes and stumbled backwards, bumping into the table behind her. "I apologize, my lady, but he is a man. He will recover easily from the pain." Her voice turned desperate as each word made Evelyn's eyes narrow. "I merely wished to show you how effective one second of pain could be, so you would feel reassured that this research will prevent rebellion in the mines. Your mother said it was your greatest priority!"

Evelyn stepped back. The woman's voice quivered as she covered her head to protect herself—to save herself from Evelyn. It made her realize how this must look. She had just slapped one of her mother's best researchers to protect a slave!

"I apologize, my lady," the woman whimpered. "I could tell he was a slave so I assumed you wouldn't mind." Her voice cracked. "I beg your forgiveness."

Evelyn watched as the armored guard retrieved a glass bottle and some cloths from a different table and started pouring a liquid onto Francis's hand. He grit his teeth as it covered the fresh burn, looking away to avoid panicking. His breathing was getting dangerously fast.

What was she to do? Evelyn had brought Francis out of the mines to protect him. Now he was in pain again and this time it was because of her.

There were six witnesses who had seen her blatant protection of him too. Even now, the researcher was staring at her, eyes wide. They would tell her mother and Evelyn's feelings for Francis would be exposed.

Evelyn turned her back on the woman. She shouldn't have punished her simply for doing her job. Harming slaves was allowed if it furthered research. Men were not as fragile as women and could handle the pain. That was what she'd been taught all her life.

But man or not, Francis looked ready to faint from this.

Even now, Evelyn's hands were aching with the itch to avenge him. Francis had done nothing to deserve this, and his blistering skin looked ready to fall off.

What would her mother do?

"I was wrong to react the way I did," she muttered, her voice hoarse. "Do not disobey me again...and do not touch this man."

The researcher nodded and the guard stepped aside as Evelyn yanked the medicine from her.

"Prepare my carriage," she ordered. "And leave the building until I order you to return." She wanted to help Francis without their judgmental stares.

"Yes, my lady." The researcher was clearly confused as to what she'd done wrong and likely feared Evelyn might stop funding her research. "Again, I apologize—"

"I approve of your collars," Evelyn said through grit teeth. "Start mass-producing them immediately and send them to the mines. How long will it take to distribute them?"

"Two to four weeks," the woman said, her eagerness returning. "Thank you, Lady Payne!"

The name stung. It was what her mother was called. Evelyn preferred the use of her first name. It didn't put her on a pedestal or build walls between them.

Evelyn was turning into her mother.

"Leave me!" Evelyn glared at the women until everyone exited through the back door, slamming it behind them and likely discussing what had just occurred amongst themselves.

Once they were gone, Evelyn poured the bottled liquid over Francis's wound again, being as gentle as possible but feeling her stomach clench as he grunted from the sting.

"I'm sorry," she whispered against her better judgement. "I didn't want her to do that."

"I know, my lady." He still spoke politely even though they were alone.

"It won't happen again." She didn't know how to ensure it didn't but she was determined to protect him.

"Thank you, my lady, but please don't be angry for me."

She frowned and looked up at his pained face. "Why?" She no longer cared if others thought badly of her for defending a slave. Their opinions didn't matter. Even her mother's was beginning to lose its value. "I can defend you if I wish."

He turned away, gulping. "It gets my hopes up," he whispered honestly. "That you might care for me."

The heat in her ears rushed to her cheeks and she accidentally touched his burns with the bottle. He hissed and she had to quickly pull away. "I'm sorry, Francis. I..." She bit her tongue.

How should she respond? She had already explained why they couldn't be together—why they shouldn't respond to these feelings.

She was on the council now and needed a flawless reputation amongst the nobility. If the woman in charge of thousands of slaves took one as a concubine, it would be humiliating. It was a sign of desperation. Besides, now that she had learned what happened to her father, she knew her mother would never let Francis become more than a bodyguard.

Yet, despite telling herself it shouldn't be, she found her thoughts dominated by Francis and a life with him. She wanted him.

Should she send him away? Would removing the temptation banish these persistent dreams?

Francis stared at her, watching her internal struggle, and the pain left his face as he smiled. It wasn't the playful or sarcastic smirk he normally wore. This one was sad, desperate, his eyes the same as the day she had pushed him away.

When he leaned forward to kiss her, she didn't move or stop him. She tightened her grip on the medicine bottle as he wrapped his arms around her, holding his wrist away from her but using his undamaged one to pull her close.

His lips made her forget her station, her mother, and her duties. Right now, he was the only thing in her world and she wanted him more than she'd ever wanted anything.

Once they pulled apart, her face bright red and his white from the burns, he rested his head on her shoulder. "I thought I was going to die when she burnt me," he admitted, his words muffled against her sleeve. "I didn't want to die without touching you at least once."

Her eyes welled up with tears. She couldn't push him away. Not again. "We can't tell anyone about this," she told him firmly, taking a deep breath.

"Yes, my lady."

"This is only temporary," she continued. Her mother always told her romantic feelings lasted for one or two years before fading. They could continue this relationship until then and separate after that. If they ever got caught, that's what she would tell her mother. This would be short-lived.

"I'll take what I can get," he said with a pained chuckle. The adrenaline rush from the kiss was probably gone, giving way to the burn's sting again, but he didn't move away.

"You can get off now. We need to go to the wedding rehearsal," she told him, running her fingers through his hair as he continued pressing his forehead against her shoulder. "We're already late."

"Yes." He sighed. "I'm just...savoring the moment."

"Francis," she warned, making him rise with a laugh and apologize before she led him through the front door to the outside.

As they returned to the carriage and she sent a servant back to her mansion to summon a healer, Evelyn couldn't help enjoying the immense relief she felt from finally giving in to her feelings. Even though her brain was telling her to dismiss Francis before she did something she'd regret, the warmth in her chest told her she had made the right choice.

The rest of the carriage ride was spent stealing glances at Francis and he was doing the same to her. Her entire world had changed in a mere ten minutes.

CHAPTER TWENTY-SEVENTEEN

Francis and Evelyn were late to the wedding rehearsal but they didn't miss much. The ceremony, which Francis was eager to see so he could learn how to do such a thing himself, was just beginning as they snuck in together.

The castle's entryway had once again morphed into a completely different room. The walls were covered in white and golden tapestries depicting the queen and her future prince. Blue flowers lined the stairs and matched the dark blue uniform of the priest, who stood on the third step to be slightly above crowd. She had a necklace around her neck strung entirely with black empyrean stones. Their presence now made sense to Francis, after what he'd heard about the stones connecting people to the gods. If the stones truly spoke, the priestesses would want as many as they could get their hands on.

The only people in attendance, seated on black chairs circling the priest, were the councilors and their many husbands. Evelyn's mother was seated to the far right, near the queen, and the Dalius prince Antonio was seated beside her, whispering in her ear as the rehearsal began.

"I'll be joining my mother," Evelyn told Francis as they entered the room, her blush already gone. He was surprised she could act so normal while his heart was still racing. "Stay against the wall with the other bodyguards and don't go anywhere."

"Understood, my lady." He smiled, genuinely this time, and the grin only faltered when she touched the burn on his hand. The red empyrean stone bracelet was still wrapped around his skin and she had made no mention of removing it. Her touch stung so he moved his wrist away and bowed to her. "I'll be here when you get back."

When he returned to an upright position, he saw Evelyn's mother glaring at him, ignoring the prince beside her. The woman's prying would be a real issue now that he and Evelyn were finally mutually in love.

The queen and John started descending the stairs toward the priest as Evelyn moved along the wall to reach her family. Francis tried to focus on John, but his eyes kept drifting toward Evelyn.

Her mother had glared at him a moment ago, but her entire face changed into a bright smile as she made room for her daughter. A twinge of jealousy shot through him as Evelyn sat beside the prince, who immediately started whispering in her ear. His mouth was too close.

"You should move out of the doorway." Evelyn's mother was suddenly beside him. He had been so focused on Evelyn that he hadn't noticed her approach until it was too late. "You belong with the slaves over there." She pointed at the other men standing against the wall.

"Understood, my lady." He said this phrase so often that it no longer felt like real words. "I will do as you command."

The older woman looked him up and down. Her bright purple dress didn't match the darkness in her eyes. "I see she put a bracelet on you."

Before he could answer, she grabbed his wrist and lifted it to take a better look. Pain shot through his entire body in response to her fingers gripping the burns but he grit his teeth and stayed silent, glancing at the queen to make sure no one had noticed. The rehearsal was proceeding normally, thankfully, and no one was looking at them.

"In a few weeks, every slave in the mines will wear these," Lady Payne said thoughtfully. "And I plan to put chains on every man in Clostrum someday, not just the ones underground. Then my daughter will have no cause to worry about betrayal."

Her eyes shifted from the shackles to his eyes, and he knew she had seen him freeing other slaves. He was the betrayer.

"This is a warning," she whispered, her voice so calm and collected that it frightened him more than her words. How could she smile while talking about shackling him and his friends? "We will free you and your fellow males when Clostrum no longer needs you. Until then, you will obey me and stop interfering with my daughter's life."

"Then why don't you dispose of me?" he hissed. "As you did your husbands?"

Her eye twitched. "I'll pretend you didn't just address me informally." Her grip tightened, shooting sparks up his arm. "Trust me, when Evelyn stops enjoying your company, she will dispose of you herself. She will spot your manipulations eventually and realize you are taking advantage of her position, just as my husbands did. Be glad she's taken a liking to you. If not for her, I would have killed you as soon as you arrived in the capital."

Her threats only motivated him to free his friends even more.

…But he didn't want to be taken away from Evelyn, especially after she'd just opened her heart to him.

"I understand, my lady," he said and bowed, keeping his eyes dead as John normally did. He refused to let her see the blatant dislike he had for her. He didn't hate her, since she was likely no different from Evelyn at some point, but that didn't mean he had to like her.

"And bear in mind that merely fleeing the capital is not enough for a man to be free," she continued. "How much do you know about Dalius?"

"Very little." He'd never been to the land across the eastern sea.

"Dalius breeds assassins whose entire job is hunting down runaways. Their type are silent and efficient, and I am fully capable of bringing such people under my employ. I hope you understand my meaning."

So, she was the one responsible for Estar's death. How many other people had her assassin killed?

"I understand you perfectly."

"Address me with my title," she warned.

"Lady Payne."

The lady's smile shifted into a smirk for a split second, then she walked away without saying goodbye.

The queen and John were in the midst of pledging allegiance to Clostrum and the gods when Francis joined the other slaves near the wall. The queen was dressed in her everyday black dress and John's suit matched, though John said they'd be wearing red on the wedding day. It was apparently the queen's favorite color. Francis found it strange that John knew her favorite color despite despising her.

The bodyguard next to him was a slave bearing scars on his back and bare shoulders. The two made eye contact as Francis joined him.

"You look shaken up, Francis." The older guard had met Francis a few times during the council meetings. "Did you do something to anger your mistress?"

"The mother of my mistress," he muttered. "What do you know of Dalius assassins?"

The guard glanced at the wedding ceremony, then shook his head. "Only what I've heard, and it only spreads in upper class circles," he whispered. "All I know is that some live among us, though the nobles hide their presence. You'd think they'd want to show them off to scare slaves into docility."

"Agreed. I wonder why it's kept a secret." Francis had never heard of Dalius assassins hunting slaves before.

"I know most of the middle class track down the slaves themselves. The hunters are only sent by those who can afford it."

Francis was already picturing the child they had freed, the very first slave they helped. Had he made it to Antalius? Or was he murdered?

Francis should have listened to his instincts that day. That boy's blood was on his hands. "What happens to the slaves when they're caught?"

"Some are sent to the mines." The guard shrugged. "But I think the majority are killed. The nobles can afford to replace them." He leaned toward Francis, eyes narrowing. "You shouldn't bring this up anymore. It might put a target on your back."

He already had one.

The ceremony came to a close and as the future married couple turned toward the crowd, who clapped politely, Francis caught John looking at the queen with an almost kind expression. It was the way Evelyn sometimes looked at him. Was John finally warming up to the queen? She looked quite happy now, despite barely smiling.

Francis would have to ask him the next time they met, which might be tonight.

If it weren't for her mother, he'd be tempted to spend the night with Evelyn, just talking and pretending their current stations didn't exist. Watching her sit so close to that pretty-faced prince made him uncomfortable. He hated how good they looked together.

CHAPTER TWENTY-EIGHT

John spent his last unmarried night on the roof of an abandoned building with Francis, dressed in the black uniform he wore to the ceremony that day. He'd brought a bitter, cinnamon alcohol drink and a gun he stole from one of the guards, a habit of his by this point, and Francis couldn't tell how John felt about the situation. He was about to marry the most powerful woman in the country but hardly seemed to care.

"Evelyn's mother told me it's common practice to send Dalius assassins after runaways," Francis explained quietly as he took a sip of the cold drink. The light of a few lanterns passed below, belonging to workers who had finished their shifts late. "Do you think…they killed our friends?"

"Who knows." The future prince shrugged and let his legs swing off the edge of the roof. "It's the risk you take for freedom, right?"

"I suppose." But it left a sour taste in Francis's mouth. He couldn't send slaves to their deaths with a clear conscience.

"That woman probably thought she would discourage us." John laughed. "But she accidentally gave us secret intel. Now that we know they're being hunted, we can train your friends to defend themselves."

Your friends?

"What can a few weeks of training from an inexperienced prince and bodyguard do against years of military training?" Francis sighed and laid on his back, looking up at the stars. The blinking lights matched the color of the empyrean stones: red, white, green, and yellow.

"So maybe we don't free the slaves one at a time. Maybe we should be more direct." John pointed at the castle. "Kill the rich nobles and there will be no one left to enslave the men."

"Kill your own wife? And Evelyn? I don't think so."

"Why not?"

"You wouldn't feel bad about killing the queen?"

John didn't answer for a moment. "Ivy isn't happy anyway. She's mentioned wanting to end her life before."

"Why? She has all the wealth and power in Clostrum."

The prince shrugged but it looked less genuine. "She can boss people around but knows they all hate her. She has money but has to spend it responsibly so the people don't suffer. She has no friends and her family is dead. She has nothing."

"She has you, doesn't she?"

"She knows I want to kill her."

"…You two feel very similar at times," Francis said, sitting up slightly. "Do *you* still think about killing yourself, John?"

"…Every day."

Francis bit his lip. "I'd be sad if you did."

"Yes, and you're the reason I haven't ended it yet. I couldn't leave you alone to become prey for that Payne woman."

"Evelyn? What's wrong with her?"

"You always talk about how she's a good person, but she tolerates slavery and abuse while thinking herself moral."

"That's not true. She struggles with her decisions. I can tell."

"I don't care if she struggles. I care that she lets people die." John shook his head. "Forget it. I don't want to argue today. You'll see her the way I do eventually. Then we can finally leave this place together."

"What if she proves you wrong?"

"…She won't." He pointed at the burns on Francis's arm. Evelyn had used a white empyrean stone to remove the band after the wedding, but it was still swollen. "You haven't told me how you got that burn."

Francis took the red bracelet from his pocket and showed it to John. Evelyn let him keep it, saying he deserved it as payment for dealing with the pain. "It came from this. Her mother plans to put one of these on every man in Clostrum so they can't escape."

"When?" John sat up, curiosity lighting his eyes again.

"In a few weeks. Why?"

John looked around, ensuring they weren't being watched, then leaned closer. "I've been thinking about helping the slaves escape the Valhander Mines, then blowing it up to pay those nobles back for their abuse. They set a cave-in trap, right? We can take advantage of that."

"The trap relies on empyrean stones, which we can't activate. Only women can." Francis hesitated. "But…if you found a way, I wouldn't be against it."

"You told me your mistress increased the rations and reduced the lashings a few weeks ago. That means the men are at their strongest. It's the perfect time to break them free. They can fight back without restraint. Once your girl shackles the men with those bracelets, it'll be too late. We'll never have another chance like this."

"That's true." Francis was becoming convinced. "And we could…No, hold on. If we did that, it would put Evelyn in danger. She's the one who demanded the extra rations, so she'd take the fall."

"What's the worst they can do? She's one of them. The nobles don't kill their own."

"They do." Francis frowned at the castle towers a few streets away. "The former queen was allegedly pushed off the castle by one of her own. They might do it to Evelyn too."

"You're still worrying about that selfish wench? Stop prioritizing her over your own brothers, Francis!"

"I love her!" Francis shouted, making John lean away in disgust. "Besides, regardless of what happens to Evelyn, your plan could result in the deaths of thousands if we aren't careful. Evelyn's mother has caved in mines for less, and there's no doubt she'll do it again. Plus, it's a temporary solution based on revenge. It won't change anything in the long run. If anything, the men who *don't* run will be treated worse."

"You don't know that! Besides, even if it fails, it'll be worth it to give those women a taste of their own medicine!" John's eyes were filled with gleeful bloodlust.

"So, you don't actually care about helping our brothers. You're just doing this for your own satisfaction!" Francis stood. He'd said too much. "Let's end the discussion for today, John. I don't want to fight the day before your wedding."

The future prince watched him stand, then glared at the Payne mansion. "That woman will be the death of you," he said but waved his hand, admitting defeat. "Don't worry. I won't do anything reckless so long as you're around to make me feel bad for it. I won't hurt your precious Evelyn either."

"Thank you, John." He looked down at his hands, one burnt and one bearing the final ring he had left from Evelyn's shopping trip. He had kept the ring in case he ever decided to run away on his own, but now he knew he could never leave her behind. He cared for her too much and a life of freedom would feel empty without her.

"Here." He pulled off the final ring, his last chance to leave, and handed it to John. "Keep this in case you decide to flee."

"What is it?" John received it and studied the ring. "Is this a black empyrean stone?"

"Yes." The stone was tiny, barely bigger than a speck atop the silver, but it made the ring the most expensive one he owned. "I wish you luck with your wedding, John."

"Thanks." His voice was monotone again. "Though it doesn't matter. She won't treat me any different regardless of my title."

"…When I saw you completing the rehearsal, I got the feeling you didn't hate her as much as you say you do."

John scrunched up his nose. "I don't know what you're talking about. I'm not the type to fall for an abuser."

"That's good. Maybe I misunderstood." Francis was sure he saw the hint of a smile on John's face during that ceremony. It had emerged while looking at his queen.

Francis turned, ready to leave, but before he stepped away, John spoke up again, quieter this time.

"She's lonely and empty like me," he whispered. "And she only gets angry after the stones talk to her. I've heard her conversations with them. They're one sided. I think they whisper poison in her ears, making her paranoid and saying I'll betray her. It makes me want to do the opposite and treat her well, just to spite them."

Francis remained silent, surprised he was opening up.

"Whoever is on the other end of the empyrean stones doesn't have good intentions. That or they're overprotective. I know the voices are real, though, because they're always accurate about my movements."

Francis looked at the empyrean stone ring he had given to John. "Maybe you shouldn't keep the empyrean stone with you, then. You don't know who might be listening."

"I won't. I'll lock it away until I need it." John stretched and yawned. It was almost sunup. "Regardless, part of me sympathizes with the queen but she still chooses to hurt me...Perhaps if we grew up in different situations we could have been friends, but it's too late now."

For a moment, Francis imagined a future where both he and John managed to escape with Evelyn and Ivy. "Perhaps if you took her away from the empyrean stones and her responsibilities as queen, things might improve."

"Maybe, but that's such a large undertaking that it's not worth it." John dead eyes matched his words. "And I know she wouldn't come willingly. Her duty is all she has left. There's no point thinking about it."

Francis wanted to push him to give in, envisioning a future where all four of them could live peacefully in the west, but he knew reality would never allow for it. "I have to go, John."

John just waved and continued staring at the mansion. His legs were no longer swinging.

This was the first time Francis felt like they truly connected, and it might be the last.

CHAPTER TWENTY-NINE

Evelyn had attended so many weddings in her childhood that she grew tired of them before the age of ten. When it was normal for noblewomen to have anywhere from three to twenty husbands in their lifetime, weddings felt commonplace and tedious. It was such a waste of money spent on a man who would often be treated as expendable from that day onward.

Until she met Francis, Evelyn didn't understand why women became so excited for weddings. Now, as she sat with her mother and Antonio and occasionally snuck glances at Francis, she only slightly understood. The thought of sharing such a day with him might not be so bad.

The interior of the castle was where the royal wedding occurred. Just like the rehearsal, the only witnesses were the councilors and their partners.

The queen and John both wore red and were stoic as they recited vows about loyalty and how the man should serve his wife until death. It wasn't anything out of the ordinary, other than the strange dress color and lack of smiles from the bride and groom.

The common folk were waiting outside the castle wall, civilians who came to see the queen and her new prince give a speech after the ceremony's conclusion. While Ivy wasn't the most popular queen in Clostrum's history, the people knew she was responsible for keeping them safe from intruders, so enough of them showed up to form a crowd.

As the priestess droned on and on about responsibility, Evelyn tapped her feet impatiently, only stopping when prince Antonio nudged her.

"Do weddings make you nervous?" he asked with a perfect smile. "You shouldn't be. I'm sure you'd make a lovely bride. I wouldn't mind seeing you in a wedding dress too, my lady."

His flattery was so obvious she wondered if he did it on purpose to make it clear this was a formality. The thought of wearing a wedding dress did tempt her to steal a glance at Francis again, standing against the wall behind them. She knew she could never have a wedding with him, but she could at least imagine the smile on his face when he saw her walk down the aisle.

"I have no plans to marry," she told Antonio, receiving a glare from her mother. "Not presently, at least."

"Well, I'm sure I can change your mind," he whispered flirtatiously.

She doubted it but wouldn't say anything to the contrary with her mother sitting so close. It was clear she wanted Antonio to join the family. He would make a perfect ally, bringing royalty into the Payne family line and more importantly guaranteeing protection from Dalius during any future conflicts.

Unfortunately for her mother, Evelyn had fallen in love with a slave and would therefore remain "unmarried" forever in the public's eye.

As the ceremony ended and Evelyn clapped, she looked around the room and once again tried to see everything through Francis's eyes. Instead of expensive jeweled dresses and hair that took hours to style, she noticed the slaves creeping about in the background, bringing drinks to the witnesses and holding up the queen's dress trail. Instead of viewing the many husbands in the room as nothing more than handsome males with empty minds, she saw men with dreams and aspirations that might never be fulfilled. They might be happy with their lives here, but they hadn't been given any other option.

"There's going to be a dance later," Antonio reminded her, whispering in her ear. His warm breath made her shiver in disgust. "Can I assume you'll be my partner for every song?"

"I'm afraid I'm not a fan of dancing," she answered coldly and stood as the queen and John walked out the front door to greet the public. The witnesses would follow them and Evelyn took the opportunity to slowly slip away from her mother and Antonio in the chaos. It was easy enough to join the crowd, then back out of her mother's sight and slip down an empty hallway before she had the chance to notice. The two-hour ceremony had drained her mentally and she needed a quick escape.

"Abandoning your responsibilities?" Francis asked jokingly as he trailed along behind her. She hoped he was the only one who noticed her slipping away from the cheers and applause of the ceremony.

"Weddings are always tedious," she answered. Once the voices behind them were far enough to become muffled, she opened the door to one of the guest bedrooms and peeked inside before ushering Francis in. Then she shut it behind her.

The room was bare. Other than an empty dresser and queen-sized bed with red sheets, there was nothing. There wasn't even a chair so she had to settle for the windowsill overlooking the street beyond the castle walls. The commoners walked below, carrying tall chocolate cakes and white banners to celebrate the queen's marriage. Evelyn doubted they even cared about Ivy but liked the excuse to eat and dance.

"And this wedding is especially stifling since Ivy and John are a volatile couple. I don't know what she sees in him," she admitted, her agitation slipping through.

"His face?" Francis joked as he leaned against the wall next to her, crossing his arms awkwardly and studying her instead of the crowd. "But I do think she feels connected to him, as he does to her. They relate to each other." He turned to study the people below, their lives so different from his and Evelyn's. "I think they'd get along if they weren't trapped in this castle with all its grievances."

"I suppose the same could be said for us." She watched a little boy and girl dance around each other, not caring about their genders or stations. Their laughter made her wish she could escape this stifling capital with its fake fawning and guilt.

"You don't think we get along?" Francis asked, making his mouth downturn in a fake expression of hurt. "I thought we were quite close," he teased.

"I was referring to being trapped in this capital, not Ivy and John's relationship." Evelyn glanced at him. His hands were behind his back now and he was studying every inch of her face like he was memorizing her.

She decided to copy his earlier stance and crossed her arms. "Sometimes I wish we were both born in the country," she admitted, filling the silence. "If we were poor farmers, we could marry and live together without fear of judgement." She heard slaves didn't even exist in those forests and fields.

"We could still get married," he whispered, moving his hand behind his back.

"A cute idea," she began, about to laugh at his joke. "But not a realistic one—"

When he brought his hands forward, she saw two simple red empyrean rings resting on his palms.

"Francis," she whispered, her throat closing up. His cheeks were pink and he was smiling nervously. She wished she could wear the same expression but her worries were overpowering how joyful this scene should be.

"With the way things are, we have no idea how long we'll be together," Francis explained, his calloused hands slowly pulling hers closer. "Just like when I kissed you after being burned, I want to do this now before I lose the chance. I don't want to regret it later if things go wrong."

"That's…" There was a lump in her throat. He was proposing. "We've only known each other for a few months, Francis. That isn't enough time to get to know someone…" She gulped, the lie making her bite her tongue. She felt she knew him better than anyone else in her life. "Not to mention our difference in stations."

The look in his eyes, begging her to forget all of that and do this for him, made her shut her mouth.

"A woman in the common district helped me make these from the restraint that burned me," he explained, holding them closer for her to see.

"You're willing to put these back on?" she whispered as he gently raised the ring finger on her right hand. "After they burned you?"

"I know you'll protect me," he answered softly. Women had the power to light the stones but they could also prevent someone else from doing the same. Its why women could bear empyrean weapons without risk of harm to themselves. The bullets and blades could still pierce, but they couldn't freeze or set someone alight. Certain guns also required the fire of the red empyrean bullets to travel forward. "And you'd never use them against me."

His faith in her nearly brought her to tears. He already trusted her too much. Blinking rapidly, she redirected the conversation. "How did you pay the woman who made them?"

"She took the leftover stone for herself." Francis prepared to slip one of the rings on. "If we put it on your right hand, your mother can't say it's a wedding ring, right? It can be our secret."

Now her eyes were watering. She didn't move to stop him because, deep down, she wanted this. She had wanted it for months, ever since she realized how she felt about him.

"What if we get caught? Or I get pregnant? Everyone will know and my family will lose its credibility," she continued even though her other hand remained by her side, refusing to push him away.

"I doubt your mother would throw away her grandchild just because it's the offspring of a slave," Francis said. "She kept you, didn't she?"

"…She did."

"And if she tries to harm our child, you can run to Antalius with me." He said the last part so longingly that she knew that was what he really wanted. "Just the two of us, living off the land and taking care of each other."

As the cold stone moved onto her finger, she felt the urge to give in and run away with him right now. She could abandon her mother, her home, her country, and live for herself. His dream could come true and she could finally make him happy.

But that would be selfish. Maybe someday, after her duties were done, they could finally retire in Antalius. For now, she had all of Clostrum to serve and protect.

"I have to be honest, though," Francis whispered as she put the other ring on his matching finger. "Seeing you with the prince from Dalius was the final push that convinced me to do this. I wanted to mark you somehow, so he'd know you belonged to me."

"You were jealous?" She found that unbelievably adorable and the pink that reentered his cheeks when he mentioned it made her want to tease him even more.

"I think it's natural to feel that way," he defended, turning away and pursing his lips. It was rare to see him so embarrassed. "You did the same in the mines, didn't you? John told me you stopped the night games because of me."

"Don't bring that up! I don't want to remember those games." She hit his arm lightly, then held onto him, once again relieved she'd done the right thing. "Though I didn't enjoy working in the mines, I'm glad it let me meet you."

"So am I."

She felt ready to cringe from the way he was looking at her and the embarrassing words she was uttering, so she pulled him into a hug so he wouldn't have to see her face. "We'll find a way to make this work. My mother doesn't need to know." Her body relaxed as he wrapped his arms around her back and squeezed. "I'll do everything within my means to protect this," she said. "And you. Just stay by my side and I'll keep you safe, Francis."

He hugged her back but he was squeezing so hard that she began to sense he doubted her ability to keep them together. Hopefully with enough time, he'd come to believe her.

"I forgot to say the vows," Francis said regretfully as their time ran out and Evelyn headed back into the hall. "I practiced it after the rehearsal too."

Evelyn couldn't help laughing under her breath. She remembered how invested he was in learning about wedding ceremonies before. Now it made sense. "If it's important to you, we can do it tonight, after the reception is finally over."

"I'd like that," he whispered, then reverted into his servant form as they entered the foyer. Evelyn hoped her excitement didn't show on her face, though she was sure the tedious festivities would be more than enough to dampen her spirits by the end of the day.

CHAPTER THIRTY

The coming weeks were the most peaceful he'd ever experienced. Francis was able to spend all day by Evelyn's side as a slave, then in the privacy of the evening, they could act like a real husband and wife. He also got to see John occasionally in the dead of night. For the first time in his life, everything flowed smoothly and without worry. To make matters even better, the creation of the empyrean stone restraints had been delayed by a month due to poor weather, so Francis didn't have to worry about its implications just yet.

For just a few weeks, Francis could pretend he was a normal man. He wasn't a slave ignoring the struggles of his brothers. He was just a husband spending time with his wife and finding new ways to make her smile. Even John smiled on occasion now and despite Ivy still treated him poorly, his attitude toward her was improving.

Life was starting to feel good.

Then, on the final day of the second week, the calm ended.

Winter was fast approaching, so on her day off, Evelyn took Francis into the capital's shopping district again to buy him a pair of winter coats. Even though red empyrean stones were enough to keep houses warm, they were risky to bring into carriages where thieves were tempted to steal them or fires could start.

As his wife shopped inside one of the buildings, its front window filled with a variety of colorful furs from the western woods, he waited at the front door, enjoying what little good weather they had left.

Francis was letting the sun shine on his face and thinking about nothing in particular when he heard a scream and turned to see a small boy running down the street toward him. The child was dressed in rags, not dissimilar from the clothes Francis wore in the mines, and he had blood running down his chin.

There was a woman chasing after the boy and she had a whip in her hand, which she was attempting to use on the child's heels. He barely looked five years old.

Francis didn't push the boy away as he hid behind him, sobbing and begging Francis to protect him as he clutched the back of Francis's pants.

"What's going on?" he asked the child, panicking as the woman marched toward him with a look that could kill. "What happened?"

"She wants to kill me," the boy whimpered. "I burnt the bread. I didn't mean to."

Francis studied the woman. Judging by her white uniform and tied back hair, she was a baker. If she worked in this part of the city, she must be moderately wealthy, likely owning at least five to ten slaves. Looking back at the little boy, he could tell the whip had struck its mark and left a cut on the boy's forehead, chin, and jaw. It would leave a permanent scar and might become infected.

"You!" The woman pointed at Francis. "Step aside! That boy is my property!"

It was Francis's responsibility to do as she said. Regardless of who he served, this woman had authority over him.

But he could feel the child's shaking hands cling to the fabric of his pants. The warm blood on the boy's face soaked the fabric as he pressed his small face against Francis's clothes. The woman kept fiddling with her whip, eager to use it on the child, and he felt like he was in the mines again, about to receive a lashing.

"My mistress will buy him off you," he told her. "Assuming he's an orphan." He wouldn't want to separate the child from its parents. "She can pay you double his asking price."

"I said, step aside!" The woman grabbed his shoulder, her nails digging into his skin, and tried shoving him but he refused to move. She was weaker than him. "Slave! Obey me! Step aside!"

"I'm afraid I cannot." He shouldn't do this. He had no authority here. "My mistress is Evelyn Payne." He shouldn't bring his wife into this and soil her name. "She will pay for the slave."

"I don't even care that he burnt the bread," the woman sneered, so focused on snatching the child that she didn't hear his words. "He tried to run from me. Disobedient brats need to learn their lesson."

Francis's eyes narrowed and when the woman grabbed the child's hand, he lost control and shoved her back, making her fall onto the cobblestones and drop her whip. Everyone in the street who had previously been watching in silence gasped.

"Francis?"

He froze, then turned slowly.

Evelyn was standing in the door of the shop behind him, purse in hand. She was staring at him with fear in her eyes, fear for the consequences of what he'd just done. He had laid hands on a woman, using his bodily advantage to harm the weaker sex. Even if he was her husband and bodyguard, he had no excuse in the public's eye.

What made it worse was everyone in this street knew who she was. Whispers began among the shoppers and sellers, waiting for Evelyn to respond accordingly.

"Evelyn," he whispered, still feeling the child latched onto him. "I'm sorry, I—"

"My lady," she sharply reminded him to address him appropriately, stepping past him and opening her purse. He watched with bated breath as she pulled several gold coins from her purse and dropped them in front of the woman. "This should be more than enough to pay for the child and damages. I apologize for any injury my slave has given you. I assure you he will be summarily punished."

The woman spat at his feet but took the coins anyway. She could buy ten more slaves with all that money.

For a moment, Francis feared Evelyn might send the child away but to his surprise, she ordered both of them to enter the carriage and took them home without bothering to retrieve the coats she'd just bought.

The start of the ride to the Payne mansion was silent, as Evelyn stared out the window with a pale face and wrinkles between her eyebrows. Then, she finally spoke without making eye contact. "Francis, you do realize what you've done, don't you?"

"Yes. I'm sorry. I couldn't just stand by and watch him get whipped. He's a child."

She shot him a glare, not angry at his actions but at the risk he had taken. "My mother will hear of this and might dismiss you. She's done the same to others for less. How am I supposed to defend you without outing myself?"

The child listened to them with tears streaming down his cheeks. His hands were covering his forehead defensively.

"What would you have me do? Watch a little boy die when I know I could protect him?"

"I would rather lose a child I don't know than the man I love!" she shouted, shocking him.

"How could you say that, Evelyn?" Francis whispered.

His wife turned away, biting the top of her finger nervously. "Don't do this again," was all she said as they arrived home and she stepped out. "Send him to the kitchen. The cook needs an assistant anyway."

He hoped that was the end of it but as expected, the next day while Evelyn was bathing, her mother summoned Francis to her office. It was located at the other end of the mansion, far away from the slave quarters and Evelyn's bedroom.

Everything about the office represented power and control. There wasn't a speck of dust on the books, not a single creased page. The papers on her desk were organized and labeled. The letters were enclosed with gold wax. The empyrean weapons hanging on the walls were spotless. Even the large window offered her a complete a view of the streets, gardens, adjacent mansions, and castle. She could see everything from up here.

Lady Payne was waiting for him at her desk, her hands crossed over one knee and the right side of her face raised with a smirk. She knew how uncomfortable she made him and wanted to keep it that way.

"Take a seat, slave," she told him, gesturing toward the wooden chair in front of her desk. "I think you know why you're here."

He didn't answer, focusing instead on hiding the ring on his finger. He kept his left hand over the right to keep it concealed.

"Two weeks ago, I entertained the idea that you'd given up your immature escapades about the city. I noticed you stopped freeing slaves after the queen's wedding. Isn't that right?" She waited for him to nod, treating him like a child.

What she said was true. He hadn't made any efforts to help anyone in the last two weeks, though he wasn't happy about it. He knew he was still being watched every time he left to visit John, so he hadn't done anything risky yet.

After he nodded, she continued. "I hoped, for your sake, that you finally gave up on soiling my family name." She pursed her lips. "But it appears I was wrong."

He shifted uncomfortably. She must be referring to what happened today with the baker.

The ring felt heavy on his finger as she sneered at him, her friendly façade she used in public gone.

"This is your final warning, boy. Stop destroying my daughter's reputation or I will kill you. My daughter may have taken a liking to you, but I can frame you any way I like and make you the villain before ending your life. I could even convince her to kill you herself."

Bile rose up his throat. He wanted to talk to this woman about the potential she had to save generations of children in the future. He wanted to speak to her as a son would to a mother, rather than a slave to his mistress. There was so much good she could do. All of her apparent anxiety and difficulties would disappear if she would fight for good rather than progress and wealth.

But this woman wasn't like her daughter. While Evelyn wanted to understand and sympathize with the slaves and was willing to grow, her mother was set in her ways. She was practically begging him to open his mouth and give her a reason to execute him.

So, he stayed silent, like every other coward he used to judge.

"Don't get cocky," she finished, looking surprised that he wasn't talking back. "Prince Antonio is the man I have chosen for my daughter. Marrying him will protect her from enemies you barely know exist. Once I see them married, I can die without regrets. If you can't stand by and watch, I suggest you speak up now."

Her words stung and he couldn't help clenching his jaw, silent.

"And one final thing. I know you were curious about what happened to the slaves you freed a month ago." She stood and grinned down at him. "I had my assassin recapture them and return them to their mistresses but, unsurprisingly, the women didn't want them back, so I was given permission to execute them."

His eyes welled up with tears and it took everything in him to stay seated. This woman was taller but he could still wring her neck. If only his conscience and the consequences weren't hold him back.

"If they hadn't tried to escape, they would still be alive." She leaned forward, her face a breath away from his. "I want you to remember their faces every time you consider doing something stupid."

"I just wanted to help," he whispered.

"It's time you acknowledged that you can't help anyone, Francis. All you can do is obey. Doing otherwise only brings harm to others."

Maybe she was right.

"What will happen to the boy Evelyn bought yesterday?" he asked.

"The baker's boy? We'll take him, but the public opinion of Evelyn has shifted, so if the boy slips up even once, I am within my rights to finish his previous mistress's actions."

"…Thank you, my lady."

There was no hesitation, no doubt, in her eyes as she told him to leave. It was clear by the look on her face that she knew she had broken his spirit.

He didn't tell Evelyn what happened. As she exited the bath, he put on a smile and made a joke about seeing her in a towel, pretending his entire world hadn't just fallen apart with only her remaining. She looked concerned, aware his smile was fake, but likely assumed it was related to what happened yesterday.

It was better that she didn't know. She was too stressed already.

CHAPTER THIRTY-ONE

"I have a question," Evelyn said one night as they lay together in bed. She had spent the last hour teaching him to read Clostrian and by this point, his eyes felt ready to fall out.

"Go ahead," he said, eager to put the book down and avoid picking it up again. He couldn't understand how she read books for hours on end without a break.

Evelyn took the children's book from him and placed it on the nightstand. She thentook a moment to rid the blanket of wrinkles, keeping him in suspense, before finally resting her head on his shoulder. "When you were growing up, did you ever think about having children?"

"More often than you might think," he admitted. Even though he had little chance of leaving those mines, he had still dreamed of it often. "I wanted to have two girls and one boy. One of them would enjoy gardening, one would enjoy hunting, and the last one would have an unhealthy obsession with books like you do."

"I don't have an obsession!" She gasped as he laughed at her outburst. "I'm being serious here."

"So am I." He giggled for a few more seconds, then stopped so she'd calm down. Teasing her was one of his favorite pastimes and she knew her reactions only encouraged him. "How many children do *you* want, Evelyn?"

"Enough to guarantee my cousins can't inherit the business," she grumbled. "So four, maybe, though with each child, the risk of death in pregnancy increases."

He hadn't considered that until just now, since this was his first time with a real woman in his life—one he wanted to make a family with. "Why are you bringing this up?" He grinned. "Is there something I should know?" Was she hinting at something? They'd only been together less than a month but he'd heard of women bearing children less than a year after marrying.

"No." She turned away, rubbing her nose and filling him with disappointment he wasn't expecting. "I was just curious, since you sometimes bring up that family in a cottage you dream of. I wanted to hear more about it."

Even though they both knew it wasn't possible, she still wanted to hear about it. He didn't deserve her. "My friends would make fun of my dream when I was younger," he admitted. "When they heard I wanted a daughter, they insisted I name her Remmington."

"Remmington? The knight from those foolish novels?" She scrunched up her nose, still playful. "That's a terrible name and it's a male one too!"

"Yes, which is why they said it. They sought out the silliest name they knew. It was that or Bim."

"What does Bim mean?"

"Nothing. It just sounded silly. Really rolls off the tongue, doesn't it?" he teased.

"Well, I can guarantee neither of those names will ever be spoken aloud by me," she huffed and pulled his arm closer. "If we did have a daughter, what name would you choose?"

He paused. "You're really set on this topic. It's making me think you might be—"

"I'm not," she insisted, though she refused to make eye contact. "I was just curious. If you don't want to say it—"

"I like talking about this," he cut in, enjoying it immensely. "But to be honest, I couldn't find a name that I liked. There are so many nice ones and I can't choose the right one until I see her for myself."

"That's not how naming the baby works," she said but he could see her smiling now.

"And what about you? What names do you like?"

"Never thought about it," she muttered. "Which is why I asked."

As they went to bed, sharing the blanket now instead of forcing him to sleep on the floor, he stayed up late trying to think of a suitable name. He could already picture the child, a little girl with blonde hair like her mother's and dark eyes like his, running through their garden in Antalius and bringing flowers to her mother.

"When you're pregnant," he whispered to his sleeping wife. "I'll tell you the name I want. I'll make it a surprise." And if he was dead by then, likely at the hands of her mother, she wouldn't have to feel guilty for using a different one.

CHAPTER THIRTY-TWO

Evelyn had mixed feelings as she reentered the mines for the first time since she left. On the one hand, she had an eerie sense of nostalgia when meeting the commander, who hadn't changed at all. On the other hand, the sound of metals burning in the empyrean pots and the stench of filth made her want to retreat to her clean mansion.

She was here to inspect the mines and ensure they had followed her guidelines, which she didn't doubt the commander did. She also wanted to judge the effectiveness of her own rules and see what changes needed to be made. That was mainly why she brought along Francis, against her better judgement. He had a keen eye and people were willing to reveal their secrets to him. She needed him here even though he might react poorly to the location.

The only consolation of being here was that no one here would judge them like the citizens in the capital would. She could treat Francis kindly without worrying about it getting back to her mother. The only people down here were slaves and convicts. Any rumors were unlikely to spread to the surface.

"You look lovely," the commander said to Evelyn as she entered the mines. Evelyn was wearing a blue and silver dress with a high collar. Her makeup and hair were perfect, intentionally styled to ensure the guards knew she was in charge now.

Francis wore a similar outfit, though the colors were toned down. His hair was also growing and almost long enough to tie in a ponytail, as was the current fashion for noblemen.

However, despite his improved appearance, his expression had worsened. He'd been sullen ever since he pushed down that baker in the street. She hoped his change in attitude was merely guilt from ruining her reputation and not the symptom of something worse.

She'd avoided asking him, though. Overseeing the empyrean stone construction and visiting prince Antonio so her mother wouldn't be suspicious had stolen all of her time. By the time she went to bed, she was unwilling to discuss anything with her husband that might lead to a fight.

"Just one more week until the collars arrive, correct?" the commander asked as she led Evelyn through the familiar foyer toward the kitchen. The slaves looked noticeably healthier but not happier in any way.

"Yes. I have overseen the entire process," Evelyn said, smiling from relief. Soon, all the pain and worry would be gone.

"That's a load off my mind," the commander said, stepping aside so Evelyn could look at the kitchen herself.

To her disappointment, the cripple she had encountered when she worked here was still in the corner but instead of sitting on a chair, he was standing with crutches. He was still handing out bread to his fellow slaves while balancing on straight but useless legs.

"He's able to stand without help now," the commander commented, following Evelyn's line of sight. "And if his legs continue to heal properly, he may be able to walk someday."

"That's good news." Evelyn smiled and glanced at Francis to see his reaction.

His gaze was focused on the far end of the room. What was he looking at?

She followed his gaze and saw a young man around their age sitting on a pillow in a different corner. He had a scar over each eye and his jaw was purple from bruises. The young man's legs were broken and twisted under his body incorrectly, just like the other cripple across the room used to be.

Evelyn paled as she realized who it was.

This was the slave who had tried to run twice—the one Evelyn had given the commander permission to break.

The disgust was obvious on Francis's face and when he turned, it was aimed at her. "You own this mine," he said, interrupting the commander mid-sentence. "I thought you were trying to end this practice."

She shouldn't have brought him after all. She'd been so preoccupied with her marriage and meetings in the capital that she'd forgotten the punishments she'd granted over a month ago.

Evelyn glanced at the commander, who was listening with a questioning expression, then grabbed Francis by the arm and pulled him to the slave barracks. They should be empty at this time of day and were soundproof.

As they walked, Francis continued talking in a low hiss, his eyes wide and arms shaking. "You promised me you would defend my friends. That was the least you could do. You own these mines, Evelyn."

Once the doors were shut and they were alone in the dark room, its floor covered in significantly more blankets and pillows than before, she finally spoke.

"The crippling of that one man was a necessary evil," she told him, shushing him until she finished. "Once we have the collars on the slaves, they won't need to fear physical punishments again!"

"Because they'll have to fear death instead, a painful death in which you burn their throats! How can you feel good about this, Evelyn? This is what you wanted, after everything you saw here? This is your solution? To place collars around the necks of children and threaten to burn them if they question you?" He gripped her arms, shaking her as though that would knock some sense into her. "You're not your mother, Evelyn!"

"It's better than the alternative! I'm doing what I can, Francis! Why do you expect perfection?"

"I don't expect perfection! I expect human decency! After you saw what a single second of fire did to my wrist, you thought it was okay to do the same to countless others? You removed my collar but placed it on others without hesitation?"

"You think I didn't hesitate?" She was shouting now but no longer cared. No one could hear them anyway. "I don't feel good about this, Francis. I wish the world didn't need slaves and the gods weren't demanding we dig, but the reality is that until we find what the gods are looking for, I have to choose the kinder of the two."

Francis loosened his grip on her. "So, when I thought you were becoming sympathetic to the slaves, you were only looking at me and no one else? I assumed your protection extended beyond a single man."

"You're ignoring what I just said—"

"If the gods require children to die for their will, perhaps they aren't really gods!"

She put a hand over his mouth, worried his voice might carry. There could be black empyrean stones in the walls for all she knew. What if the gods heard his blasphemy?

"You're living in the moment, Francis. Think of the future. Right now, I have very little authority but in the coming years, when my mother is gone, I will be in charge. I can give commands without restraint. You must wait until that day comes."

"I'm sure there are thousands of women who said the same when they were young, before they had power. Then when they gained control, they refused to give it up and became just like their mothers."

"You don't think I can maintain my morals?" she asked, choking on her own words. "You think I'll become power hungry? I thought you knew me better than that!"

"Look what you've already stooped to! At the slightest pressure, you crippled a man! His legs will never heal. He will never walk again! If you can't stick to your morals now, you won't do it later when there's more pressure!" He released her arms. "You've always viewed me and my vision as unrealistic but I'm not as foolish as you assume. I know how easy it is to give in. With each step in one direction, it becomes harder to change your path."

Blood was pounding in her ears and her eyes were watering. He made her feel like a monster. After everything she'd done, all the risks she had taken for him, it still wasn't enough! He would never be satisfied.

"If you don't like how I act, why did you marry me?" she whispered.

"Because I loved you and still do! But that doesn't mean I will sit by and watch your mother corrupt you. You have so many chances to improve the lives of thousands, Evelyn, so much potential. I want to see you—"

"So, you're in love with a future version of me you made up in your head?" she hissed. "All you see when you look at me is an illusion. I'll never live up to your standards."

"You know that isn't true." He paused to step away from her and paced around the room to rid himself of his anger. When he returned to her a few seconds later, he was calm again. "I know it's hard to go against your mother but I'm asking you to do it for me. The common folk of Clostrum don't care about slavery. Most people can't afford slaves and I've heard there are many who wish slavery didn't exist. There are many willing to help you free my people. They just need to know someone as powerful as you is an ally. If you speak up, they will follow and defend you."

"I'm not trying to please the public," Evelyn said. "I'm trying to please the women who are willing to hire assassins and kill both of us. I want to avoid seeing you kidnapped and used as blackmail against me."

"I'm not afraid," he said.

"I am!"

Her breath echoed in the quiet room as he stared at her. "Evelyn—"

"I'm not going to lose you," she said. "Call me selfish if you like or cowardly or any number of names, but I will fulfil your wishes on my own. I won't back down from my mother, but I will not act rashly and endanger you. I can make change without bringing injury to those I love. You need to trust me."

He didn't speak and that was answer enough. She knew he disagreed, but this was the point where they couldn't stand on the same side. She wouldn't give up her life for these slaves, even though he was willing to. She couldn't be as selfless as him.

She hoped with time he would come to understand. Many years from now, when slavery was finally abolished, he would look back on this moment and understand why it was a necessary. The path to the freedom he craved would be a harsh one but would lead to it regardless.

As they left the room and she sent him to the surface so she could finish the inspection on her own, she continued telling herself this was the right decision. She *could* end the torment of these men and preserve her own family at the same time. It would take time and patience, but she would prove Francis wrong.

This was what she kept telling herself as the commander completed the inspection. Francis didn't speak during the three-day carriage ride home. Even when Evelyn addressed him, he remained silent.

"We'll discuss this another time," she finally said during their second day on the road after sleeping separately. "Let's spend a week apart. I'll hire a temporary bodyguard so you can focus on your training." She could even bring Antonio in to defend her. Any prince of Dalius was more than capable.

"Very well, my lady." His formal tone infuriated her, but she hoped this rift between them would disappear with a week or two apart. It would clear their heads and help him face reality.

CHAPTER THIRTY-THREE

For the following week, the couple continued sleeping separately.

Instead of lying beside her or on the floor as he normally did, Francis placed a pillow outside her door and slept there instead. She understood why he did it and couldn't blame him but when she woke in the middle of the night, disturbed by nightmares of a future without him, the empty side of the bed where he normally slept felt cold.

The emptiness wasn't enough to overcome her pride, though, until the fifth night.

After spending the entire day with Antonio, attending a parade to celebrate Clostrum's independence from their neighbors, Evelyn came home to a different welcome than normal. Instead of seeing Francis waiting by the door, her mother was there instead. The older woman spent several minutes gushing over Antonio and how good he looked beside Evelyn, insisting on a proposal by the end of the month.

It made Evelyn sick to her stomach and she dismissed the man early, eager to find Francis instead. Part of her feared he had finally left her. The head maid informed her he was still in training and would return by midnight, but his absence made it difficult to fall asleep that night. Perhaps seeing the mines again made him change his mind about their marriage and their love for each other.

Once sleep stopped eluding her, she dreamed she was underground again, serving as a guard and overseeing Francis and John as she used to. It almost made her smile to return to a simpler time but then Francis turned on her, shouting the words he said to her a week ago in the barracks. He was cursing her, wishing death upon her, and then he was wrapping his hands around her throat, crushing her windpipe under his scarred fingers.

Evelyn struggled against him, but he was no longer the weak and tired slave her mother had created. He was powerful, strong enough to snap her neck with little effort, and as he did so with a loud and painful crack, she awoke.

Tears filled her eyes as she sat up in bed, drenched in sweat and panting. Her hands leapt to her throat, feeling for bruises and finding none. The dream had felt too real.

"Francis?" she whispered at the closed bedroom door. Had he returned from his training? "Francis?" Her voice turned to that of a child, begging.

His shadow shifted under the door, filling her with relief, then there was a click and he stepped inside, his eyes red. Had he been crying?

"Can you come to bed?" she whispered, reaching for him. "Please?" She needed to feel him, to confirm that he would never harm her.

She could see hesitation and confusion in his movements. She'd been so cold to him after their fight. But he came to her anyway and wrapped her in his arms, comforting her by gently stroking her hair. "Did something happen?"

She pulled him closer, wishing she had never let him go. "Don't leave me," she whispered.

"I won't." He continued running his hands through her hair. "Are you okay? Did the prince do something?"

"No." She wiped away her tears. "I'm sorry I can't meet your expectations, Francis."

He didn't answer but she could tell by his sloped shoulders and low breathing that he had no plans to fight again.

"I will do what I can to protect your friends," she promised. "I swear it. Please, just give me time. Don't give up on me."

He caressed her cheek. "I won't."

"I love you," she added, pulling away and searching his eyes. There was no resentment in them. Only hurt.

"I know. I won't leave you, even if you fail."

She nodded. This was the real Francis, the one who didn't abandon people even if they were flawed.

"But I will never lie to you," he continued. "If I think you are becoming like your mother, I will tell you honestly. I don't want to see you turn into her."

"I know."

He pressed his forehead against hers for a moment, sighing, then smirked. "On second thought, it's impossible for you to turn into your mother. She's much taller than you."

"Oh, you had better watch your mouth," she warned, letting a chuckle escape. It was a welcome change from the sobs.

"Your father must have been exceedingly short," he continued, placing a hand on the top of her head to demonstrate how much shorter she was.

She sucked in a breath, allowing herself to relax before retorting. He used humor to escape his pain and she was more than happy to do the same tonight. "You're one to talk. When you stand next to John and Antonio, you look like—"

"How cruel of you to compare your husband to other men," he interrupted with an unrestrained smile.

The tense mood gone, he leaned forward to kiss her and as she kissed him back, she prayed for every argument to be resolved this way. Otherwise, she didn't know how to keep him by her side. The thread of fate holding them together felt ready to snap at any moment.

How pathetic that the richest heir in Clostrum had become so desperate to retain the attention of a mining slave; And how ironic that she'd become more reliant on him than he was on her.

CHAPTER THIRTY-FOUR

After the weekly council meeting, Evelyn was held back by the queen for yet another private conversation. These sometimes ranged from personal to professional talks, usually centered around the mines and how close they were to finding this so-called "weapon" the gods had mentioned. As far as Evelyn could tell, there were only more empyrean stones and relics like knives, shields, and armor to be found. No unique items had stood out to her or her mother.

Today, however, the queen seemed focused on something else, something Evelyn had unfortunately forgotten about a month ago.

"Have you found any potential women who can give birth to my heir?" The queen was seated on her throne with one leg propped up on the arm rest, wearing black tights under her dress to combat the winter winds. "Remember that they must look like John or I."

Evelyn gulped and took a moment to cross her legs, delaying the conversation. "I assumed you wanted to wait a little while longer, giving the honeymoon a few months so the pregnancy seemed more natural."

"I don't have time to waste on such things. The ruler of a country is always in danger so it's reckless to delay. Besides, if John becomes the father of the future queen, the public will finally view him as a valuable asset, as I do." The queen turned away, focusing on the door at the other end of the room where they knew John, Francis, and a few other soldiers were waiting in the hall. "You have nine months to find a suitable newborn."

"I will begin right away," Evelyn said. The distribution of restraints in the mines would finally occur at the end of the week, so she would have the time and energy to focus on something new soon after. "I'll find a suitable mother and hide her in one of my family's labs." Those were the most secure locations in the city. Someone could live there for years and never be seen by the public. "Bear in mind that a few months from now, you will have to hide or wear clothes that give the impression of pregnancy."

"I don't mind. I rarely leave the castle anyway."

Evelyn smiled. "That is true." She wished she could do the same at home. She could spend all day with Francis, just the two of them. Maybe once all this work was over, they could finally have a break together. She could take him to the country and let him finally enjoy the flowers and forests he raved about. "Is there anything else you require, my queen?"

Ivy raised her chin and looked down on Evelyn, tilting her head. "You have been very close to that Dalius prince lately."

Against her will. "Yes."

"You haven't mentioned the empyrean voices to him, have you?"

She avoided telling the prince anything, political or otherwise. "About the weapon the gods want you to find?" she ventured.

Ivy's eyes narrowed. "Yes."

"No, I have not."

For some reason, Evelyn felt like the queen didn't believe her. If anything, the answer seemed to make Ivy's countenance darken even more. "I have received word that he was spotted near one of your mines."

"I was not made aware." Had her mother sent him there?

"The Mines of Valhander are where the gods wish for us to dig. I fear he may know this and is spying for his mother."

"If he is, I have nothing to do with it. I can launch an investigation on him if you wish." Evelyn had assumed he was merely here to pursue a marriage, as her mother wished.

Was Queen Ivy becoming paranoid or was she right about Antonio? The prince always felt guarded, hiding his true feelings behind all his flattery. "Doesn't the royal family in Dalius have empyrean stones of their own?"

"Yes. My mother sent them years ago to prevent a war. I wish we could take them back." The queen turned her glare toward the window, staring at the shores of the eastern sea.

"Perhaps the gods have told them about the weapon already," Evelyn offered, pointing at the black stone hanging from the queen's neck. "There is a chance the weapon may be for—"

"Do you *want* the gods to speak to those savages?" Ivy leapt from her chair and pointed accusingly at Evelyn. "Spending time with that foreign prince has made you forget the Dalian's violent nature!"

Evelyn frowned, confused by her sudden outburst. She didn't particularly like prince Antonio or his people but he hadn't acted violent or barbaric in their time together. "The gods do not discriminate among us. That's why I suggested they may speak to the Dalius rulers as well as yourself. You speak as though Dalius and Clostrum are still at war. That was nearly a hundred years ago."

Ivy was in front of the table now, her fists poised to punch its surface. "The gods only speak to those who are worthy!"

Ah, so Ivy assumed only *she* was worthy. Evelyn wasn't surprised. If only a few people could hear the voices from the stones, those who heard it would predictably assume they were special.

Sighing, Evelyn stood from her own chair so they were on the same eye level. "My queen, I hold no allegiance to Dalius. I am loyal to you and you alone." The words tasted foul on her mouth but she didn't want to risk the queen's wrath. "If you suspect prince Antonio is trying to work against Clostrum, I will launch an investigation."

Ivy's lips twisted. She was thinking things through.

Then her eye jerked to the side, as though she heard something behind her. The silence made Evelyn wonder if the stone around her neck was speaking to her right now.

"My queen," Evelyn started, glancing at the stone on the queen's throat, then back at her. "I will take care of this."

"You won't investigate anything," Ivy whispered, sounding resigned to something Evelyn wasn't allowed to hear. "You'll let him steal what is ours and send it to Dalius so they can finally retake our land."

Evelyn stepped back, not liking this three-sided conversation. She couldn't defend herself if someone she couldn't hear was speaking against her. "Then I will send him back to Dalius so he cannot steal anything." Only her mother would protest.

"No. He knows too much." Ivy started toward the door, shouting for the guards. The throne door opened and Evelyn saw John and Francis standing there, alongside prince Antonio. He must have come to pick Evelyn up, likely at her mother's request.

As soon as the queen saw the prince, his handsome face lifting as he smiled at both of them, the queen redirected her path toward him. Evelyn could see her pulling a bracelet off her wrist, strung with red rings. If that was empyrean stone, she could wrap it around his throat and burn him then and there.

Evelyn had to stop this. The queen's insanity was rearing its ugly head and could start a war. If Queen Triana found out her innocent son had been murdered in cold blood, she would retaliate within the month.

"Ivy!" She ran to the queen and grabbed the arm holding the bracelet. All three men froze when she shouted, though none moved to defend either lady.

"My queen," she whispered, glaring at Antonio as she spoke, hoping he would take the hint and run. "Doing this will create a war. I assure you, if there was anything to find in that mine, I would have found it by now. He knows nothing. Send him back to Dalius before you make a rash decision."

Ivy struggled against her grip but was thankfully no stronger than she. "Unhand me before I tell my guards to lock you up," Ivy hissed. The guards in question were running down the hall toward them now, their boots pounding on the stone floor. "I'm doing what I can to protect my country."

"This will not protect us. It will create a war." Evelyn shook her head, confused. Ivy had always seemed somewhat intelligent and logical, albeit a little prone to anger. She had never acted this manic before. However, based on the bored expression on John's face, this wasn't a first for him.

"Antonio, leave us," Evelyn commanded before the guards could reach them. She then glanced at Francis, who had one foot toward her but looked afraid to interfere.

"This is my final warning to release me," Ivy growled and Evelyn finally let her go. As soon as she did, Ivy shoved her, then hit her across the face with the bracelet. The stone cut her cheek and had enough weight to knock her even further.

"You are letting your feelings get in the way of what's right!" Ivy shouted, ignoring the blood running down Evelyn's cheek. "Whoever gets the weapon first will have the power to win any war! Are you so focused on the present that you ignore the future?"

Evelyn didn't know how to answer anymore. She had never been struck by the queen before, and judging by the look on Ivy's face, she planned to do it again if Evelyn said something wrong. The queen eyes were still darting back and forth from Evelyn to the walls and ceiling. Were the voices shouting at her as she spoke? It certainly looked like it.

"The gods are giving us a gift and you are wasting it to appease the wishes of people across the sea that care nothing for us or our people! If you cannot keep our country safe, perhaps you should not be a member of my council!"

Evelyn's own temper flared. She saw Francis shake his head at her, warning her to keep it at bay, but it was too late. "Just a minute ago, you were placing the identity of your future heir in my hands. Now you dare to call me a traitor!"

Ivy sneered at her, then raised her hand to strike Evelyn again, this time with both the bracelet and a fist. Evelyn tried to step back and cover her face with her arms but she knew her skin would be burned either way. The queen wouldn't hold back the stones' power this time and Evelyn was afraid of countering the control of the stones, lest she anger Ivy more.

She prepared herself for the pain, reminding herself that if Francis could take it, she could too, but it never came.

Breathing heavily, she lowered her hands and looked at the queen. Why had Ivy stopped?

The queen still had her hand raised but John's fingers were wrapped around her fist, his grip unwavering despite the glowing stones burning his skin. He didn't even flinch from the pain.

As soon as Ivy saw the stones burning her own husband, she gasped and made the glow disappear.

The stench of burnt flesh filled the room as Francis grabbed Evelyn's elbow. "We need to go," he whispered, pulling her toward the door. "She'll kill you if we stay."

Evelyn was still staring at John, shocked he had protected her and hurt himself in the process. She thought he hated her and every other woman in this country.

Francis was breathing heavily, panicking, but she refused to leave until she'd resolved this. She would not let her entire life be thrown away because of a single woman's insanity and stubbornness.

"Ivy," she began, brushing Francis off as he continued tugging her arm. "I have friends and family in Clostrum that I want to protect. I am not going to help Dalius or anyone else destroy the country I love."

Ivy had looked rageful a moment ago but now, with John holding her back, the anger had finally faded and it looked like the voices had too. "And if you find the weapon, you promise to hand it over to me?" she asked, almost desperately. "So no one else can use it against us?"

Evelyn didn't believe there was a weapon. She was beginning to think the voices in Ivy's head were imaginary, a symptom of Ivy's insanity. The queen was a child raised by a thoughtless mother, tasked to prevent a war at the age of ten and rule a country alone. Paranoia was what protected her growing up and it had become all she knew. The councilors who acted suspicious or questioned Ivy were viewed as enemies and banished or executed. Many of her mother's friends had died from this over the years and even though the queen had become less violent recently, it seemed to be returning.

If the weapon was real, queen Ivy was the last person who should have it.

"Yes," she lied with a smile, nodding confidently at the ruler. "Of course I will. You are my leader."

The queen smiled in relief. Her smile was very pretty. It was a pity Evelyn had to lie to see it. "Thank you, Evelyn. I'm sorry for hurting you. It won't happen again, so long as we continue working together."

Evelyn gripped Francis's hand a little too tightly, trying to keep her façade up. "Thank you, my queen."

If this weapon really existed, whoever had hidden it had the right idea.

There was an idea solidifying in her mind now, that she might need to bring Ivy out of power. Such a violent person wasn't fit to rule. Hopefully the insanity would eventually cause her own downfall. If it didn't, Evelyn would deal with it later. That, or John would.

Evelyn jumped when the blood from her cut ran into her mouth, its bitter taste reminding her she was still angry about being attacked. "Francis, let's go," she whispered, turning away from Ivy. "Before I lose my temper."

But Francis wasn't looking at her. He was staring at John, who was still gripping Ivy's hand with pursed lips. John was looking at his wife like he wanted to wrap the empyrean stone bracelet around her throat and strangle her with it.

"John," Francis said cautiously.

John looked back at him, blinked a few times, then released his wife. Only then did Francis pull Evelyn out of the room and into the hallway, heading for the stairs.

"We will speak of this to no one," Evelyn told her husband as he wiped the blood from her face. "I'll deal with her later." After the mines were no longer a concern.

"I thought she was going to kill you," Francis whispered, his hands rough against her smooth skin. His voice was cracking from fear and paranoia. He had felt death's touch three times this month.

"I'm lucky John protected me," Evelyn said with an astonished laugh. "He surprised me."

"I don't think he did it for you," Francis replied quietly, his breath still shaky. "He may have been looking for an excuse to…"

"To do what? To kill her?" Evelyn asked and the immediate fear in her husband's eyes confirmed it. He had accidentally exposed his friend for wanting to murder the queen. John could be executed for the mere suspicion. "Well, I'm glad he showed restraint, for his own sake," she said, silently assuring him she wouldn't report John.

"Yes, this time," Francis whispered. "But how long will he last?"

A traitorous thought filled her, a hopeful one. If John finally snapped and killed Ivy, they would be free of her and her accusations. "I'm sure he's smart enough to run away if he *does* kill her," she answered, meaning it.

"But he'd be hunted," Francis said.

"The council might let him go," Evelyn whispered, knowing her words could get her killed but Francis wouldn't tell anyone. "If she proves herself a danger to the council, John can kill her and no one will try to stop him."

She thought her words would encourage Francis and lessen his worries about his friend but instead, he turned toward her with wide eyes and an open mouth. This was the third time he'd looked at her this way. "Why are you talking like this? I thought she was your friend."

"She was." Evelyn stopped at the top of the stairs and looked down at the castle foyer where so many parties and weddings had occurred. "Then she tried to kill me." Why was he always looking at her like that, like she was a monster? "Are you defending her after she tried to kill me, Francis?"

"No."

"Then what's wrong?"

"…I don't think killing people will solve anything," he said. "Revenge only causes more pain."

He was always so idealistic, wanting to believe everyone had potential to be good. Even after everything he saw in the mines, he was still unwilling to make sacrifices. "Francis, I know what I'm doing. If I ever do something as extreme as harming someone, it will only be as a last resort. Trust me."

"For your sake, Evelyn, I hope that is true."

But she could tell he didn't believe her anymore. This wasn't the first time she'd acted like her mother. Perhaps Evelyn had always been like her and was just too young to see it.

CHAPTER THIRTY-FIVE

"You look as ready to leave this miserable city as I am," John said to Francis with a chuckle.

They were on the roof of a closed tavern, discussing what happened in the throne room.

Francis still felt like they were being watched. As he glanced at the black empyrean ring on John's finger, he wondered whether the eyes he felt from the gods in that stone or if it was one of Lady Payne's assassins.

"I saw a side of Evelyn that scared me," Francis admitted. "And I want to know whether it's *her* or her mother speaking. I want to know if the woman I love can prevail over this city's influence."

"You're really trying to convince yourself she's special and unique after everything she's done," John scoffed, "And ignoring the fact that she was raised here. The corruption of these nobles runs through her veins. She is no different from all the pathetic, miserable women she shares a table with. She just tells herself she's better and you believed her."

That couldn't be true. She had been trying to help people, to be merciful. These temporary things she'd been doing were just that: temporary. She could see the same future he could...couldn't she?

"I find it increasingly ironic that you seemed happier in the mines than you do here," John said with another laugh.

"I *was* happy…for a few weeks." When it was just him and Evelyn celebrating a honeymoon in secret. He had let his love for her distract him from the slaves serving their food and washing their clothes. He ignored the ring weighing down on his finger. It was stained with the blood of his brothers. He had known Evelyn for nearly five months now but nothing had changed for the better, other than living conditions. Not even *she* seemed happier.

"We can still run away," John offered, as though reading his mind. "We still have a few days before the slaves are shackled. We can go to the mine together, bring as much gold and weapons as we can, sneak in, and help them flee."

"You talk about sneaking in as though there aren't guards with empyrean guns at the entrance," Francis said hopelessly.

"You bear the armor of Evelyn Payne now. Take her ring, claim you are there to deliver a message, then walk inside without issue." He shrugged. "That's the least violent option but the riskiest. I have a better way."

"And what way is that?"

"Those guards have never been attacked from the outside. They're used to shooting down defenseless men. Their armor is often discarded because it's uncomfortable and their laziness leaves them exposed," John began, speaking energetically. Once again, he only got excited when talking about rebelling against Clostrum. More specifically, he was excited about spilling blood. "You've been trained with a bow and arrow and I've practiced enough to shoot too. We could take them out from the cover of the trees, then stroll right in. We know how many nightguards there are and where they're stationed. They should be easy enough to kill."

"I don't want to kill them," Francis cut him off. "Most of the guards used to work with us."

"By the time they recognize us, they'll be dead," John answered.

"It's not about being recognized. We grew up with some of those women and you know as well as I that some of them are kindhearted. They're just trying to pay off their debts."

"They're paying debts for crimes they committed." John scoffed. "Are you trying to make me care about the criminals who gave us lashes and raped us? Who stood by and watched as we collapsed from exhaustion?" John shook his head in disgust. "If it makes you feel better, you can try the simple infiltration on your own and if that fails, we can use my plan. Either way, we'll find our way in and free our brothers."

"There has to be another way."

"Your other way was convincing your wife to free all the slaves, which failed, so this is our only option."

"She might do it eventually."

"When? In a year? Ten years? Fifty? How many men are you willing to watch die before it's enough? The children being raped down there won't live long enough to see your lovely Evelyn free them. I bet she'll expect them to thank her for being so merciful too."

"…Doing this won't help anyone, John. The nobles will retaliate by punishing every slave who didn't make it. Evelyn will never be able to outlaw slavery if you prove them right."

"That's the sacrifice one has to make," John sneered. "I would rather save a hundred men and let a thousand die than stand by and watch from the castle as every one of them dies a slow, painful death."

It was clear nothing Francis said would stop him. John had clearly thought about this for a long time. "I can't leave my wife," he said quietly.

The veins popped out on John's neck. "You never will, will you? No matter what she does."

"It's only been a few months. Permanent change takes consistency and patience."

"And I suppose you'll stop me from going to the mines because your precious wife will take the blame?"

"No, I won't." He refused to choose between the woman he loved and his best friend. "But I will ask you to rethink it."

"If I continue with this life, I'll eventually snap and kill Ivy, probably in self-defense ironically. I'd rather leave this place alongside our brothers than alone and on the run for murder."

"You plan to kill her?"

"…Not unless I have to." He turned to the west, toward the mine three days away. "So long as Ivy doesn't hit me, I can leave her behind unharmed and let her tear herself apart."

"She'll send people after you," Francis warned.

"That's what the weapons are for." John smirked. "And if I'm recaptured, I'll just break out again or die and take Ivy with me. She would prefer that, I think. I already told you she wants to end her own life."

Francis felt a tear slide down his cheek. Was everyone around him losing their minds or was he the one who had gone mad? The only things his friends talked about were killing each other or committing suicide. Why choose to end everything prematurely when they could walk away from it all and try to build the lives they wanted?

He didn't speak as John patted him on the back. "I'll be at the western city gates tomorrow night. If you want to join me, meet me at sundown. Just know that if you decide to stay here with your heartless wife, I won't wait. I'm tired of waiting for you to see what is so obvious to me."

"Very well." Francis wanted to go. He had been happy with Evelyn for that brief time and was glad he married her. Even though the illusion of happiness had been so brief, he would never regret it. But he had always known their relationship would be temporary. Either her mother or their circumstances would tear them apart. He wouldn't leave her on his own, though. "I will never leave her until she dismisses me herself." Or until her mother threatened to kill him.

John nodded. "I knew you'd say that. You're loyal to a fault, even when the person isn't good enough for you."

"I'm sorry, John."

John forced a laugh, clearly trying to hide his raw emotions. "If you ever change your mind, I'll meet you in Antalius."

"Thank you. Maybe I'll bring Evelyn with me."

The prince scoffed but didn't reject the idea. He likely didn't care either way. Francis wasn't even sure if John wanted to leave. He was more focused on revenge than freedom. A peaceful life in Antalius might bore him and drive him back to Clostrum for vengeance.

CHAPTER THIRTY-SIX

After arriving home late, Francis crawled into bed with his already sleeping wife and watched her face. Creepy as it was to study her sleeping form, he found himself doing it often. He never knew when it might be his last chance to see her.

They hadn't discussed what happened in the castle, as she'd gone to her mother's office immediately after and talked for a while, then she had to meet with prince Antonio and a few other Dalius diplomats to discuss the trading of empyrean stones. By the time she returned home, she had fallen into bed and hadn't woken since.

As he stared at her, he allowed himself a few minutes to imagine stealing her away from this mansion.

He had heard stories of Antalius, how they had leaders like Clostrum did but each leader only oversaw a small community. Every commander knew each woman and man in their community personally. If a leader was corrupt or selfish, it was difficult to hide from the villagers and the ruler would be replaced. It wasn't a perfect system, but it seemed far better than this. Evelyn didn't know the names of the women and men whose lives she controlled. She hadn't even met most of them in person. How could she make life-changing decisions and decide their futures when she didn't even know them at all?

He wanted to believe in her. He knew there was good in her, just as there was good in many other women in this country. He saw the conflict within her, the guilt and doubt that plagued her as she worked. All she needed was someone to counter her mother, to give a voice to the doubts she already had. He could be that voice.

The only problem he foresaw in that regard was how long he could keep up that hope and conscience. The more death and betrayal he watched and felt powerless to stop, the less he wanted to fight for what was good. He wanted to hide. He sometimes looked in the mirror and saw the same empty, soulless eyes John always had.

When Evelyn first met him, Francis would sometimes dream of a future with her. In his dreams, she was always happy, free of her past, and with children she cared for and loved as much as he did. He still had dreams like that now, but instead of living happily in Antalius with children of their own, he saw a copy of her mother, hardened and so focused on her duties that she ignored her own daughters.

The thought of watching her turn into that kind of person filled him with guilt, because he knew that was the last thing *she* wanted. But could his presence really prevent that from happening, or would he end up just as broken as her by then?

The sun peeked through the curtains of the window and he was about to climb out from under the blankets and return to the floor where he was supposed to sleep when the bedroom door suddenly opened. Candlelight filled the room, revealing him in the bed with Evelyn—a slave with his mistress.

Francis leapt from the bed, cursing himself for not locking the door as they often did nowadays, but it was too late. Evelyn's mother was standing in the doorway. She had seen him lying beside her daughter.

As he stepped away from the bed and bowed, she grabbed his hand and held it up, bringing his red empyrean ring into the light.

"Come with me, Francis," she said. "It's time we discussed the situation you and I have found ourselves in."

CHAPTER THIRTY-SEVEN

Lady Payne's private office felt even more horrifying in the dark, with candles casting shadows on every corner of the room. As Evelyn's mother shoved him into the room, not saying a word until they were inside, he spotted a figure standing in the corner, someone tall. Francis couldn't see the person's face but could smell strong perfume, something only a noble or royal would wear.

"Take a seat, Francis," his mother-in-law said as she shut the door behind him and locked it.

Francis did as he was told and as Lady Payne walked around her desk to sit before him, her candle revealed the identity of the figure in the corner. It was Antonio, looking just as clean and proper as he did in the castle. He was standing like a soldier, though, with his hands behind his back and head high. He didn't make eye contact, even as Francis stared at him.

"I knew about your relationship with my daughter from the beginning," the woman began, calm and collected except for her twitching eye. "If it was a brief romantic experience, I would have waited for it to play out and for her to tire of you. Then I could send you into the country to serve on a farm for the rest of your life without bringing disgrace to the family."

He lowered his chin, waiting for her to continue. Best not to risk saying anything yet.

"And if you were a simple boy using my daughter to escape the mines and the miserable life of a slave, you wouldn't be standing here now. Those kind of men don't try to impact their surroundings, as it would jeopardize the comfortable life they've obtained. I almost wish you were using her for her money, something she always feared growing up. At least then you wouldn't interfere with her duties. Instead, you're using her for far more nefarious reasons."

"I'm not using her," he began and she raised her hand, as though to slap him.

"You are. It's not just money you're after. You're after something far worse, something that will bring ruin to this country if you have your way."

"Freeing slaves will not destroy Clostrum," he corrected quietly. "If the loss of a few slaves is enough to bring down a country, it wasn't a strong one to begin with."

Lady Payne grinned and he realized he should have kept quiet. She wanted him to talk back. All the more excuse to kill him.

"You are correct, boy. Clostrum isn't a strong country. If it weren't for the empyrean stones, Dalius would have taken over decades ago," she said. "But the stones do exist, and with them Clostrum has evolved into a peaceful society. Did you know that before the downfall of the former kings a hundred years ago, all of Clostrum was a giant city? The mines you grew up in used to be halls of a castle three times the size of the capital. The empyrean stones we currently have are only a fraction of what they owned. There is potential for so much more and Dalius knows it."

Francis glanced at Antonio, wondering why she was saying this in front of him.

"If we gave you and your friends a choice to work in the mines or work elsewhere, two things would happen. First, those who are honest and value their lives would refuse to work. Then we would be left with only the desperate ones willing to steal the stones for themselves."

"You don't know that," Francis said. "People are willing to work if they receive an equal reward in return."

"A cute belief to hold, though unfortunately that isn't how the real world works." She sighed, reminding him of Evelyn. "The gods were kind to grant us empyrean stones that only women could wield. They allowed the weak to finally defend themselves against the strong—"

"And dominate them," he cut in, knowing he shouldn't argue but she wouldn't let him stay regardless. Not anymore. He could tell she was telling him all this because he was about to be either banished or killed.

"But there may be more stones we have yet to find and some of them may not be for women alone. Can you imagine what would happen to Clostrum if men were able to wield the stones?" She paused even though they both knew he wasn't supposed to answer. "It would create chaos, destroying the delicate balance of our society. If men regain power, they will wreak havoc on the peace we have worked so hard to preserve."

Francis could already picture John doing such a thing, even without the empyrean stones. "So to prevent violence and chaos, you tortured and killed young men," he said quietly, "and just hid it underground."

She bristled, though he could tell she knew what she'd done and no longer cared.

"I have seen a woman kill a man because he couldn't please her in bed," Francis whispered. "I have seen a child lose an arm because he wasn't deemed strong enough to carry a stone twice his size. My back is covered in lashings because when I was a child, *you* feared I would become strong enough to defend myself. You punished me for something I never did."

"The loss of a few men is a small price to pay for the lives of thousands."

He clenched his fists. "You're a coward. You murder children because of a mere chance that they might disagree with you!"

She looked at his fists with raised eyebrows and grinned. He was proving to be as violent as she claimed all men were. "Men like you are a threat to my daughter's safety. If I allow you to remain, you will become her undoing."

"I want to protect her," he defended. "From becoming a guilt-ridden monster like you."

"Once you leave this room, you will go to her and beg her to let you leave," she continued, ignoring him. "Once you convince her to release you, as I know you can, Antonio will escort you to the city gates."

"Where he'll kill me?" Francis whispered, glancing at Antonio. The prince still refused to look his way.

"That is what he was bred to do." Lady Payne smiled at the young prince.

"Why is he doing your bidding?" Francis asked.

"He is the last in a line of princes. He has no chance of inheriting the throne in his home country, so he chose the second-best thing, to marry an heiress who is set to inherit an empyrean kingdom." Those who held the stones, held the power. Not even the queen had complete access to them.

"Wouldn't the queen be a better option?" he asked, directing the question at Antonio, not her.

"The queen is slowly losing her mind and is the last in her line," the lady answered for him. "After she dies, Evelyn will take control in her absence, so long as there is no rightful heir to the throne. Antonio knows this so he came to me, offering to betray his country in return for a kingdom that rivals his own."

"And you trust him?"

"Show him your collar, Antonio."

The prince did so, revealing a red empyrean stone collar around his neck. There were some blisters around it already, likely from it being molded onto his skin with an opposing element.

"He put it on willingly," Lady Payne said. "And unlike you, Francis, he does what needs to be done to survive and thrive. Not all men need to be slaves, if they act intelligently and serve the right mistress."

Francis shook his head. "All the wealth in the world will not protect him from the nightmares and guilt he will suffer. You will stain his hands with the blood of children. I wouldn't wish that on my greatest enemy."

"Not everyone feels guilt as you do," Lady Payne said, rising from her chair.

"Perhaps not in life," he answered quietly. "But when you are old and dying, left with only your thoughts and the impending judgement you know will greet you in the afterlife, the consequences will finally catch up with you." He stood and looked her in the eye. "And I pity you for it."

The woman's jaw clenched and for a moment, he felt like he was getting through to her, even if it had to be done through fear. Perhaps fear for her own life would be enough to change her ways.

Then she nodded at the door. "Do as I have commanded. Convince my daughter to let you go free so she can marry Antonio and live a fulfilled life without your distractions."

"And if I tell her what you've done? That you are forcing me to betray the woman I love?"

"If you do that, I will call you a liar, take you to the mines of Valhander, and force the lash into your hand so you can carry out my punishments on the men you care so much about."

He could tell she meant it. It wouldn't be her first time. She might even enjoy it.

Francis regretted saying Evelyn would turn into her mother. She was nothing like this woman and he prayed she never would be.

"And if that isn't enough, when I orchestrate the queen's death, I will force you to kill the prince you spent so many nights talking to."

His eyes widened. She would even threaten John. "How long have you been watching me?" he asked.

"Antonio has since the beginning. He carried out the murder of each slave you freed and he will do it to your friend as well. Do I need to threaten more people close to you, like the boy in the kitchen that you brought here, or is this enough to make you obey?"

"It is." He now acknowledged that no matter what he did in this mansion, nothing would ever change. This woman could not be moved. He could at least prevent the deaths of those he loved.

Besides, he'd become resigned to this reality weeks ago. He always knew he'd be replaced and taken from Evelyn. That was why he married her so prematurely. He just didn't expect to lose her so quickly.

"Now go." The mother looked victorious and almost gleeful at her victory over him. However, as soon as Antonio opened the door for him to leave, her smile vanished and she returned to the composed noblewoman he had become familiar with over the year. She concealed her true nature expertly. Evelyn would never know what her mother was capable of.

Francis stepped toward the door, ready to obey, but as the salt of fresh tears touched his lips, he imagined how Evelyn would react and knew he couldn't bear to see it—the pain in her eyes as he told her he didn't love her and wanted to leave her behind.

He had promised to serve her forever.

He wanted to keep that promise. He wanted her to know, even if he was gone, that he still cared for her more than anyone else in this world.

Even if he left, he wanted to plant the smallest bit of doubt about this place and all it represented. He also wanted her to believe that he still loved her and was waiting for her in Antalius. If she had hope, perhaps it would be enough to make her change, to help her see beyond this narrow path her mother was putting her on.

"May I write a letter instead?" he asked desperately, not caring that his voice was wobbly and his eyes red. "I can't say it to her face."

"And if she doubts the letter?" His mother-in-law crossed her arms and shook her head. "She would realize it was my doing."

"I'll make it as believable as I possibly can," he promised. "And I will leave my wedding ring here." It was all he had of her.

Perhaps if he could escape Antonio once they were outside the gates, he could reach the Antalius border. He could wait for Evelyn there and hope she realized the letter was a lie.

"Besides, even if I said it in person, she still might suspect I was being forced." He held out his shaking hands and she studied his tear-streaked face. "I'm not a good liar. Not when she's right in front of me. Please."

If he could reach Antalius and became stronger, both in body and situation, he might someday be able to return to Clostrum as a different, more powerful man. He could save Evelyn from her mother and bring her to a cottage he built with his own hands. They could spend their final days together with food and clothes that weren't created by others and he wouldn't have to fear raising his children in this hell.

The mother tilted her head and glanced at Antonio, then narrowed her eyes. "I suppose you wouldn't be very convincing looking like that." She pulled a few papers from a desk drawer and slid them toward him. "I will be watching and read it over before giving it to her. Do not try to deceive me, Francis. Your death will not prevent me from killing your friends."

"I know. I will not deceive you." He didn't plan to.

He spent ten minutes writing the message, weaving truth into the lies. He told her why he married and loved her, then explained why he had considered leaving. He talked about how she tolerated so much evil that he worried she might become the type of woman he feared. He confessed that he was beginning to doubt he'd ever taste true freedom in his lifetime—not while he was with her. He feared that nothing would ever change.

These were all honest words, but these doubts had never been enough to drive him away from her. Not completely.

"Do not guilt her," his mother-in-law ordered, reading over his shoulder. "Do it again." She burnt the paper on the nearby candle and handed him a blank sheet. "Criticize her. Lay bare all the anger I know you feel toward me and the other women I represent."

"I don't hate you," he whispered as he wrote it again. "I just know you could be so much more."

The letter he ended up writing was short and to the point, most of it the words of Evelyn's mother rather than his own. He tried to weave the truth and doubt into the sentences, and did at some points, but eventually had to end it prematurely so his tears wouldn't stain the page and give him away.

Then Lady Payne pulled the ring from his finger and placed it atop the page. "Thank you, slave. This is goodbye. I pray the afterlife treats you better than this one."

He wondered if she meant it.

As he was escorted out of the mansion, his shoulders and head concealed by a cloak Antonio gave him, he knew he wouldn't miss this building or the mistress who owned it. The food was tainted because the slaves who served it were forced to do so.

All he would miss were the men and women who had treated him so kindly…and his wife, who he truly believed loved him with all her heart.

He hoped she wasn't too sad in his absence. He didn't want her heart to break because of him.

But he also hoped she would miss him. Even if she slept next to a different man, he wanted her to dream of him so the five months they spent together would be remembered years from now.

The most important thing, however, was that whenever she looked a slave in the eye, she would no longer see a mere tool or pawn. He wanted her to see him instead, so it would make her think twice before hurting them.

CHAPTER THIRTY-EIGHT

Even though John spent the entire night outside the castle, stealing gold and weapons to hide in the castle catacombs, he was back in bed beside the queen before she woke up. When she rolled over to face him, still asleep, he studied her pretty face. She so rarely smiled and he wished he could see it one more time before he left.

He wanted to leave but no longer wanted to kill her, despite everything she'd done.

John had hated every woman he came across. They were selfish, condescending, and overthinking. Those who treated him kindly in the mines were often the worst, as they would lash out the most when he did something wrong or didn't react gratefully to their brief kindness. There was always a reason for what they did. If they acted sweet, it was because they wanted him to view them as better than the other women. If they let him sleep in their bed, it was because they wanted him to admire them and make them feel good.

At first, the foolish child he used to be believed they genuinely loved him and wanted to help. Then, when he was tired or in pain and asked for a merciful night of sleep—mistakenly believing they would give up their own pleasure for him—they would scream, calling him selfish and worthless.

He learned to stop reacting after that, perfecting the mask he wore over his eyes and face so no one could ever understand what he was thinking. If a woman was sweet, he wouldn't believe it. If she was cruel, he felt no surprise.

While showing emotion brought out the women's true intentions gradually, showing no reaction at all revealed it almost immediately. The women didn't want a boring man who refused to pretend he loved them.

If anything, showing no emotion gave him pleasure because of how it frustrated those guards. Some of them viewed him as a challenge, as a man who just needed to be broken or loved enough to break down his walls, but they eventually gave up and took it out on him immediately after.

Then he met the queen, who made no effort to hide how selfish she was. If anything, he could tell she forced herself to act more cruel on purpose. There were times she would reprimand one of her subjects, then show signs of remorse once the woman's back was turned.

She had unlimited power and could command John to do anything, yet she demanded nothing more than his presence. He never had to share a bed with her unless he wished, so long as he remained in the same room. She never forced him to speak or show emotion. Even after months of complete silence, her attitude toward him never changed. All she did was look at him longingly and vent to him when no one else was around.

The only times she changed was when there were others around or she spoke to the stones.

The queen was an insecure woman, a type he was all too familiar with. The stones preyed on those insecurities, whispering in Ivy's ears until she could do nothing but lash out. She said they only stopped taunting her after she threw something or hit him.

She usually apologized afterwards, which he was nearly willing to forgive, but the next day she would do it again and the apologies rang hollow after a while.

"Why don't you get rid of the stones?" he asked eventually in a moment of weakness. He wanted to be with the woman he had come to enjoy tolerating, the one who wasn't plagued by the voices.

"They're the only ones who speak honestly," she answered, not understanding how he felt. "And they tell me things no one else knows. They tell secrets that release my worries."

So they brought the *queen* peace about her country but gave *Ivy* herself ceaseless panic in her personal life. It didn't feel like a fair trade.

He didn't know why the gods continued telling Ivy about his escapades. A god shouldn't care about a singular slave and what he did. Perhaps the stones were overprotective, acting like the mother neither of them had growing up. If that were the case, he could almost accept the paranoia the stones created, but the cynical part of him knew the stones were just creating chaos for reasons unknown. Perhaps it was merely to make the two of them miserable.

As John stared at his wife, her face so peaceful for once and free of the wrinkles that always covered her forehead, he considered yanking the empyrean stone necklace from her neck. He could tie her up and carry her to Antalius where they could live together in hiding like a true married couple. It might allow the genuine person he saw within her, and almost liked, to come to the forefront. He might even fall in love with her over time, like Francis did to Evelyn, but it couldn't happen.

He would be chased by Clostrum soldiers until they found and killed him for kidnapping their queen, creating a scapegoat for the public to hate so they wouldn't realize the nobles already wanted her dead.

Plus, Ivy would crave the empyrean stone's voices again, he was sure. She wanted the power they granted her, the knowledge she believed would help her fulfil her duty and make up for all the mistakes her mother made.

No one held more guilt than Ivy. When she was in one of her bad moods, she would often mock the nobles who blamed her for her mother's mistakes. They used to constantly taunt her by listing how many innocent women and children died due to barbarian invaders and starvation. This ensured Ivy could never be happy at any point, so long as her mother's shadow hung over her.

The queen was a slave like him. The only difference between them were their chains. While his were made of stone, hers were concealed under gold and jewels.

"If you want me to free you," he whispered, "I will."

His heart stopped when she opened her eyes and looked at him, her sleep ended. "What did you say, John?" Her eyes were sweet and loving, crinkled because she was happy to see him.

"No," he whispered, pushing himself off the bed. "I didn't say anything." He wasn't the kind of man willing to dedicate his life to freeing her. He wasn't good like Francis. The last shred of kindness had burned up years ago.

John could tell she wanted to talk to him. It was rare for him to speak and she craved it like air. But he got out of the bed and dressed himself to avoid doing so. Her empyrean stones would start speaking to her soon anyway and their voices always overpowered his.

As predicted, by the time he had royal robes on his shoulders and turned back to her, she was staring at the ground and focusing on whatever the stone was saying. Her fingers traced its surface, something she only did when hearing a particularly horrid statement. What had the gods seen this time?

He looked down at his hands, at the ring Francis had given him, and as he studied the black stone resting in the silver band, he realized they had seen and heard everything he said to Francis about the mines.

The gods knew he was planning to run away.

Feeling genuine panic for the first time in a while, he looked back at the queen and immediately knew he'd been snitched on.

There was a tense silence as she stared at him and he regretted not hiding any weapons in this room. He didn't want to kill her but wished he at least brought something to defend himself. He shouldn't have allowed his weakness for her to get in the way of survival.

"You are planning to destroy the mines," she stated, rising from her bed and moving toward the dresser near the window where her jewelry was kept. "And you plan to leave me."

He narrowed his eyes. Killing her seemed unavoidable now. "Yes."

She opened one of the drawers, revealing all the empyrean stone jewelry inside. "How long have you wanted to leave?"

"Ever since I was born," he answered, wondering if she would pull a gun from the drawer to shoot him. He was surprised when she instead pulled out some gold and red empyrean stone necklaces and stepped toward him, holding them up to his face.

"This is more than enough to get you to Antalius," she said softly. "To get *us* there."

"Us?" He had considered bringing her not a moment ago.

"Take me with you." She was a breath away now, standing on the tips of her feet so they were nearly the same height. "Save me from this place."

He knew he shouldn't. She would make him miserable. They would be at each other's throats and could never be happy. Their problems would follow them across the border. But…

He let her kiss him and for the briefest moment, felt something new in his heart: a warmth more intoxicating than the joy he felt while planning the murders of nobles. It made him feel good, like he was a child still able to feel true emotions and happiness. He wanted to bring her with him then, despite all the bruises and cuts she had left on him.

Then she draped the red empyrean stone necklace over his head and tightened it around his neck.

"What are you doing?" he hissed as she pulled away, keeping one hand on his neck. Her soft skin was cold.

"I can't let you leave me," she whispered.

"You can come with me," he reminded her.

"You want to kill me." She gripped her black necklace with the other hand. "Don't you, John?"

He grit his teeth and sneered, the warmth in his heart gone and never to return. Perhaps he should attack her—force her to burn his throat and end this now—but the thought of killing himself scared him enough to keep him still. He didn't want to leave Francis alone in this world. It would feel like a willing betrayal to his only friend.

"You're never leaving me," the queen told him, leading him from the bedroom.

She later placed several empyrean stone collars on him, just as Evelyn was about to do to the miners. It hurt to put on and he was sure it would make many men lose what little hope they had to be free. For John, however, it only fueled his hatred. He wanted to place a collar on the throat of every woman on the council so they knew how it felt.

He didn't wish it on Ivy, though. A merciful death was enough for her. The councilors who tortured her were the ones who needed to be punished. By killing every woman in this castle, including Ivy, he would avenge her. He would avenge them both.

CHAPTER THIRTY-NINE

As Antonio escorted Francis through the city, draped in black to hide their faces and bearing the insignia of the Payne family so no one would try to stop them, Francis tried to avoid imagining how Evelyn's face when she read the letter. It would only make him angry and he didn't want his final moments to be filled with hatred.

The dark streets were empty, the ground muddy from the damp air and beginning of snow, and the air was colder now that they had no empyrean stones to warm them. Lady Payne hadn't given Francis a warm coat to protect him from the cold, as Evelyn would have. A walking corpse didn't need a coat.

"Do you plan to betray Evelyn once she marries you?" he asked Antonio as they approached the city gates. Once they passed it, Antonio would kill him and bury his body in the nearby forest.

"I won't betray her," Antonio said, his words sounding genuine. There was no reason to lie to a dying man. "My former mistress is no different from my current one."

"You refer to your mother as a mistress?"

"You don't know much about Dalius culture, do you?" Antonio chuckled, a dark laugh he had never used while socializing with noble ladies. "I wasn't the youngest brother until recent years. I used to have two twin brothers born after me, both of them bearing weak legs. One died from weakness and when it became clear the second wouldn't be fit to serve in the army, my mother 'sent him away', which was the official term for killing him."

"Why would she do that?"

"Dalius is not filled with the greenery and lakes of Clostrum. Resources are not as plentiful. We have to take what we want if we are to survive. Women cannot be weak and men who can't protect them are considered useless. The weak become a burden on the strong, stealing their food and drink by contributing so little."

The female guards at the city gates stopped them and only let Antonio through when he showed the signed letter from Lady Payne granting him access, sealed with her ring insignia. They were then free to walk down the snowy plain leading to the tree line. Antonio wouldn't kill Francis until they were out of sight.

"You sound like you resent your mother," Francis said as they walked, trying not to slip on the wet, dead grass. "Is that how you feel about Evelyn too?"

"Are you trying to ensure I won't hurt her?" Antonio removed his hood so Francis could see his face. Wrinkles were already forming around his eyes from smiling so much but it didn't age him. He was still as handsome as ever, even while looking at Francis with a similar look John often wore. "You really do love her."

"Of course."

"Why?"

"Because she's a good person."

Antonio smiled sympathetically. "I'd like to think I am too." He stopped next to the trees, the tall pines rising far above their heads. "Now that we're free from the prying eyes of the capital, I can speak freely."

Francis waited for him to explain himself, shivering from the breeze. He wished he could stand among the trees, even in his final moments. They smelled minty and bitter, not sweet like he'd imagined.

"I don't want to kill you, Francis, and based on what I've heard about the mines, the men living there are tortured as much as I was growing up. Is that correct?"

"It is." Francis's spirits rose. "Do you want to help them?"

"I do," he admitted without expression. "I have done nothing but obey the orders of women, murdering those no different from myself, and have received nothing in return." Antonio crossed his arms and smirked. "Listening to that women talk her way around tormenting children only fueled my desire to protect them."

Tears pricked Francis's eyes as he realized his words may have meant something after all. "I'm glad." He glanced at the city gates where John had said to meet him. "Prince John will be here tonight. He can help us."

"I'm afraid we have no time to spare. It will take several days to reach the mines and if we are too late, the men will be shackled and there is little we can do to protect them," Antonio warned.

"Very well." He didn't want to leave John behind but was sure they would encounter him later regardless. "Do you have a plan?"

The man nodded confidently. "This is what I was trained for. It's the perfect irony that my skills in combat were meant to help women fight wars. Now it will be turned against them."

Francis nearly cried then and there. He could finally free his friends, his brothers, and would finally see Antalius with his own eyes. He could build his cottage and return for Evelyn as a stronger and confident man.

For once, his perseverance had paid off.

CHAPTER FORTY

The bed was empty when Evelyn woke and when she rolled over to check Francis's blanket on the floor where he normally slept, it was empty too. Thinking she slept in, she moved the curtains to see where the sun dangled. Strangely, it wasn't any higher than it normally was when she awoke.

She hadn't slept in, so where was he?

"Maid!" she called, opening the door and shouting down the hall. A moment later, one of the male maids cleaning the rooms down the hall peeked his head out and asked what was wrong. "Where is my bodyguard?" she demanded.

"I apologize, my lady, but I don't know where he is." The maid bowed meekly, then awaited further commands.

Confused, she turned back to her room without addressing the man again. Francis never left the room unless it was an emergency and when that was the case, he often told the other servants where he was going.

She started dressing for the day, planning to ask her mother about his whereabouts, and she was about to cover her face in makeup for the day's events when she noticed an out of place paper on her dresser.

Resting on top of it was Francis's wedding ring, identical to the one on her right hand.

Panic flooded her chest as she picked up the letter and started reading, clutching the ring in her other hand.

It read:

I'm sorry, Evelyn, but I can no longer stay here with you. I cannot watch as you willingly hurt myself and my fellow slaves.

Evelyn frowned. He often referred to the other slaves as his friends or brothers. The handwriting was his but it felt off, stilted and awkward. Had he really written this?

I am leaving for Antalius and taking my people with me. I am sorry if this hurts you, but it must be done.

Taking them with him? Was he referring to the slaves in the mines? Or John?

I will be happier in Antalius as a free man, away from your control. I thought I loved you but my love for freedom is stronger and more important.

She knew being free was his dream and he'd been horrified by her decisions in regard to queen Ivy and the mines. Had her actions made him rethink his love for her?

Her heartbeat pounded in her ears as she dropped the letter. He would have spoken to her about this in person. He wouldn't have abandoned her before begging her to go with him. He would have given her a final chance. She likely would have said no but he would have tried regardless, as he had before.

No, he asked her in the past and she rejected him. He knew her answer.

"Mother!" She marched out of the room, hiding the letter in the pocket of her dress and slipping his ring onto her left hand finger.

If Francis planned to leave her, he'd have to say it to her face. He had to be heading west and was potentially picking up people in the mines, so she could still intercept him and hear the words from his own mouth. Otherwise, she would be plagued by doubt that perhaps this letter was fake and he was in danger. She would never forgive herself if it was a trick and she willingly fell for it.

"Mother! I am going to the Valhander mines!" she announced as she entered her mother's office. "I won't be back for several days."

"What's wrong?" her mother asked, rising from her desk with worried creases under her eyes. "Has something happened to the slaves? Is there an uprising in response to the changes you're implementing?"

"No, but there may be soon." Evelyn held her hands behind her back, hiding both rings. "I want to oversee the changes myself, in case something goes wrong."

Her mother smiled softly. "I'm glad you're so willing to take responsibility for your decisions. The other nobles would be lucky to have half as much dutifulness in a daughter. Come." She wrapped an arm around Evelyn's shoulders. "We'll go together."

Evelyn didn't want her mother to come but knew it would be suspicious if she refused.

CHAPTER FORTY-ONE

Antonio bought two horses in the nearest town, then he and Francis spent most of the coming days on horseback, riding to the mines of Valhander. They ate as they rode and only stopped to sleep for a few hours at a time. Their window of opportunity got smaller with each passing hour, so Francis didn't mind how Antonio hurried him.

"I will take care of the guards," Antonio said, showing Francis the bow and crossbow he had hidden beneath his coat. "Give me ten minutes and all the women will be dead...or unconscious, if you please."

"Every single one? Against one man?" Francis was impressed and grateful that Antonio didn't plan to murder them all as John did. He knew all those women personally and not *all* of them were cruel.

"I was trained to kill my mother's political opponents without leaving a trail. Doing so in a country that is no longer accustomed to war should be much easier." Antonio smiled at him. "It will be your job to convince the men to leave. I know some may be too afraid to face the repercussions of fleeing."

"And you'll come with us to Antalius?"

"Yes. I pray it doesn't start a war, though I know Antalius is capable of fending off an army, as long as it's small enough and the battle occurs in their forests where they have control. Antalius would have the advantage in the winter as well, since it gets colder there than the east." Antalius was further north than Clostrum and Dalius, and the winters could be harsh depending on the year and the will of the gods.

"I just hope the rumors of equality in Antalius are true," Francis said and didn't speak on it again. He spent the rest of the ride talking to Antonio about his family, though the prince wasn't too keen to speak on it, and what Antonio planned to do once they were in Antalius.

"I can train the people of Antalius to defend themselves," Antonio answered. "If Dalius ever tries to control Clostrum, they will invade Antalius as well. I would like the westerners to have at least a fighting chance."

"Do you ever wonder if we are romanticizing Antalius?" Francis asked. Reaching that border was his lifelong dream but perhaps the land was full of the same selfish people he had encountered here.

"Perhaps a little, but I hear it is better than Clostrum and leagues better than Dalius." Antonio shrugged. "As long as I can build a home and family there, I don't care. I can defend myself from a few hunters and forest dwellers."

Francis smiled, feeling heard. "That's what I want too." He could already imagine the look on Evelyn's face when he brought her to a home he built from scratch.

CHAPTER FORTY-TWO

The Valhander mine was as Francis left it—the towers in front of the entrance were unchanged and the guards wore loosened armor as John described. Francis hadn't noticed it on his way out but he could now tell the guards weren't on high alert. They didn't expect someone to venture this far into the country. They also didn't expect the slaves to flee; not when the last one's legs were broken.

Antonio stopped the horses out of the guards' earshot and tied them to trees where they wouldn't be found. He then instructed Francis to hide in the bushes, out of sight.

"If I die, you can take the horses and flee." Antonio scanned the towers and surrounding clearing, then pointed at the mine's doorway in the hill. "Do not go inside until I exit and tell you everything is safe. Understood?"

"Understood." Francis was glad he wouldn't have to participate. What little skills he gained as a bodyguard were nothing when compared to a Dalius soldier.

Lanterns hung from the mine doorway and several torches lined the road toward it, which Antonio avoided as he snuck toward the towers. There were more lights in the wooden towers, reflecting off the long-barreled guns the women atop them held. Francis saw one of them turn toward Antonio for a moment, spotting the movement among the shadows, but she eventually went back to talking to her companion and didn't look again.

Francis watched as the prince snuck within range of the towers, then loosed two arrows, both meeting their mark in the women's throats. One of the guards fell from the tower immediately, landing on her back with the arrow still protruding from her neck. There was a loud crack as her bones broke on impact and the other female shouted before collapsing too, alerting the women in the tower on the other side.

A horn sounded but the only people who could hear it were those inside the mines. The nearest town was miles away and, according to Antonio, it had next to no soldiers stationed. The poor farmers living there would not come to defend the Payne family's employees.

The soldiers turned their guns toward the now empty tower but Antonio had already slipped back into the trees. He took his time circling around as they panicked, then after a few minutes, killed both of them as well. By the time three more soldiers rushed out of the mines to see what was going on, there were no guards alive to greet them.

"I thought he was going to let them live," Francis whispered in despair, wishing he was brave enough to stop Antonio. Doing so would require stepping into the open and being shot, and as much as he wanted to protect these women, he was afraid of dying, especially when he was so close to freeing all the men inside.

He couldn't help hearing Lady Payne's voice in his head, mocking him for his inaction. *Coward. Selfish. All men only care for themselves.*

The lives of a few are a worthy sacrifice to protect the many. That's what she said to him not a few days ago. Now he was enacting those words.

The guards from inside the tunnels were a little more prepared for the attack, emerging with shields and forming a defensive group, but Antonio had already climbed onto the second tower and loosed on them from above, hitting their shoulders and other open spots in the armor before striking their necks as they fell. Antonio took his time and every guard who exited didn't stand a chance against him. If they knew he had a empyrean collar around his neck, they would have had the advantage, but without that knowledge, there was little they could do but run back into the tunnel, which none of them did.

By the time Antonio entered the mines and returned a few minutes later to proclaim the mine safe, Francis had resigned himself to the deaths of those women. There was nothing he could have done and he couldn't let himself become distracted by things he couldn't change.

He would have to use that same mindset when thinking about Evelyn and her mother too.

"I have taken out the women guarding the slave barracks," Antonio told him, not a speck of blood on his clothes. Only the knife in his hands had been stained. "I will take care of the remaining ones sleeping in their rooms. I am sure some didn't hear the horn or ignored it. They might try to sneak up on us later."

"Please don't kill them," Francis begged as they ran down the steps together. "They don't need to die."

"It will be risky to tie each one up," Antonio said. "And I have heard terrible things about these convicts. Why do you wish to spare them?"

"Because it isn't our job to pass judgement. If there is a god and afterlife, he can pass judgements." Some of these guards might be like Evelyn, wishing they could do differently. Not every woman in here enjoyed harming others. "I thought you said you could do this without killing anyone."

Antonio shrugged and motioned for Francis to continue. "I shall do as you command. Once the risk is gone, I'll inspect the rest of the mine to ensure there are no stragglers."

That struck Francis as odd, since the mine wasn't active at night. Could Antonio be looking for the ancient weapon, as the queen feared? No, Francis wanted to assume the best. Besides, as Evelyn said, if there was a weapon here, she would have heard about it by now.

"Thank you for your help," Francis told Antonio as the scent of blood, stone, and mud filled his nostrils. It made his heart race, recalling the sting of the lash and the pain in his throat, but it also reminded him of familiar faces and smiles. His friends were within reach.

"I wish you luck," Antonio replied, smiling sadly. "You are a good man, Francis."

Then the two parted ways. Antonio headed for the guard barracks and Francis went to the slaves. Francis had never imagined one of his greatest allies would first appear as a rival, but he was glad things had turned out this way.

As he opened the door to the barracks and saw the sea of terrified faces change from frightened to overjoyed as they recognized him, he knew he had been meant to do this from birth. It was his destiny. All his years of suffering and turmoil finally had meaning. His dream was within reach.

CHAPTER FORTY-THREE

Evelyn bit her fingernails as the carriage carried her and her mother through Clostrum, the horses being changed at each passing town so they could ride through the day and night. They only stopped for a few minutes at each location to buy food and even that felt like too much of a delay.

Evelyn's mother spent most of the trip reading and answering letters she brought. She only bothered to discuss their goal during the last hour of the trip.

"I always hated bringing down that mine on your father," she said as Evelyn bit off her last nail tip. "I should have thought about different solutions, as you did, but I was so stricken with grief that I didn't bother. I'm glad you're building upon what I taught you."

"Thank you, Mother," Evelyn said unenthusiastically.

"In just a few days, we will never have to resort to that again." Her mother was smiling proudly. The child in Evelyn wanted to enjoy her mother's praise but she was too worried about Francis to care.

What if he really was trying to free the slaves? Evelyn and the commander had prepared the mines to cave in easily by strategically placing red empyrean stones among the wooden supports on the ceiling. They would burn away if activated. She had also installed empyrean stones on the outside of the hill to prevent the slaves from digging their way out if they survived the cave-in. If the slaves were trying to rebel with Francis's help and couldn't be contained, she would have to use the last resort on her own husband, just as her mother did. He would die under the hill he grew up digging.

She wasn't sure she'd be able to do it when the time came. She might cave and refuse to kill him, disappointing her mother and releasing hundreds of men to enact revenge on the surrounding villages. Then the queen would send her armies to wipe them out, leaving Clostrum's borders unprotected, and it would endanger the entire kingdom.

All of this would happen because of *her* weakness—because she allowed herself to fall in love with a slave and let him weaken her resolve.

Her mother was oblivious to this, to how close they might be to disaster. She was writing a letter with a slight smile on her face, occasionally glancing up to comment on something the letter said. Evelyn was almost jealous of how little she knew.

Evelyn spun the red rings on her fingers as the mine entrance came into view. Her stomach dropped as she saw the ground covered in blood and spotted a corpse hanging from one of the towers with an arrow in her throat. Had Francis done this? He couldn't have.

"What's going on?" her mother asked, dropping her letter to look out the window. "Stop the carriage!"

Evelyn's entire life flashed before her eyes as she stepped from the carriage and saw the pile of female bodies in front of the door. All of her work to improve this mine's productivity had led to this moment.

Her mother continued shouting at the soldiers and bodyguards she'd brought with them. They moved to defend Evelyn and a few others approached the entrance to investigate.

They didn't need to look for long, as the sound of male shouts and chants echoed up the stairs.

"Stay back, my lady!" the bodyguards shouted at Evelyn as tall figures ran up the stairs toward them. Evelyn feared it might be men, ready to hurt them, but instead she saw the commander and a few other guards whose names she barely remembered fleeing the mine. The commander's hair was down and she had a bruise over her eye.

"What is going on here, Fiona?" Evelyn's mother asked the commander while motioning for the soldiers to surround the exit.

The commander was breathing heavily and wasn't wearing her full uniform. She must have been asleep when the attack began.

"The slaves have broken free," she told them, bowing as she spoke. The guards who came with her did the same. "They killed the other women and are planning to do the same to us if we do not run."

"Was Francis with them?" Evelyn asked desperately, ignoring the strange look her mother gave her.

The commander gulped, then nodded. "They will be upon us any minute. We need to burn the supports before we are slaughtered, my lady."

"No." Evelyn pushed past the bodyguards trying to prevent her and looked down the steps into the mine. "I can't," she whispered. "I can't do this."

"Evelyn, if they get free, you will be the first to die. Get away from there!" her mother shouted.

She had to see him with her own eyes to know if it was true. "Francis wouldn't kill anyone!" she insisted, squinting into the darkness. The torches on the walls of the stairs revealed too little.

"Look what they have done already!" her mother insisted, joining Evelyn and pointing at the corpses lying a few feet away. "Are you willing to let them harm others just because you know one of the slaves personally?"

"He's not just a slave!" Evelyn shouted, panicking. She could hear the male voices getting closer. They were chanting a name. "He's my husband." They were chanting Francis's name.

Her mother didn't look surprised by Evelyn's admission. She must have already figured it out. "Look at all you have done for him, Evelyn. You took him from this horrid place, gave him a home in a mansion, gave him new clothes, food, jewelry. You sacrificed our family's reputation to take care of this slave and this is how he has returned your kindness!"

"That's a separate matter," Evelyn whispered. "He doesn't care about wealth or comfort. He cares about protecting others."

"We are the ones protecting others, Evelyn. We must protect all of Clostrum from this attack!"

She could see movement at the bottom of the stairs. The men were coming.

"These men will be thirsty for blood. They will plunder and rape any women they find. They will kill any who try to oppose them. Are you willing to unleash such monsters into our villages?"

"You created the so-called monsters," Evelyn hissed. "When you raised them without sunlight and beat them for existing."

Her mother growled and turned away, addressing the commander. "How many women are still down there?"

"None. We're all that's left. The rest were killed," the commander answered and Evelyn felt her heart burn.

Perhaps her mother was right. Maybe the slaves had become a mob, unable to be controlled, but that couldn't be Francis's fault. He wouldn't murder others, even if he was angry at them. This wasn't like him. He must have told them to let the guards live and they wouldn't listen.

But as the ascending slaves stepped into the light, she saw Francis leading them, a wide smile on his face that she hadn't seen in a while. After murdering all these women, people no different from her, he was still able to laugh. Had she been wrong about him all this time?

Francis stopped as soon as he saw her and for a moment, the rest of the world faded away until only he remained. Her mother's shouts became muffled, the edges of her vision went dark, and even the voice in her head went silent for a moment. All she could do was stare at him, wanting to ask why he had done this. Was it her fault? Had her actions driven him to violence? Spending his entire childhood down there hadn't broken him, but her breaking his trust had.

He opened his mouth, his lips moving to form her name, but her mother suddenly grabbed her shoulder and shoved her to the ground.

"They have weapons, Evelyn!" her mother screamed, pushing her from the entrance. "Everyone step back! I'm burning the supports!"

Evelyn scrambled to her feet, seeing the look of terror on each man's face. She screamed for her mother to stop, for Francis to run up here, but with a snap of her mother's fingers, the entire mine began to emit heat. The mine's ceiling glowed red and within seconds, the beams holding the entire mountain up began to collapse. Men screamed and scrambled toward the entrance, trampling each other in their rush to escape, but as the commander pulled Evelyn away, she saw the entire mine collapse on the slaves.

A second ago, Francis was staring at Evelyn, looking desperate to say goodbye. Then he was gone, crushed under stone.

"No!" Evelyn shoved the commander away and ran toward the remains of the door, trying to dig through the shifting dirt. The stone dug into her fingers, cutting her and drawing blood. She thought she could still hear voices within. "Help me! They might still be alive." Tears stung her cheeks and a second later, her voice began to sting from her sobs.

Her mother was staring at her in disbelief. "Evelyn, get away from there. You could get hurt."

"You killed them!"

"I did what was necessary to protect my daughter." Her mother grabbed her arm and pulled her away, motioning for the bodyguards to retrieve the rods of red empyrean stone stored nearby. They would be used to cover the entrance in case any survivors tried to dig their way out. If anyone got that far, the guards would activate the stones and burn them alive.

Evelyn struggled against her mother but the reality of Francis's death was already sinking in, and it was taking all strength from her legs. She was close to collapsing, and her darkening vision was threatening to put her to sleep.

"Commander! I assume you can take care of this?" her mother asked as she dragged a stunned Evelyn away. "I will send reinforcements and supplies to you from the nearest town."

"Yes, my lady." The commander bowed again, then stared remorsefully at Evelyn. She looked like she wanted to apologize, though Evelyn didn't know why. Did the commander regret letting them die?

"With time, Evelyn, when you have a child of your own, you will understand why I did this," her mother said as she shoved her into the carriage and climbed in behind her. Evelyn placed her palm on the carriage door, ready to leap back out and keep digging, but she could barely breathe and knew she'd just get yanked back again.

"I know seeing so much death at once can feel traumatizing, Evelyn," her mother continued calmly, "But you'll get used to it with time. You must remember that far more deaths have been prevented this way."

Evelyn glared at her, the skin on her hands hot. When her mother activated all the empyrean stones, she had made the rings on Evelyn's hands burn too. Even now, the pain was almost too great to bear. She was biting the inside of her cheeks to tolerate it, filling her mouth with blood. The rings had only burned for a second before Evelyn blocked her mother's control. How had Francis survived a burn for twice as long without lashing out?

"I'll have to send extra soldiers to the other mines to ensure the same doesn't happen there," her mother said casually as the carriage moved away from the mine. She was already picking her most recent letter off the floor of the carriage and studying it as though nothing had happened, as though she hadn't just killed a hundred innocent men.

"We didn't even talk to them first," she whispered, making her mother's eyes snap back to her. "They would have surrendered. They wouldn't have hurt us."

"You saw those corpses," her mother said with a frustrated sigh. "Do you really think you are special in their eyes? To men, all women are the same."

Evelyn tapped the rings with her bleeding fingers, wondering how quickly they would kill her mother if pressed against her neck. "…Were you always this hateful, Mother, or did I only see it after I met Francis?"

The courteous and professional look her mother had been wearing vanished and she instead glared at Evelyn with the look of a mother reprimanding her child. "You are prioritizing a man who abandoned you over the woman who raised you. I will never leave you, Evelyn. Could he say the same?"

"He didn't abandon me. He just wanted to be free."

"He knew the queen would persecute you for this mistake," she hissed. "And he did it anyway. He proved that he didn't care about you. I do!"

A year ago, Evelyn would have believed her without question, but now, after seeing the world through his eyes and knowing people were not as black and white as her mother believed, she thought differently. Francis didn't hate women. He wouldn't kill them unless it was in self-defense.

"Give it a few days. Think about what we saw and the people he killed, and you will come around to my way of thinking," her mother said quietly, returning her attention to the letter.

No. No amount of time would change this. "You expected this to happen, didn't you? You were waiting for Francis to do what my father did so you'd have an excuse to finally be rid of him. You wanted him gone so you could marry me to Antonio for your own political gain."

"How would I force your lover to enter a mine and start a rebellion? Years of progress have been buried now. Do you really believe I would do that when I could just kill the boy instead?"

"No." Not unless her mother wanted to send a message.

"I am all you have left, Evelyn. Don't make an enemy of your last remaining ally."

That was where she was wrong about her. Evelyn didn't mind being alone. She would rather stand alone than live alongside a murderer, one who would likely interfere every time Evelyn tried to do good from now on.

Her mother may have been able to heartlessly murder her own husband, but Evelyn was not the same. She was nothing like her and never would be.

CHAPTER FORTY-FOUR

The following days passed in a blur.

There was no point returning to the mines since all that remained were corpses and memories of Francis, reminders that she couldn't protect him. So Evelyn spent most of her days attending parties, sitting through meetings, and walking through the capital districts she had never bothered visiting before. She was mindless, hiding within routine to avoid the reality of her loss. When her days were filled with activities and responsibilities, Francis's absence couldn't haunt her.

Prince Antonio accompanied her every time she left the house. She didn't mind his presence anymore. He rarely spoke and when he did, it was about the work she was doing. His empty flattery stopped after Francis's death, either because he no longer had competition or he pitied her for her loss. Regardless, he never mentioned Francis and she was grateful for it.

But on the third day, she was tired of wearing a mask and faking smiles, so Evelyn locked herself away in her bedroom, rereading Francis's letter over and over to search for some deeper meaning behind his words.

In the end, she always came to the same conclusion. He had tired of waiting for her to act and tried to free his brothers on his own. He must have felt there was no other option. Killing the guards had become a necessary evil to protect himself. If she had helped him as she should have, his hands never would have been stained with blood.

In the end, she placed the blame on herself. She should have been more forceful and proactive when addressing her mother.

Perhaps when he looked at her, he saw her mother reflected in her eyes. The thought terrified her. She never wanted to resemble that woman in any way now. After watching her only parent end a hundred lives without blinking, all Evelyn felt when they crossed paths was disgust.

Evelyn only put away Francis's letter and left her bedroom once her mother's carriage carried her off the mansion grounds. Once she was gone, the young woman finally exited her bedroom and went to the kitchen.

As she instructed the servants to cook something for her, she took a seat on one of the wooden tables and listened as they whispered amongst one another, chatting about what had happened at the market today. It wasn't common for nobles to sit inside the kitchen. They usually waited in the dining room instead. This break in etiquette was likely why the servants looked so nervous around her.

As she listened with her head down, the little boy Francis had saved walked past with a bag of potatoes in his little arms. He bowed to her as he went, eyes full of terror, and it confirmed her fears. She looked just like her mother.

"What is your name?" she asked him quietly, aware that the other servants stopped what they were doing and stared when she spoke. The little boy looked equally surprised. She had never attempted to make conversation with him before.

"Peter," he whispered, adjusting the bag in his arms. "My lady."

"Just Evelyn is fine," she muttered, rubbing the back of her neck and feeling the tightness loosen slightly. "Do you like living here, Peter?"

He nodded, though it was clear he was saying what he thought she wanted to hear.

"Do you have a family?" she asked.

The boy shook his head. "My pa died of a fever and my ma sold me to pay for medicine."

"I see." She patted his head, feeling him tense as she did so, then she walked away with a slice of bread in her hands. "If you ever need anything, please tell me, Peter."

The way his face lit up slightly when she said his name filled her with a prick of pain and joy. It was time to start learning the names of the people around her. She should have done it as soon as she left those mines months ago. It was the least she could do. Francis knew all their names, after all.

"Are you all right, my lady?" one of the servants asked as she passed. "I heard you vomiting in your room this morning. Do you need some medicine?"

"No." It was just the reaction to her nightmares, in which she relived Francis's death. "I'm fine…Thank you for your concern."

The woman smiled and nodded, though her worry was still clear. "If it continues, please let me know."

This woman who served under her spoke more like a mother than Evelyn's biological one did.

CHAPTER FORTY-FIVE

Antonio arrived that afternoon and caught her in one of the sitting rooms, talking to one of the male maids as he dusted the bookshelves with a bucket of water and cloth. She was enjoying the conversation, listening to him talk about his daughter, but as soon as the Dalius prince entered the room, the maid made a quick escape and left her alone with him.

"I'm glad you're talking again," Antonio told her quietly as he sat on the chair across from her.

The book on her lap, which she'd previously ignored so she could talk to the maid, was back in her hands by the time he sat down. She didn't want to talk to him. "I'm not going out today, Antonio, so there's no need to escort me. My mother is away as well so there's no—"

"I don't come here because of your mother," he interrupted. His voice was so different when he was serious, and much easier on the ears. "I have always come for you and no one else."

She didn't believe him and showed it by turning to her book instead.

"I think it's time we talked about more than idle gossip or tedious policies," he continued, catching her attention. "I know you and your mother are very different people. While she focuses on accumulating wealth and power, you strive to do more. You want to make real change."

"I don't," she lied, not trusting him. "Francis wanted change and look where that got him."

The prince picked the book off her lap and closed it. "Francis didn't have someone who could protect him. You do."

"You insult me," she mumbled.

"No. I am finally being honest with you. With me by your side, you can make the changes Francis wanted without having to fear assassination or Dalius."

He was quite brave to take her book and speak so bluntly. She was already on the edge of snapping. He shouldn't test her like this. "You speak like you knew Francis. You didn't. I don't think you even spoke to each other directly."

"I knew enough." His eyes looked raw and genuinely sad about his death.

"And what can you do to protect me? You said you prefer flattery to using a sword. If I anger anyone in the capital—"

"I lied about that part," he admitted. "I was hoping to escape my mother's expectations and country's legacy when I told you those things. In truth, I worked as an assassin for the crown before I came here."

She sighed. Was there a single person around her without blood on their hands?

"I would rather use my skills to protect people instead. I want to help you, Evelyn." He leaned forward, her book dropping to the floor. "I'm tired of being used by women for their own gain. For once, I want to be with someone who puts the well-being of others before herself."

She should push him away. She didn't want to rely on anyone ever again and there was no point going against her mother now. Francis was already dead. There was little point in bringing about change now because he wouldn't be around to see it.

"If we don't do anything, Francis's death won't have meaning," Antonio whispered.

With that one sentence, Evelyn could feel Francis's presence again in the back of her mind. While he may be gone, his words and the impact he left on everyone around him remained. He had helped a lot more people than he hurt, and it was Evelyn's job to continue that.

It didn't matter that he left her. He had been doing the right thing, placing himself above everyone else.

It was time she learned from it, rather than run away or try to remain the same.

"Then I'll be relying on you from now on," she told Antonio, rising from her chair and pulling her hair from its braid. "I think I will go out today after all. Wait in the entrance hall for thirty minutes."

"I will accompany you," he said, referring to staying in her room as a bodyguard like Francis used to.

"No." She didn't want anyone else standing by her side or sleeping beside her bed ever again. That spot was reserved. "Wait for me outside the door if you must."

CHAPTER FORTY-SIX

By the end of the week, Evelyn was summoned by the queen to discuss what happened in the mine a week ago. She went despite not feeling ready to face Francis's best friend. She knew John would be by the queen's side, looking as dead inside as Evelyn felt now. Luckily, her mother came with her so she wouldn't have to do any of the talking. Antonio came as well, as he always did.

"You'll come to appreciate him with time," her mother would say about Antonio. Little did she know he wasn't on her side anymore.

The throne room felt empty without the council to fill its empty chairs. The queen was seated on her throne in a dark grey dress and her husband was next to her with red bands around his neck and hands. He looked miserable but as Evelyn entered the room, he didn't break eye contact. She knew he was silently asking where Francis was.

The door closed behind Evelyn after they entered and no one spoke until the three of them were standing before the queen in a line. There was a small table covered with plates of chicken and tomatoes beside the queen, likely the remains of her lunch, but most of the food was untouched.

"Evelyn," Ivy said, ignoring Evelyn's mother as she spoke. "I heard there was a collapse in one of your mines."

"Yes."

"The Mines of Valhander. The one I told you to prioritize," the queen clarified.

Evelyn knew she was referring to the location of this illusive weapon they had yet to see. "Yes, my queen."

"And what caused this collapse?"

Surely she already knew. "There was a rebellion."

John raised his head, listening intently. "Was he there?" he asked Evelyn. They all knew who he was talking about.

"You are addressing a noblewoman, slave," her mother told him. "Do not speak unless spoken to."

"And you are addressing the prince of Clostrum," Ivy interrupted her, rising from her throne. "You will mind your tone, Lady Payne."

Evelyn couldn't help feeling glad that someone else shared her distaste for the murderer.

"Did he die?" John asked again, narrowing his eyes at Evelyn.

"He…" Her voice cracked.

"Evelyn! Did he die?"

A tear slid down her cheek. "Yes."

John nodded, his eyes welling up with tears of his own, then she watched as he grabbed a knife from the queen's dinner table. Evelyn knew what he planned to do and could prevent it by activating the collar around his throat, but she couldn't kill someone Francis cared about. John and the rings on her fingers were all that remained of her husband.

Her mother shrieked as John drove his knife through the queen's throat, finally ending her suffering.

Evelyn saw Ivy's eyes move toward his collar, able to kill him with her final breath, but as he removed the blade from her neck and allowed the blood to flow over her grey dress, Ivy smiled at him and reached out to touch his face. She didn't try to kill him and as she fell to the ground, she looked grateful.

Evelyn turned away from the dead body but couldn't wipe the queen's face from her mind. She finally looked at peace. All the voices in her head were finally silenced.

"Antonio," Evelyn's mother whispered, stepping closer to the Dalian prince so he could protect her from John. She was smiling, though. This was what she wanted. The queen was out of the way and couldn't endanger them anymore. Now Evelyn could ascend the throne, if they played their cards right.

John turned on both of the women. "Who destroyed the mine?" he asked Evelyn. Her answer would determine his next move. "Did *you* kill him, Evelyn?"

She glanced at her mother, who was trying to hide behind Antonio. The woman didn't look the least bit worried about John. Instead of activating John's collar, her mother was waiting for Evelyn to talk John down herself. They needed someone to take the blame for the queen's death, after all. Besides, Antonio could overpower John if he tried to kill her.

Evelyn could lie and say the commander brought down the supports, casting the blame elsewhere as her mother always had, but she didn't want to lie to John or protect her husband's killer. Her mother needed to face consequences for her actions.

"My mother did it," Evelyn whispered. "She killed him."

John turned the knife around in his hands, a look of mutual understanding in his eyes, before he approached the hateful woman.

"Antonio!" her mother shouted. "Restrain him! Prove your loyalty to the Payne family!"

"I thought I already did," the man replied quietly and to no one's surprise but her mother's, he stepped aside so John could reach her.

Lady Payne screamed, her eyes that of a child, and raised her hands to activate the collar around John's neck but instead of seeing the runes light up and burn him alive, nothing happened.

"What's going on?" her mother screamed, stumbling backwards. "Why isn't this working?"

She realized too late that Evelyn was using her own mind to keep the stones from burning, protecting John so he could end her mother's life.

"No!" The woman turned to run for the exit.

"Hateful wench," John hissed at Lady Payne as he drove the knife into the back of her neck. He then released her with a sigh and let her fall forward into a pool of her own blood.

Evelyn had hoped to feel some weight fall off her shoulders as she watched her only family member die, but she felt nothing. If anything, she was sure Francis would be disappointed in her.

"Evelyn," her mother gasped, blood flowing from her open mouth. "You were all I had…"

But the daughter's heart was closed to her, never to be opened again. Her love for her mother had died with Francis. She didn't respond, clenching her teeth as the woman suffocated in her own blood.

"Are you going to kill me now?" Evelyn was standing between two men who were both capable of ending her life in seconds. The only thing stopping them were their collars and consciences.

John had grabbed a second knife from the table and was pointing it at her, but he hadn't moved and his eyes were as empty as ever, though he was breathing heavily from the adrenaline.

"Go ahead," she told him. "I have nothing left to live for anyway."

John considered it but eventually shook his head. "As much as I want to kill you, you just saved my life." He lowered the weapon. "And Francis wouldn't want me to. I owe him that much."

The prince of Clostrum then turned to Antonio. "What's your part in Francis's death?"

"Lady Payne told me to kill him, but I let him go," Antonio explained. "I hoped he would flee to the west. I didn't know he was planning to reenter the mines and get himself killed."

Both Evelyn and John listened carefully for any lies, but the man was completely serious, his normal façade of the perfect gentleman gone.

"I wish he didn't have to die," Antonio added quietly, turning toward Evelyn. "If you wish, I can return to Dalius. Your mother was the one forcing me to stay so if you wish to dismiss me, I am under your command."

John didn't look ready to kill him and she wasn't either, so she didn't answer. He already knew what she'd say.

"Remove these bonds," John ordered, holding out his arms to Evelyn. "Then my debt to you will be paid and I can leave this hateful place."

"You will be hunted for killing our queen," she warned him. "And I won't protect you."

He scoffed as she used one of her white empyrean rings to remove the bracelets, then the collar around his neck. "I may have let you live but I don't want your help. There is no one to hold me back from killing every woman who has ever wronged me now."

Once he was free, John rubbed his scarred arms and yanked his wife's empyrean stone necklace from her dead body. "Be warned, Evelyn, that while I will not kill you for his sake, I will still make your life a living hell. Everyone you love will die by my hands."

"There's no one left that I love."

"Then we are finally equal in that regard." Sneering at them both, John exited the throne room, never to return. He left a trail of blood in his wake but by the time the guards noticed, he would be gone.

"What should I do, my lady?" Antonio asked, speaking with the voice of a soldier instead of a royal or future husband. "Should I alert the guards that the queen has been killed?"

"No." She studied queen Ivy's face. Only in death could the queen look her age. "Ivy requested I find her an heir." Acid climbed up her throat and she forced it down. "We will keep her death a secret for nine months, then we will tell the people she died in childbirth."

"Why nine months?"

"It gives us enough time for her to realistically produce an heir, one who can inherit the throne under my guidance." Evelyn had promised to give Ivy a fake heir. She intended to keep it.

"And where will this heir come from?"

Another tear slipped down her cheek. "From me."

She had realized she was pregnant a mere day after Francis's death. If he had known, she doubted he would have left. "But before we do this, I need to know your allegiances. Will you help me rule this country, Antonio, and make Francis's dream a reality?"

He bowed without question. "As long as I can serve by your side, my lady, I will do everything I can to protect you. My life is yours."

She would be the judge of that. If he showed any signs of deceit, she would send him back to Dalius, though he hadn't given her any reason to disbelieve him. He was yet another victim of his upbringing, like her and Francis.

Evelyn was determined to be different from the paranoid queen who expected the worst from everyone. She had to act more like

Francis and give everyone she met the benefit of the doubt, including this prince.

"Summon every castle employee," she commanded, staring at the two bodies. "And ensure they are sworn to secrecy. Any who try to flee will be locked up until I decide what to do with them."

"Understood, my lady."

It stung to hear him call her what Francis used to. "If you remain loyal, you will become the eventual stepfather of Clostrum's new ruler," she told him, knowing it would be more than enough motive to gain his allegiance.

"…Understood."

She remained stoic until Antonio left, only letting the tears flow once he was gone.

In less than a week, her entire life had fallen apart.

She was standing over the bodies of her last family member and friend. John had been set loose in the city and would likely murder all the women her mother had tried to protect. Clostrum was left without a monarch and could be invaded at any moment.

Her world was on the brink of destruction…but that left it in the perfect position for change.

Her mother may have killed Francis thinking it would ensure the country remained stagnant, but it had instead become the final nail in a new foundation Francis had spent months trying to build. He had wished for Evelyn to finally stand up against Clostrum and make a change. While he may not have wished for it to happen this way, he had succeeded.

With a hardened heart and carrying the future ruler of Clostrum inside her, she stepped over Ivy's body and sat on the throne, resting her hands on the cold black stone and setting the two red rings on her fingers alight for a brief moment, just so she could feel something again.

As the tears stopped and she was left with nothing but silent emptiness, Evelyn heard something else.

"You need to be careful. You can't trust anyone in this castle."

It was a female whisper, one that was both quiet and loud at once, speaking next to her ear but also echoing around the room. She couldn't identify the person speaking until she looked down at the black empyrean stone necklace hanging from her neck. The voice originated from there.

The queen was right after all. The gods did speak from the stones, and they sounded female just as she described.

However, as it continued to speak, the female voice morphed into a different and far more familiar one.

"Evelyn," the voice greeted her, whispering intimately in her ear. *"I'm here to protect you."*

She refused to acknowledge the voice as it deepened, turning male and staying that way. She could already tell whose voice it was trying to emulate and she wouldn't believe it for a second. Its deceit had been Ivy's undoing and it wouldn't become hers too.

However, despite putting up her guard, the voice it used filled her with warmth and comfort. It belonged to the one person she would give anything to hear from again. Perhaps it was the grief or insanity finally taking its hold or maybe the gods used the voice of someone you loved so they could put you at ease. That was the only way to explain why she could hear Francis's voice coming from it.

Even in death, he was still with her.

"I know you're using his voice to take advantage of my weakness," she told the stones coldly. "I won't believe a word you say. I won't let you turn me into Ivy."

But she couldn't bring herself to tear the necklace away. She had longed to hear this voice for days.

I wish you hadn't killed her, it continued as she looked down at her mother's corpse. *She could have changed and done some good.*

"She killed you," Evelyn whispered spitefully.

...Everyone deserves a second chance and even a third. As many as it takes for them to change.

"She didn't deserve any more chances," she hissed. "Nor did she deserve my forgiveness."

No one deserves forgiveness...but they need it. It's the only thing that can save them. It saved you, didn't it?

As the voice continued, she didn't interrupt again. Its icy words filled her with loneliness, so she blocked out the words and listened only to the sound. Francis's calm tones and slow pace soothed her. Her mother couldn't steal him from her side, not even in death.

The red rings on her fingers warmed as she closed her eyes and forced herself to relax. Francis continued warning her of the dangers as she did so, and after basking in the voice for several minutes, she decided she would never rid herself of this empyrean necklace. She would let his voice act as a motivator, a constant reminder of what she almost became. She would never heed its warning, choosing to only rely on herself, but that didn't mean she had to discard this last reminder of him. It could grant her the illusion that she wasn't alone.

No, that wasn't right. Neither the voice nor the rings were Francis's remains.

Her hand went to her stomach, where the final piece of Francis was growing. The child they had created would become his legacy and with it, he had ensured she would never be alone.

Francis may have never seen the free world he envisioned, but she could try to ensure his daughter did. It was the least she could do.

CHAPTER FORTY-SEVEN
SEVENTEEN YEARS LATER

The sun peeked through Evelyn's bedroom window, stinging her eyes and giving her a rude awakening.

As soon as she sat up in her bed, trying to forget the dream she'd just experienced, she heard a comforting voice in her ear wishing her a good morning. It was Francis. The mimicry of his voice was sometimes the only thing that motivated her to leave her bed.

After dressing herself in a purple dress and pinning the family crest above her chest, she did her best to cover the dark circles under her eyes with a white powder, then touched the wrinkles forming around her mouth. She wasn't forty years old yet, but life's agitations were already creating creases along her face.

The first hour of her morning was spent patrolling the mansion to ensure every servant was awake and in fine health. They were all happy to see her, as serving in her household was now a highly coveted spot thanks to the high salary and gracious treatment. She then headed to the dining hall where breakfast was to be served. Today's meal consisted of a small plate of oats and fruits. Long gone were the impressive plates of meat and pastries that went untouched. Evelyn wasn't a fan of wasting food she didn't plan to eat.

As she emptied her plate, her baker Peter walked in, wearing a light blue uniform and carrying a small, paper box full of pastries. He had grown from that cowardly, bruised boy Francis rescued into a fine young man with a wife and child. He had also claimed on multiple occasions that he considered Evelyn a godmother, since she had given him a home in her household once slavery was outlawed. He was one of the few servants who knew about Evelyn's daughter, which was why he always prepared the girl's favorite sweets for her every morning.

"Thank you, Peter," Evelyn said as she rose from her seat at the head of the long, empty table and peeked inside. The pastries for today were covered with strawberries and sugar, making her stomach roll over from the overpowering sweet scent. "Are you trying to addict her to sugar at such a young age?" she asked jokingly, making Peter chuckle. He had come to joke around with her nearly as much as Francis did once it became clear Evelyn didn't look down on him.

"On the few occasions I've met her, she has informed me you never let her eat anything sweet unless it's a gift." He gestured toward the carefully wrapped box. "Hence, I remedied that."

"Very sneaky," Evelyn commented with another chuckle. "I'll send her thanks to you and tell her to give you something in return." Back in the day, it was unheard of for a woman to give an unrelated male a gift, but times had changed in the last ten years or so.

"Oh, no, I—" Peter's reacted as he would have before the law change, but then he quickly thought better of it and smiled. "A mere thank you would suffice. This is good practice for my own daughter, after all. She'll be old enough to eat solids in a few months."

"When that happens, I'll prepare a feast for her," Evelyn commented absent-mindedly, ready to head out. She had bought Peter a house as soon as he spoke of marriage. Francis would have wanted that. "Until tonight."

After saying goodbye, she left the mansion in the care of her maids as always and rode her carriage to the castle. Most of her days were spent there now, despite technically not being a member of the royal family. The current queen of Clostrum, Rem, was an orphan, so it was Evelyn's responsibility to step in and act as a mother in the former queen Ivy's place. That's how the public perceived it, at least.

The castle walls had been repainted a warm and welcoming cream color, something Evelyn herself had requested so the dreary black stone could be hidden. There were curtains and tapestries of bright pink, yellow, and green above the windows so her daughter could grow up with warmth around her.

Evelyn's husband was waiting at the castle gate and accompanied her up the stairs as he did every morning. Unlike her, Antonio had barely aged a day. His dark skin was still smooth, his jawline sharp, and his smile perfect with white teeth. He still drew stares when they walked down the street. Time had been kind to him.

Though the eighth prince of Dalius was her husband in name and on paper, neither of them acted like a couple. This was a professional friendship on good days and barely an acquaintance on bad ones. Evelyn wasn't capable of falling in love with anyone again, no matter how many days passed, so Antonio lived in his own separate home. She couldn't move on from her dead lover and Antonio had learned to expect nothing from her besides responsibility and protection.

Despite their unromantic relation, Antonio never complained and often acted as Evelyn's bodyguard when they were in private, but as soon as they entered the castle, like today, and young Queen Rem ran toward them with a grin, he would shout her name with a huge grin on his face and pull her into a hug like a true father.

Rem had grown up to look just like her mother, with blonde hair fashioned into perfect curls, but the dark eyes were inherited from her father. She was shorter than Evelyn but as she was only sixteen, time would tell what her true height would be.

Because Rem looked similar enough to John and Ivy, no one questioned the young queen's appearance and her similarity to Evelyn. The former queen Ivy's death in childbirth also went unquestioned, as no one missed her *or* her husband, who mysteriously disappeared immediately after.

Evelyn watched sixteen-year-old Rem hug Antonio, then smiled as the girl turned toward her and the box of pastries in her hands. Evelyn made sure to warn her about eating too many sweets as she handed over the box, then she patted her on the head and told her all the things she'd be expected to do today, including lessons and sitting in on the weekly council meeting. The council met three times a week now, taking charge of the kingdom until their queen was old enough to take over.

"I heard one of the mansions across the street was attacked by the rebels," Rem told Evelyn as she munched on a sugared strawberry, pointing out the window at the mansion in question. "Do you think they'll try to kill me too?"

"No." Evelyn glared at the window. It had become normal for noble homes to be invaded and the head of the house killed, particularly if they didn't have sufficient security to protect them. "You're the one person they won't kill, Rem."

"You never bother to explain why," Rem said suspiciously.

"Because you're still young," Evelyn lied, knowing the true reason. John, the leader of the self-proclaimed Knights of Retribution, would never kill Francis's daughter. John enjoyed killing, from what witnesses had said, but he would never break his one rule. He knew

Rem's true identity and would never carry her blood on his hands. "And the guards will protect you."

"As will I," Antonio added, smiling at Rem, then at Evelyn. Evelyn didn't return it.

"Now why don't you change out of your sleeping wear while Antonio and I go to the throne room?" Evelyn asked, giving her husband a knowing look. They had to discuss the threat Dalius was posing to Clostrum, since he was her main connection to the foreign country.

"Very well, Mo…Lady Payne."

Evelyn's heart stung at the girl's slip up. Rem had no idea who her real mother was and since Evelyn and Antonio were the only role models she ever had, it was normal for Rem to view them as family. Sometimes she wished she could be honest with the child. She wanted to talk about Francis again, about how Rem shared his smile and optimism. The girl would finally have someone to blame for her odd name too.

Evelyn had been tempted to tell the truth on several occasions, but it was too risky. Rem might accidentally reveal it to the public and then she'd lose her claim to the throne. If that happened, all the changes Evelyn brought about would be reversed, including the outlawing of slavery.

So Evelyn and Antonio kept it to themselves.

However, the secret didn't stop Evelyn from raising Rem like her own daughter. Evelyn would do anything to protect her innocence and give her the childhood Francis never experienced.

Waving goodbye, Rem did as she was told and charged down the hall to her bedroom, the box of sweets clutched tightly in her arms. As she ran away, the couple headed upstairs to the remade throne room. The walls were golden now and the council table was white with golden pillows atop the seats. The black empyrean throne was the only thing unchanged.

"I'm worried about the rebels," Antonio said as Evelyn took a seat on the throne. "You should send *me* to hunt them instead of inexperienced soldiers. I can wipe them out in less than a year."

He wants to kill John, Francis whispered from her stone necklace.

"I need you here to watch over Rem," Evelyn answered, studying the long council table and its empty seats.

"Don't you fear the civilians siding with him? It could cause a war," Antonio warned. "The same happened in Dalius when I was young."

Antonio wants to be hailed as a hero, the stone hissed.

"I have spoken to Clostrum's citizens over the years. None of them view the rebellion positively. John's people rape and pillage without discrimination. He has made enemies of the people and it makes them appreciate Rem more."

Antonio grit his teeth but didn't frown. He had too much facial control to show such emotions. "I have more news from my mother."

"And?"

"Your hoarding of black empyrean stones has them convinced you know some secret about the gods. They suspect you've found some way to utilize the black stones as a weapon." As far as everyone knew, the black stones were still useless, unless one counted the venomous voices they hid.

He's not telling you everything. They are thinking of invading. I have heard it.

"Keep me informed," Evelyn said, ignoring the voice. "I'll alert the military if I fear an invasion. For now, just focus on keeping them appeased."

The Dalians want access to the mines. They are tired of waiting and begin to suspect Antonio has betrayed them. They're paranoid and we've seen what paranoia has led to before.

"I will do my best to convince them, my lady." Antonio looked her in the eyes and she could tell he was waiting for her to speak honestly. She had long suspected Antonio genuinely cared for her, which would explain why he stayed by her side all these years. The stone claimed he still sided with Dalius and was serving as a spy, but she couldn't be sure.

"I will write a new letter to my mother tomorrow," Antonio continued. "Is there anything you wish for me to add?"

"No. There is nothing I want to say…Just assure them I am not hiding anything. The reason I hoard the empyrean stones is to ensure they cannot torture anyone again, as they did the former queen." And she didn't want to share Francis's voice with anyone. "There is no weapon to be found. Tell them that."

"Yes, my lady." Antonio bowed and walked away, leaving her alone on the throne—the true ruler of Clostrum and mother of the future queen.

With Clostrum no longer relying on slaves for manufacturing and mining, the country was vulnerable to attacks from their neighbors and even from within, but what happened in the future didn't matter to Evelyn. There was always a chance someone in the future might ruin all her progress, making all her efforts obsolete. It's what her mother always feared and tried to prevent. But while there was no guarantee for the future and Evelyn couldn't change the actions of others, she could still make her own decisions. Even if others refused to take up Francis's cause in the coming years, she had to remind herself she was helping others *now*. The slaves she had personally escorted from all her mother's mines had thanked her. She still received letters from former slaves, updating her on all the good her laws had brought about. Their children would never know the pain of a lashing or the burn of stale air in their throats. That was all that mattered.

She just wished Francis was here to see his efforts come to fruition.

EPILOGUE

SEVENTEEN YEARS AGO

Francis ran out of oil for the lanterns in the mine two days ago and the piece of wood currently burning at his feet was the last remaining piece from the tunnel's supports. Once this fire went out, Francis's world would be plunged into darkness for good.

When the tunnel collapsed, the men who hadn't died managed to dig their way back to the deeper tunnels, which hadn't been destroyed. The woman who had brought the supports down on them hadn't bothered activating the ones further into the mine, which meant some of the tunnels didn't cave in and it was the only reason some of them survived.

During the first three days, some tried digging new tunnels toward the edge of the mountain in the hopes of escaping, but all they reached were the indestructible red empyrean stone bars that had been placed around the exterior of the mountain to prevent them. Empyrean stones couldn't be broken unless one had a white empyrean stone, which only women could activate, so there was nothing they could do. They were going to starve to death here.

The only place left to dig was down. Many gave up. Francis was the only one who begged them to keep going. He remembered what the queen had said about an ancient weapon hidden beneath the mines, waiting to be discovered. It might be their only way out.

So, the men used their final days alive to dig deeper into the mountain that would become their tomb.

By the end of the week, rations ran out and the toxic air choked the weakest of them. The bodies started piling up. Francis and his friends tried to give all twenty-seven of the dead a burial but as his energy waned, so did his hope, and he eventually lost the strength to even move the dead bodies out of sight.

Finally, after digging and finding nothing but more empyrean stones they couldn't use, there was only Francis and one man left— the young rebel Evelyn had crippled.

On their final night together, the man thanked Francis for what he'd done and prompted him to keep going. Francis felt guilty as he was handed the final ration and he could only watch as the last survivor crawled away to die elsewhere so Francis wouldn't have to move him.

Then he was alone, trapped in this tunnel with nothing but regret and eventual anger toward every being who had wronged him. He had spent his entire life believing that if he persevered and tried to see the good in everyone, even the most hateful person, it would bring him peace and happiness in the long run. Instead, it had left him with nothing but loneliness and regret.

He missed Evelyn and would give anything to see her just one more time.

"This is it," he whispered with a dry throat to the air as he tried raising the pickaxe high enough to strike the wall. He had stopped feeling hunger days ago and barely had the strength to breathe. "This is what my life has led to."

What should he have done differently?

He swung his pickaxe down, knocking another red stone from the wall.

If he had been more forceful or ruthless, would he be in Antalius right now?

A second strike knocked down a white stone.

"I should have tied Evelyn to my back and dragged her to Antalius kicking and screaming," he said with a tired laugh.

He struck a black stone and watched it fall at his feet. He could have sworn he heard a voice from the rock when it hit the ground. His thirst must have finally driven him insane.

He sighed, lowering the pickaxe. If he hadn't married Evelyn, would he still be serving her now?

"No. That is the one thing I won't take back." He was glad he married her, regardless of where it led. He still loved her even now, despite the doubts they'd both had.

As the fire fizzled out behind him, he used the last of his strength to strike once more.

Francis's entire body jolted as metal hit stone, but instead of having nothing to show for his effort, he felt the wall before him fall away and a hole emerged with a blue glow behind it. It almost looked like sky.

Had he found an exit?

"Impossible," he whispered and started hacking at the wall with renewed energy. He was sure he had been digging downwards, but perhaps…

In a few minutes, the wall was gone and with it, his hope. He hadn't found an exit to the surface. Instead, he entered a small room with curved black walls and glowing blue runes curved into them.

Had he found what the queen was searching for?

In the center of the room were two objects. The first was a book lying on the floor, its words the same color as the runes and written in an unfamiliar script. The pages were brown from age; The book had to be over a hundred years old, from before society destroyed itself with war.

Behind the book and striking fear into his heart was a female statue posed like a soldier. It had hardened skin like the black empyrean stones he spent his entire life mining, and glowing white lines traveled across its naked flesh.

The woman had a human body but her limbs were too long and her hair wrapping around her arms like snakes. Her face looked normal, and perhaps even beautiful, but her eyes were empty and currently focused on him.

Francis was tempted to run but knew there was nowhere to go. He was at the end of his life anyway, so he had nothing to fear.

Looking down at the book and unable to read it, he reached for the stone figure, wondering if this could be the weapon the gods had described. All this time, the queen had been searching for a statue?

Before he could touch the thing's hand, its head swiveled toward him, its pupil-less eyes boring into his. As each limb turned to face him, the white runes began to glow red, yellow, and green, lighting up the entire tunnel behind him.

Francis leapt backwards, falling to the ground in his weakness, and watched as the creature stepped toward him. When she spoke, her voice was feminine but devoid of emotion. Her tone sounded even more empty than John's.

"Francis Noke," it addressed him, stopping a foot away from him and holding its hands out in what it likely assumed was an unintimidating stance. "Thank you for finally freeing me from my prison."

He shivered. Had he released a monster? No. Whoever this was had not been freed. The tunnels were still blocked.

"What are you?" he whispered. "A god?"

"No," it answered calmly, continuing to stare. "I am a servant of the Aeyai, a race of beings your kind *refer* to as gods. I was sent here to observe and assist your kind, though I have lain dormant for the last hundred years due to my imprisonment."

"Who locked you up?" It had to be for a good reason. "And why?"

"Your people feared me," it answered with no hesitation. "My power can cause chaos if placed in the wrong hands. Thankfully." She gestured toward him. "You are one who is worthy of wielding such power."

He was beginning to understand why this being had been hidden away. "You said you assisted my kind. How?"

"I fulfil your wishes, if they are within my ability to grant." She smiled at him but it felt soulless. "One of the last wishes I granted was a hundred years ago, to a young girl. She was a slave, like you."

He didn't understand her or how she knew so much about him.

"What is your wish, Francis?"

"Mine?" It was the first time someone other than Evelyn had asked him.

"Yes. What is your wish?"

"My wish…is to see my wife again." It was the only motivation he had to escape the tunnels. "I want to be with her again and raise a family together."

The creature tilted its head. "I cannot take you from this mine," she said thoughtfully. "You are on the brink of death and if I summoned someone, they would not arrive in time."

"So you can't do it?"

"There is something else I can do," she said.

The hairs on his neck stood as she reached a long arm toward him. "I will grant your wish," she told him even as he crawled away. "Do not resist, Francis Noke."

"I don't want to do it if it means someone gets hurt," he said. "I would rather die before I let that happen."

"I cannot harm people," she assured him, grabbing his arm. Her skin was as cold and hard as stone. "Your kind kill each other so often that I don't have to."

"What?" His vision darkened and he felt the last bit of life inside him fade away. At the same time, he could feel something else in his brain—a new presence. It was hers. "Wait. I don't want this," he whispered breathlessly.

"I must grant your wish," she repeated calmly and as her voice faded, he felt his consciousness return, though this time he felt different. All the warmth and energy he possessed a moment ago was gone. His heart was cold, empty, like he had never experienced love or sorrow before and never would again.

When he looked down at his hands, they were black as stone and reflected the glow of the walls. He could read the words written on the pages now. And when he closed his eyes, he could see even more.

Behind his closed eyelids, he could see the trees and flowers of Clostrum, the cottages of Antalius, the barbarian pirate ships on the northern sea, and the black castles of Dalius. Anywhere a black empyrean stone existed, he could see. The stones became his eyeglasses, granting him vision beyond his body.

Once he realized this, Francis became possessed by the needs of his wish and spent what felt like hours searching each location, obsessively scouring each peephole into different parts of the world until he finally found what he was looking for.

"Evelyn."

He found his wife sitting on a black throne in the queen's castle. There were two bodies on the ground beneath her, people he recognized as the queen and Evelyn's mother, but he only cared about his wife. She looked just as she had when he left her. Seeing her brought a spark of life back to his stone heart.

His wish had been granted. He could see her again, maybe forever.

As he opened his eyes and she disappeared, he felt the love vanish with her and its absence left an ache in his chest.

Horrified at what he'd become, he stared his stone hands, turning them over and missing the sensation of warmth on his fingertips. He had been transformed into whatever this stone being was. In order to see the woman he loved, he'd lost a piece of himself and might never get it back.

…But it was all worth it to see her again.

Francis, or whoever he had become, sat down in the small black room and closed his eyes again, ignoring the female voice of the Aeyai in his head and the book sitting before him. They could wait. Right now, he needed to see her again, to hear her voice and tell her he was still here.

"Evelyn," he whispered and saw her react ever so slightly. It brought back that flood of emotion again and he felt like a human once more. "Evelyn," he repeated, wishing he could cry with this new body he inhabited. "I'm here."

THE END

AUTHOR'S NOTES

This book's original form looked nothing like the story you just read. Francis and Evelyn didn't exist until later drafts and the entire plot was completely different. However, despite nearly ten drafts and five years, I'm pretty happy with how everything came together.

The original story, named *The Queen's Concubine*, was about a male slave who was essentially kidnapped by the queen, who had fallen in love with him. The slave's name was Daysee and the queen's name was Rem. (Their origin would eventually turn into Ivy and John's romance story, though theirs ended with a happy ending unlike John's.)

At the quarter mark, I created a male maid who would serve as a 50-year-old mentor for Daysee. I named him Francis and he was only there to be a father figure who would eventually die.

I also created a leader of the rebellion who was a former prince. That was John Rygiel, though his character was morally good and not as complex as the current John. Ivy was created and named alongside him and his backstory.

The final main character from this current book was created in the second draft of that one. When I decided to make the queen become good, I needed an antagonist, so Evelyn was created. She was an evil, money-focused noble who was betrayed by her past lover. That form of Evelyn acted almost exactly like the mother in this story. (It offered an alternate reality of what would happen if Francis genuinely left her and didn't die, I suppose.)

So, we had these four middle-aged background characters who acted as roadblocks or mentors to the younger characters. In the third draft, I decided to connect Francis and Evelyn's stories, since Francis was the perfect age to be that former lover who betrayed her. Then in the fourth draft, I added the twist that Evelyn was Rem's biological mother.

After that, I became so interested in these backstories that I decided to flesh them out with some genuine flashbacks, which turned into half of the story by the fifth draft. The tragic love story of Evelyn and Francis ended up becoming a lot more enjoyable and straightforward than the rest of the book's current day plot and my beta-readers agreed. By the time I was on the sixth draft, I was considering scrapping the whole main plot, focusing on the past story of Francis and Evelyn, improving its flaws, and starting fresh with the future story of Daysee and Rem.

That's how we ended up here.

Overall, I'm really glad that I stuck with Evelyn and Francis's story and scrapped the rest. It helped me avoid getting stuck in the disjointed, broken plot from before. It also let me go over the Evelyn/Francis story with a fine-toothed comb until I had it just the way I wanted it. Now the sequel won't be bogged down by past outlines and plots, and this current book leaves plenty of room to go wherever I want.

If you're hoping for more like Chains of Stone (it does say "trilogy" on the cover, after all) then rest assured that there will be more. Rem (Evelyn's daughter) will be the main character in the next story. That slave Daysee from the original story will also be in the sequel, though he will be an entirely different character from that old one.

It might be a while before this second story is released. I've already written the first draft but am not happy with it and don't want to release something I wouldn't want to read myself. So, it might take a bit. It will come out, though, unless something happens to me between then and now.

To wrap this up, I have some people I'd like to thank who walked with me through this entire book's lifespan:

First of all, thanks to Victoria, who did all the beta reading through nearly every draft. She also went on to make the covers for the story. She stuck through it all, gave her honest reactions, and kept me motivated.

Thanks to Anyaeleh, one of my best friends who read both the original and current forms of this book. She always had the most wild and emotional reactions to the plot and characters. She made it a blast to listen to critiques.

Thanks to Bella and Ole, who read one of the middle drafts and gave me the push to scrap the original story and pursue this one. The book may not be perfect, but I think they both helped immensely to improve it and refocus.

And to anyone who bought this book, thank you. Putting anything you made into the world is a scary thing, especially because I myself am a picky reader so I would feel like a hypocrite if I churned out something crappy and expected people to read it. If you enjoyed this, I'm exceedingly grateful and hope to see you again soon. Writing has been my passion ever since I was seven and if this story was able to help you escape reality or inspire you in some way, I'm glad.

If you want to see more stories like this (or are just into genres such as: romance, fantasy, science fiction, or horror), then keep a lookout. I have written a lot of other stories while editing this one, so they'll be coming out soon (or at least eventually).

Until next time.

COVER CONCEPT ART

By Victoria Chevalier

Francis

John Rygiel and Queen Ivy

<u>TO STAY UPDATED ON JAYSEE'S PROJECTS:</u>

Tiktok: https://www.tiktok.com/@jayseejewel

Instagram: https://www.instagram.com/jayseejewel/

Cover Artist's Instagram: Victoriarose_art7

www.ingramcontent.com/pod-product-compliance
Lightning Source LLC
Chambersburg PA
CBHW021136310726
48971CB00002B/355